I0616026

OUTLAW

OF

SMOKE

THE IRONFIRE LEGACY
BOOK ONE

JANEEN IPPOLITO

First edition © 2017 Janeen Ippolito
Second edition © 2018 Janeen Ippolito
Third edition © 2021 Janeen Ippolito

All rights reserved. No part of this publication may be reproduced, distributed, or transmitted in any form or by any means, including photocopying, recording, or other electronic or mechanical methods, without the prior written permission of the publisher, except in the case of brief quotations embodied in critical reviews and certain other noncommercial uses permitted by copyright law.

This is a work of fiction. Names, characters, businesses, places, events, and incidents are either the products of the author's imagination or used in a fictitious manner. Any resemblance to actual persons, living or dead, or actual events is purely coincidental.

Copyediting by Sarah McConahy

Cover Design by Christian Bentulan

To Kathy Anischenko.
Love ya, Gram!

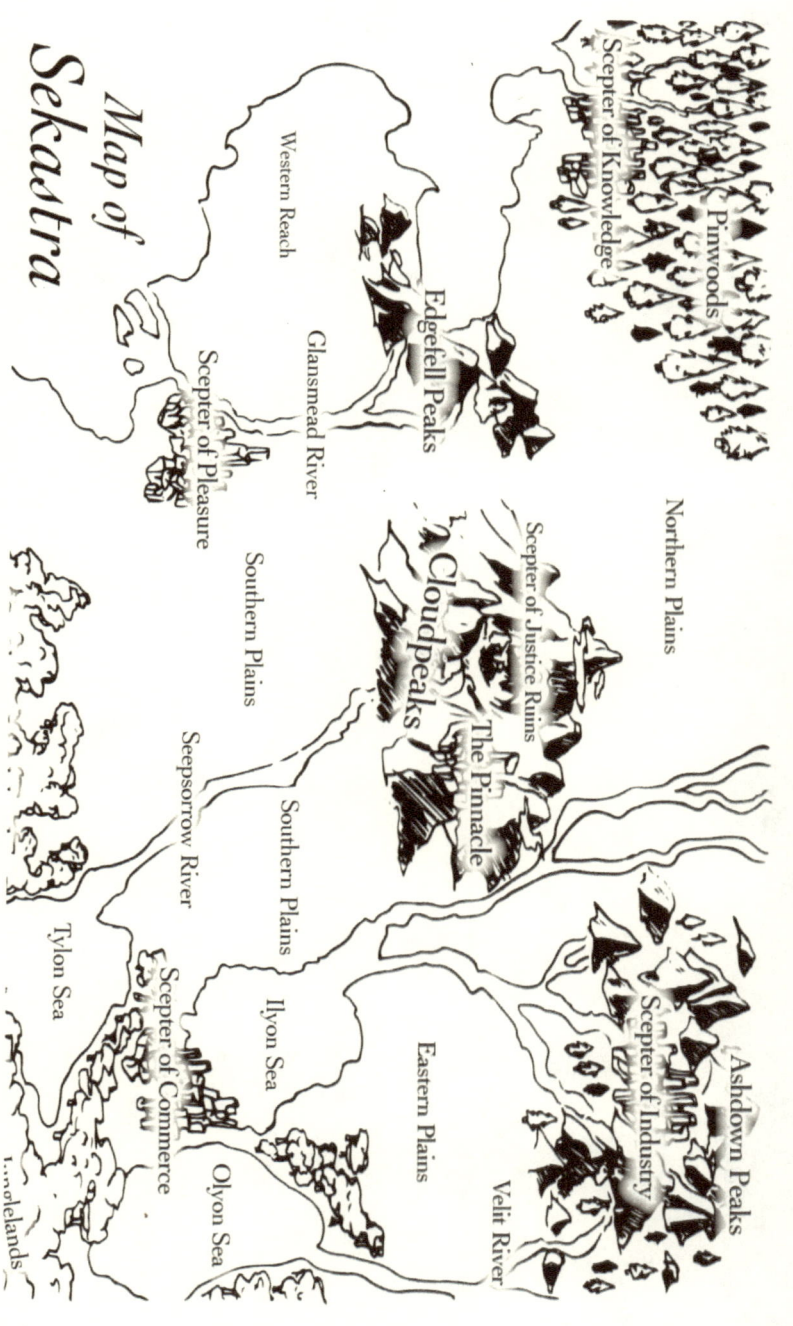

Map of
Sekastra

Scepter of Knowledge

Pinwoods

Western Reach

Edgefell Peaks

Glansmead River

Scepter of Pleasure

Northern Plains

Southern Plains

Scepter of Justice Ruins

Cloudpeaks

The Pinnacle

Southern Plains

Seepsorrow River

Ashdown Peaks

Scepter of Industry

Tylon Sea

Scepter of Commerce

Ilyon Sea

Eastern Plains

Velit River

Olyon Sea

...ndelands

CHAPTER ONE

ONE BENEFIT OF ILLEGAL MISSIONS: there were no high and mighty leaders questioning everything you did.

<Remember: in and out quickly, don't disturb anyone, and don't destroy anything.>

But beware fleetwings who tried to fill the gap.

Kesia huffed a stream of smoke at her tactical partner. She thought back, <Ruin all of my fun, hm?>

<Is any of this supposed to be fun?> Zephryn fixed her with a fierce glare, his cobalt eyes flaring with red fire. He was a vision of lethality. His long, serpentine body and midnight wings imposed themselves in her view, obscuring the starlight. Which was what they needed this night. Kesia adjusted her flight pattern to fly closer to him, further within the protection of his Cloak—part of Zephryn's Talent that allowed him to bend light around himself and others.

His Talent was the only reason she was alive. An ordinary soldier caught on an illegal mission would face severe punishment. A criminal like her would face immediate execution. Unless she brought home reconnaissance, something to earn her enough respect for her past to be erased.

Something like spying on the Congruency's newest airship and prized captain.

A thread of panic stirred her. No more thinking, or else she would never do it. She flapped her wings, coming close enough to Zephryn to flick her long tail across his back. <I won't take unnecessary chances, I promise. Thank you for helping me.>

<For you? Always.> His stern look softened for a moment. He nudged the top of her deep red head with his snout. A flush of warmth immediately erased much of Kesia's fear. <Now, go quickly! I will stand guard against other sentinels. Satisfy your curiosity, and see what you can learn.>

<With all speed.>

She glided in slow circles beneath the ship, smelling the acrid scents of oil-fuel and smoke. Airships had once been vessels of beauty and artistry, used for pleasure excursions and merchant expeditions. After the war began, the Scepter of Industry had made new advancements, ones that stung the eyes of dragons and corrupted the air.

Kesia brought her attention back to the mission.

What should she be? Stifling a bubble of laughter, she closed her eyes.

Raven.

She shifted. Her dragon form shrank and was consumed by paper-thin skin and feathers. Kesia fought dizziness at the sudden loss of mass and angled her body to adjust for the night winds that buffeted her far more than before. Zephryn's Talent could get them perilously close to the airship, but hers would allow her to hop aboard.

Kesia shook off the thoughts and flapped her wings harder. She enjoyed this form. It was fast and fleet.

<Really? You chose a form that is a symbol of death for the humans, Rose-Wing?>

She croaked irritably. <Or perhaps a symbol of flattery, hm? After all, you're raven-hued.>

Kesia could picture Zephryn's peevish look, one with a faint undertone of playfulness that made her enjoy teasing him more. <I would not have you needlessly jeopardize yourself. And what was our bargain about disturbances?>

<What disturbance? Croaking is a perfectly appropriate action for a raven. You always seek to ruin my fun. But if it will appease you...>

She closed her eyes and shifted again, this time to another, smaller bird. By the time she reached the top-most mast of the ship, she had gained control of her new sun-dove form. Kesia landed gracefully on a crosspiece and settled her wings about herself, fanning the brilliant yellow plumage underlaid with pale blue feathers. Zephryn couldn't possibly object to this choice. Sun-doves were migratory birds that followed winter across the land of Sekastra. All human travelers saw them as good omens.

Dragons like her saw them as snacks.

<Far better. Now if only I can resist eating you...>

Kesia chirped again, this time in a fluting tone. <I would like to see you try. Even Old Master Rulland could outfly you easily, so why should I have any problem?>

<Oh, really?> Zephryn tilted his head in challenge, and a thrill raced through Kesia.

<Yes, especially if you kept slowing down to tell others how to behave.> He chuckled at that. Another rush of warmth flowed through her. She wasn't sure if others had a similar rapport with their fleetwings, and she never dared ask, lest the question alter

Zephryn's behavior or draw outside attention to it.

It was one of the few joys she had as a Pinnacle prisoner, and she was loath to lose it.

<Now quiet, good sir. I need to focus.>

She released her grip on the crosspiece and flitted lower, veering around the smaller sails and taking in each aspect of the ship. It was an archaic one, made entirely of wood. Most modern airships were made using some kind of alloy. Using masts and sails was a vanity custom, as useless as jewels on a dragon's wings. All the real power came from the masked but foul-smelling engine.

"Oye! There's a sun-dove. Good fortune on us all!" An answering chorus arose from the deck, and out of the corner of her eye, she spied numerous hands pointing her out or raising mugs in her direction. She spied a few tables laden with food and beverages, and most of the crew seemed relaxed. A few of the humans had even loosened the collars of their tunics.

<A party?>

<A maiden voyage,> Zephryn said. <A human military custom to celebrate the first launch and sail of a new ship.>

<I see.> Kesia felt a pang of jealousy for her fleetwing's knowledge. Criminals were highly limited in their education. Why waste time on a dragon who could be executed at any moment? She studied the ship further. Wings spread out on either side of the silver-toned masthead, which was crowned with— <A dragon? Why would there be a dragon masthead? We're their enemies!>

<That, I have no answer for, other than humans are irrational. Don't get distracted by irrelevant matters.>

<Who are you to say it's irrelevant?>

<Your partner who is cloaking you. Consider the time, Rose-Wing.>

Kesia made an annoyed squawk. Zephryn had a point. They had sneaked far away from the Cloudpeaks on this excursion. This airship was within the territory of the Scepter of Commerce. All the more reason for Zephryn's worry. They were on enemy turf.

Yet, he had allowed her to coax him into the mission, sneaking her out of her cell after the tactical lockdown. Zephryn didn't have to abide by the lockdown. His freedom was one of the few benefits allotted to the only remaining member of the old royal family. But freeing her was still a risk. He could be sentenced to days of discipline in the flay-room. Her fleetwing managed to avoid punishment with astonishing ease, but direct disobedience of the law on behalf of a convict?

Not even a prince could dodge that.

She had better make this worth his trouble. Kesia flitted closer, chancing a perch on the railing of the ship. It was finely polished, making her grip difficult until she dug her nails in.

Another cheer rang up from the crew. Her feathers fluffed in pity. If only they knew who she was. This war made dragon and human friendship impossible. But right now, she was a sun-dove. She would enjoy people desiring her company, for once.

"Ack, be gone with you!"

Or not.

Kesia fluttered her wings in protest, skittering away from the gray-haired woman who swatted at her.

"None of that, Virna." Another voice spoke up, this one with a light, pleasant cadence that was far more cultured. "A sun-dove is always a gift. The railing is all the better blessed for her claw marks."

"Begging your pardon, Cap'n, but the shipbuilders spent days shining up that piece." Virna gestured around vaguely. "All these here pieces! And you'll let some common pigeon muck that up, will you? Spit on the Congruency's generosity like that, will you?"

The other speaker walked into her field of vision, a tall man with blond hair and a finely-trimmed beard. "I appreciate all the efforts the Congruency has made on behalf of this vessel and all of their favor on me. And that is why I will not curse *The Silver Streak* by showing unkindness to a simple bird."

<A simple bird. Hm.> Kesia gave the captain a second look. Fitted tan pants, tall brown boots, and a plain black waistcoat over a dark blue long-sleeved shirt. The standard attire for an airship captain. It was the silver insignia fastened over his right shoulder that drew her attention. Not simply a captain, but an elite squadron leader. It explained the extravagance of the ship.

"A'right then, Cap'n Windkeeper. It's as you say." The gray-haired woman brushed off the sleeves beneath her black waistcoat and gave Kesia a last glare.

A Windkeeper? Their entire line featured humans Talented with manipulating the winds. She had happened upon one of the most powerful individuals in the enemy camp. Never mind that Windkeeper was a dragon surname. Whatever ties he and his forebears had had with dragons had been lost long ago to gunfire and bloodshed.

The captain nodded to her sharply, then turned back to Kesia with a wry look, the authority dropping from his gaze like an unwanted mask. "Sometimes I think you have it a lot easier, my feathered friend."

<I doubt it.> She gave a trill. Hopefully that would win his affections even more and allow her free range of the ship.

He laughed. "Perhaps not. After all, dragons go after you, don't they? I remember reading that in my studies. It seems like we're on the same side."

Kesia resisted the urge to bristle. Sun-doves made a good treat; every dragon knew that. It wasn't like the humans cared for sun-doves any more than dragons did, except as meaningless symbols. Though Captain Windkeeper seemed more sentimental than most.

She could use that. With another trill, she hazarded a quick flight to his shoulder. In turn, he cautiously stroked her head.

<Is he making a pet of you, then?> Ah, there was the disapproval from Zephryn. Although she couldn't imagine why this human would arouse any ill-will, other than the issue of his race. Zephryn wasn't the sort to go for that kind of prejudice. Humans were the enemy, and that was all.

<No, I am earning his trust, as I was taught. You should be so proud, Fleetwing.>

<Just acquire the information and leave. There is an uneasy stirring in the breezes. Take care.>

A shrill chirp escaped Kesia. <Very well.>

She surveyed the ship. Three levels: a central bridge, the poop on one side, and cabins on the aft. More like a pleasure ship than a warship, but appearances were deceiving. She spied the gleaming bronze multi-fire guns on either side of the railing, sixteen total. In the masts, more pipework coiled around the beams. Some new kind of weapon?

Kesia tweaked at the captain's hair around his ear, earning a gentle look of reproval and another head rub, this one angled around her neck. Giving her delicate skin a scratch in just the right place. A coo escaped her. He was certainly an animal lover.

Unless those animals were dragons.

Her enjoyment cooled. This man had killed her people. Not her father, though; Kesia had taken care of that herself.

She fidgeted, hoping Captain Windkeeper would move. Something was coming out of the pipes, and it smelled even more foul than the oil fuel. At least the fuel was a known factor, one that she had almost become used to, but this was sickening. Just a few breaths made her lightheaded.

Time to fly.

Then the pipes exploded in a fury of flames and bilious green stench.

<Kesia!>

CHAPTER TWO

HE HAD TO SAVE THE SUN-DOVE.

Shance shoved away the absurd thought. The bird had flown away the moment the blast broke through the ship. His next thoughts involved more important matters: keeping *The Silver Streak* from ripping in half and making sure his crew didn't die.

He took a deep breath and mentally reached out for the winds that always came at his command. Only faint breezes drifted around him. He frowned and extended his hand, calling with his Talent to every part of the fetid air.

A whisper of pressure on his palm was the only response.

"Oh, Fiarston," he cursed. Not that he believed in the sky god or any of the others whose temples peopled the four Scepters. No one could count on gods to come through.

Right now, *Shance* had to save his crew. And he couldn't.

What devilry was this smoke? Dragon made? But there was no evidence of dragons using weapons in their aerial attacks. They preferred flames and complicated sky maneuvers. Could a Talented dragon make nauseating green smoke bombs?

He forced down the panic knotting his chest.

Time for option two.

"Get to the parachute boats!" He coughed on the noxious green smoke, gripping the side of the plummeting airship. "All hands to the parachutes! I want you whole for our next mission!"

A pause.

Shance could sense the unspoken question; why wasn't he saving their asses?

There was no time to explain what he himself didn't understand.

"That's an order! Now!"

"Aye!"

Crewmen and officers ran across the deck, stumbling toward the craft at the bottom of the vessel. Soon the small tan blimps of the parachute boats floated into view.

Relief flooded him. At least they would be safe. The ship was close to the Scepter of Commerce. If his crew used their parachute boat propellers well, they might land in one of the Trebbian Seas that surrounded the city.

Virna's gray eyes crinkled, and her mouth was a sharp line. "Sir! R'spectfully, yer needed in those boats just as much as the rest, if not more!"

Explosions seared his ears into senseless ringing, and wood bits splintered his fingers as he grasped the tilted railing. So much for Virna's concern over the polish.

"There are other captains—"

"Yer a Windkeeper!"

"There are other Windkeepers!"

The planking split and cracked beneath their feet, and the ship careened in a haphazard, dizzying spiral.

Virna's solid figure skidded along the deck. "The captain must take care—"

"The captain is ordering you to the parachute boats! Question me, and I'll have your hide for insubordination!"

Virna clenched her hands into fists, then nodded and gave a quick salute, the bent finger joints of her right fist touching her lips. "Aye, sir!"

She ran toward the parachute boats. More of the small vessels floated toward the Trebbian Seas, where they would alight gently in the water.

"Ships in the water," Shance grunted. "What a novel thought."

The deck below him sagged. He braced his feet into a corner, trying to leverage his weight. One false step and the planks would slant vertical.

The pride of the Scepter's air fleet might be on fire, broken in half, and wreathed in green smoke that smelled like rotten eggs, but still, Shance had made a vow to bring it safely back to port every time.

Windkeeper honor.

"Come on! Work, you stupid ancestral wind tunnel!"

Shance flung out his hand once more, his heart beating like the parachute boat propellers. There was another sickening blast and puff of bilgey smoke from his ship, but no wind. Only the slow sinking of the deck beneath him as it finally gave way. Pieces of wood dug deeper into his palms as he desperately reached for any part of *The Silver Streak* to stop his fall. The grooved wood panels offered no purchase.

His hands were on fire, swelling with blisters. That would put a damper on his love life. Shance fell through the cool, empty air. A hoarse cry mixed with a panicked laugh escaped his throat, and he leaned forward. He may as well know where he would meet his death.

The blankness of dark earth greeted him. Even if it had been water, he would still have met his end; at this height, the waves would have offered no cushion.

Adrenaline surged through him, bringing new vigor to his mind. Shance stripped off his waistcoat, shirt, and undertunic, discarding all but the shirt. If he could collect even a small gust or two of wind, maybe he could slow his descent enough to avert death. He gripped the shirt cuffs tightly, ignoring the pain from his blood-smeared hands, and extended his arms behind him, calling any wind he could to his aid.

His velocity was too strong. The cloth only flew uselessly behind him.

"Doldrums!"

Shance released the shirt, and with it went his last vestige of hope. Death would almost be a relief. It would mean he could stop taking the lives of others. And there was a certain poetry to a captain going down with his ship. Although, in the old days, that meant drowning. Smashing into the ground would be quicker.

His thoughts wandered, trying to avoid focusing on the ground below. He hoped the sun-dove was all right. Even if flame-cursed Fiarston wouldn't help sailors, perhaps the god would protect small, innocent animals from dragon wrath.

Why in the lands were the sparkers still fighting this war? Weren't twenty years enough?

A broad shape appeared between him and the ground. A parachute boat?

A second later, he slammed into a lean body nearly twice as wide as his. Scales rubbed against his face, then started sliding smoothly against it as he sagged off the side.

"Hold on!"

The voice seemed to come from within his head more than from the air around him—but that was impossible. Then again, all of this was impossible. Shance tried to find air to breathe, but as usual, wind eluded him this night. Only a choked gasp escaped him.

The loud, surprisingly feminine voice shouted again. "Hold on, you fool, or all this will be for nothing! Don't make my trouble worthless!"

The order snapped through him. Shance managed to swing himself over the form again. His legs barely reached either side of what looked like a strange, sinuous tube of scales. He started to edge himself forward to a narrower part.

"Do you think to choke me? I'm not your enemy right now, Captain Windkeeper. Please don't be mine."

"How are you my enemy?"

"I would have thought the wings gave it away."

Shance hazarded a glance on either side of him. Through the dim starlight he could see the dark outline of wings spreading out on either side of the beast, forty or fifty feet of elegant strength and deadly power.

A dragon. He was on the back of a dragon. A dragon was speaking to him, even though they couldn't, they didn't do that in scale form. This had to be a hallucination, a side effect of the foul smoke. Any moment now the scales and wings would disappear, and he would feel the pain and oblivion of bones smashing into hard ground.

"Why are you helping me?"

The dragon's wings beat strongly as she descended at a sharp angle, the clawed edges waving up and down in the wind. "You allowed me to ride on your shoulder. I thought to return the favor."

"How did I do that?"

She laughed. "As easily as a bird."

Now Shance was sure he was hallucinating. The rich, melodic voice, layered with the many tones of dragon speech, was like nothing he had heard before. His father likened dragon voices to the sound of a choir of winds, with the depth of gold and silver bells. And Orun Windkeeper wasn't given to poetry.

A cool sea breeze hit his face. They were close to the Scepter of Commerce now, and dragons were notoriously fearful of water, especially in their reptilian form. How could any of this be real?

"Can you swim?"

He dared to remove one hand from her back and rubbed at his eyes. "Well enough."

"Good. Here is where I must leave you." Her wings beat at a curved angle now, maintaining a steady hovering position over the water. "The shore is half a league away. I think you should be able to manage."

"Aye." When would this dream be over? The taste of the briny seawater on his face was all too real. Shance stroked his hand against the scales of the dragon's back. Beneath the hard surface, there was another layer, pliable and almost soft. Details he would never have thought to make up. He could embellish a story over a few drinks, but never create one.

"Well, off with you then."

Shance began sliding off the side of the dragon's back. She certainly had a commanding edge for such a sweet voice. "I don't even know your name."

"Does it matter? You're alive. That's a comfort, I would think."

"True." Such a resonant voice, like honey and rain and rose petals. Old tales said that dragon voices were able to turn the mind of any human to their will. Shance understood. He could listen to the dragon speak forever.

He gave the dragon's scales a pat. "Until we meet again, my fair savior."

He fell into the water and immediately began treading to turn, just in time to see the dragon snort a small stream of flame through her slender nostrils.

"I hope not, for your sake, Captain Windkeeper."

CHAPTER THREE

<YOU'RE GOING TO GET US BOTH KILLED.>

Zephryn breathed a brilliant stream of fire onto the pile of wood gathered for their camp. More fire than necessary, but the cave where they took shelter was nestled deep in the northern parts of the Cloudpeaks. No one would spy them here.

They could have continued to the Pinnacle that night, but Kesia's unexpected charity had changed the situation. He needed to think, and so did she, even though currently it had yielded no results other than the certainty of their executions.

<I had a debt to repay.> She settled her wings around her, allowing her scales to heat up. <And something was wrong on the ship.>

He clicked his nails on the stone beneath him, pacing the length of the cave. <Yes. It

exploded. Something was very wrong.>

<You scented something in the wind and warned me. On the ship, I smelled the same thing, only stronger. It made me light-headed. It was a chemical bomb.>

<Only the humans use those and pollute the air.>

Kesia fixed her warm amber eyes on him, her slit pupils

20

wreathed in flames. Quiet, but clever. <Why would humans attack their own vessel? It was new and finely crafted. The Congruency will be very angry.>

<All the better.> But her words gnawed at him, more than the hunger in his stomach. They had no time to hunt tonight. Warming their bodies was far more important to ensure they didn't fall into the Cold Sleep. <There have been rumors of a resistance that opposes the war. We both know this.>

<Anarchists that want to destroy all governments. I suppose that makes sense.>

<Yes. Although this is a bold move for them.>

Kesia was silent for a moment, her eyes distant, as if searching for an answer. <The smoke. It reminded me of something.>

<What?>

<I don't know what,> she snapped. <But it's important. I need to know what it was.>

<Why?>

<Something from before.>

Meaning before he'd met her. When she had been a child who had killed her father.

They both fell silent, staring into the mesmerising flickers of orange, red, and yellow. This entire excursion had been to satisfy Kesia's drive—and his own, truth be told. A drive fueled by the brand burned into her underbelly, a single, thin slash with a jagged hook at one end.

The mark of a murderer.

She didn't talk about it much, even after ten years of partnership. The label prevented them from being acknowledged as true fleetwings, with all the rights and privileges as such. Breeding. More dangerous missions. Very likely their deaths in battle for a war that seemed endless. All of these things were a prize if only they could remove the taint of Kesia's sentence. But she freely acknowledged she had killed her father at age ten, a year before he'd met her.

Bitterness curled Zephryn's tail. Yes, he was a prince—of nothing. He wanted to do more, but as it stood, he had no one, and no way of finding help while Kesia was held prisoner. Besides, what was the point of fighting to rule a kingdom that no longer existed? Why were they even returning to the Pinnacle to face judgement?

Kesia would face judgment. Perhaps even death.

Death was unacceptable. He ground his teeth. <We don't need to go back.>

<What?> Kesia's head lifted, her nostrils flaring in shock. <Where would we go?>

An excellent question. Rogue dragons were liable to be targeted by both sides. <I don't know. But if we return, and they decide to execute you—>

<They won't.>

Naturally, she would take up this old argument. Zephryn blew a stream of flames into the fire. <How do you know this?>

<They have had ample reason and opportunity to kill me over the last ten years, yet they haven't. Besides, killing me would kill you as well.>

<The life of a single prince from a government the Pinnacle overthrew would not be valuable.>

Her eyes gleamed, matching the intensity in her voice. <Then why didn't they kill us both a long time ago?>

<You know why. Keeping a royal alive gives them some vestige of authority.>

<What does that matter after twenty years?>

Zephryn scoffed. <So now you believe you're valuable?>

<...no.> Kesia's head slumped. She rested her chin on her front feet. <I think the Pinnacle thinks I'm valuable.>

A rush of resigned despair filled him through their link, softening the aggression of their argument. Zephryn sent reassurance back to Kesia. <You are valuable, Rose-Wing. That is beyond question. But why do you suddenly think the Pinnacle has some plan for you?>

<I don't know. The green smoke ... there was something very familiar about it. I don't remember what. But I want to go back to the Pinnacle. There are answers.> Her scaled face was closed, her eyes fixed on the ground. <You could try to leave without me. I wouldn't mind. You're still worth more anyway.>

<You know I'm never going to leave you.> Studying her, curled up next to the flames, all Zephryn wanted to do was remove the frustration and self-loathing that seemed built into Kesia's heart-flame. It was easy to blame it all on guilt over killing her father, but that action didn't fit with the fair, compassionate dragon she was. Unfortunately, she didn't remember anything about the incident and precious few details from before it. He couldn't fix that. But maybe finding out more information could help.

<What brings that sad smirk to your face, Midnight?> Kesia glanced at him through eyes half-closed in sleep. <Plotting to take over the world?>

Too late. His world had been taken over first, by Garishton Razerclaw and the other three leaders of the Pinnacle who had made his family disappear, one by one over the years. He was left alone at age ten, dreading his own disappearance with quiet certainty. Until he'd met Kesia.

Perhaps she was right about her importance. Keeping him alive had little logic.

<Midnight?>

<Ah, yes. Well, one must always pass the time.> Zephryn flicked the end of his long tail, lightly smacking hers. It was one of the few ways dragons could show affection. Once there had been other ways, but those were forbidden during wartime. Dragons had two forms: scale form as great and mighty beasts, and skin form, which was indistinguishable from humans. Far softer skin, far more vulnerable to attack. Indulging in skin form would lead to a swift death during times of war. Even swifter if the Pinnacle found out.

Still, Zephryn remembered his parents holding him in arms of skin with warm, pulsing blood. His chest tightened, and a deep sense of protection and some other unidentifiable emotion came over him. The vague memory was one he clung to as strongly as Kesia held to her guilt.

<Rest is a far better way to pass the time.> Kesia edged herself closer to him, curling within the half-circle of his body. They should have remained on separate sides of the fire, but Zephryn only curled his tail around hers and rested his head on the ground.

A smokish sigh puffed out of her. <Midnight?>

<Hm, Rose-Wing?>

<Do you wonder if it would be nicer to sleep in skin instead of scales?>

He chuckled in their joined minds. <It would be far less practical. Humans require blankets and pillows and other notions. We would be far more vulnerable.>

<Yes, but perhaps in the future. Somewhere safer than this. I think … I remember it being nice, when I was younger.>

Zephryn shut his eyes. He recalled smooth sheets, the feeling of utter relaxation, and sleep deeper than the shallow resting periods in scale form that renewed the body but left the mind hollow. He remembered his parents retiring to the same room.

<I think it could be enjoyable.>

Kesia shifted even closer to him. <Once we report in and receive orders, that could be our next exploration.>

<When, Rose-Wing? You insist we return to the Pinnacle. Within their boundaries we are forbidden from even being in the same cell overnight.>

Not that he wasn't curious. But battles had to be chosen carefully when her safety was at risk.

<Maybe in the future. Sometime. When we're safe.>

Warmth filled him at her musings. Her optimism emerged at the oddest times.

<Yes. For now, we should be content with what we have.>

Lest in the morning the Pinnacle attempt to take it away from them.

Kesia's stomach roiled, the remains of the mountain grazers she'd hunted for breakfast turning violently in her gut. She swallowed and placed her hand over her belly. It was toned with muscle and as bare as the rest of her skin-covered flesh.

It was the only way one could enter the presence of the Pinnacle leaders. To ensure transparency, they claimed, a dragon must trade its scales for skin and a humanoid form and be able to walk fearlessly into the presence of the great leaders. If the dragon had nothing to fear, then being naked in front of a council of fierce, scaled dragons should arouse no concern at all.

If only she could believe that. Even after ten years of such meetings, Kesia still trembled. Surrendering everything she had before faceless monsters. No, not monsters. These were her people, after all.

She was the monster. She was the criminal.

The gray, smoothed stone chilled her feet as she crept along the corridor. The walls arched into a high ceiling, and ahead of her lay the blackness of the entrance to the Judgement Hall. For thirty minutes Kesia had ascended the incline in the great tower that rose amid the ruins of an old military outpost.

Now, there was only to enter the darkness.

Tiny bumps prickled her skin. She rubbed her arms, trying to make the traitorous sign of fear disappear. Maybe scales were better after all. At the very least, shifting into her half-form, with scales atop her skin, might make her a little warmer.

No. Full, bare skin only.

Hold to your heartflame, Kesia. Zephryn's words echoed in her memory. *Never let them taste your fear. I will wait for your return. No harm will come to you.*

Zephryn never faced the Pinnacle. After the events of the previous day, she thought for sure that there would be a reckoning for him. But that was foolish to even consider. The last prince had never received a summoning. Whatever dealings the Pinnacle leaders had with him were under strict privacy.

Fresh fear tossed her stomach. Kesia pressed her lips together, trying to distract herself with other thoughts. Like the green smoke from the explosion. It had smelled so familiar, calling up the taste of blood and death. And then the ship had gone down, even though Captain Windkeeper was supposed to have a wind Talent—it was in his name. Why hadn't he been able to keep his ship aloft?

They were thoughts she would share with Zephryn after this

meeting. If she survived. Kesia breathed out, centering herself. She had chosen to return. Running away had been tempting, but there were answers in the Pinnacle. For the first time, she had a chance to break through her memory block and find the truth.

Compared to that, what was another naked audience with ferocious dragons?

She stared into the opening, wishing for the night vision of her scale form. But a true dragon warrior would walk into any situation, scales or skin.

Kesia raised her chin and folded her loose brown hair behind her ears. She was a true warrior. She would own her actions and stand judgement for them.

One step into the darkness and then another, her pace measured and sure. As if she saw a brilliant light in front of her.

Keep walking. Just pretend she was as massive and dangerous as they. Keep walking—

"STOP."

She halted, her feet together, arms crossed over her chest. She bowed low, each muscle tight, controlled. Breath faint in the echoing space that surrounded her.

After an unknowable amount of time, light flared from four corners of the room, faint threads of illumination like the day dawning behind the mountains. The voice spoke again from the corner to her right, rich bass tones that wound their way around her heartbeat. "Rise, Kesia Ironfire. We have heard your fleetwing's report. Your actions were unsanctioned and impetuous."

<I hear and know your words.>

When the four Pinnacle leaders convened, they preferred to speak aloud to intimidate the dragon being interrogated. Kesia wasn't sure what annoyed her more: that they stooped to such petty tactics, or that the tactics worked.

The voice continued. "You were disobedient to the orders of this Pinnacle."

Kesia set her teeth, keeping her arms crossed in salute. It would be the flay-room and more scars upon her back. Or perhaps duties in the mines, unearthing the tepstone that shielded rooms from dragon mindspeak and the liquid slatesheen that protected dragon scales in battle. Both were toxic materials in their raw forms and had to be mined in skin form due to the delicacy of the process.

A week of mine work took one year off a dragon's life. As dragons only lived to one hundred years, mine work was a slow death sentence. Other criminals were sentenced to the mines as soon as they reached adulthood and could be most useful.

A heavy certainty stilled the turmoil in her stomach.

"Yet your excursion yielded surprising results." A new voice came from behind her, lighter and with a precision that held each consonant an additional moment. "We are curious about the explosion and this mysterious green smoke that erases Talents. If the rebels use it against our enemies, they may well use it against us, for all governments are their target. If the Congruency acquires this weapon, it could mean the end of our people."

"Indeed," replied a soft alto from a third corner. "But that is another matter. Your actions were unsanctioned and require punishment."

<I understand.>

It would be death after all.

The Pinnacle fell silent. She could sense their private mindspeak flitting around the farthest reaches of the room. Her heart beat loudly in her ears.

What would become of Zephryn? Tactical partners were committed for life unto death. If one fell, the other fell. But she was a criminal, which already set her apart from Zephryn. And he was the prince. The Nightstalkers were among the most powerful dragons. Perhaps he could survive without her.

It would make his life easier. The thought twisted her stomach into the tightest of knots. He'd never complained seriously. But in the end, she was a stone around his neck, dragging him down, just like she dragged down the fleet. She'd killed her father, and nothing could atone for that.

Unbidden, traces of memories snaked out of the depths of her mind. *Trapped in the cave as the monster came closer and closer.*

A monster with her father's eyes, wreathed in green smoke.

She shoved the image away. Maybe there were reasons her past was a mystery.

The deep voice intoned, "Your punishment will be suspension from fleet activities. You will be confined to your cell, save for physical maintenance activities and any summonings before the Pinnacle."

Suspension? But serving the fleet was the only way Kesia could find redemption. If she was prohibited, how would she ever lose the title of criminal?

She swallowed her questions. She was lucky to be alive. No, more than lucky. She should have been sentenced to death or to the mines. She was valuable to the Pinnacle. Somehow.

<What of my tactical partnership with Zephryn Nighstalker?>

"That, too, will be reevaluated. If he cannot be trusted to obey rules for your sake, then you may be reassigned to another who is more compliant with our laws. We will keep you both under strict observation."

Her legs turned to soft sand, and Kesia fought to remain standing. They would try to separate her and Zephryn?

It would be better for him. He would no longer be burdened with her.

Or perhaps it wouldn't even happen. Perhaps, if she was obedient enough, the Pinnacle would change their minds.

But they never did. And Kesia had no interest in obeying them any more than necessary. Her instincts had been confirmed. The Pinnacle wouldn't kill her. Harm her, yes, but not kill her. She needed to know why.

"Do you hear our words?"

She nodded, the movement slow and unnatural with the short neck of her human form. <I hear and know your words. They will be my path.>

"Good." The light voice enunciated the 'd' like gunfire from a human airship. "You are dismissed."

CHAPTER FOUR

HIGH COMMAND MEETINGS needed more beverages. Specifically the alcoholic kind, with generous portions and no ice to sully the contents. Shance had felt this many times before, but never so much as now, standing in front of his fellow captains and two Congruency generals while claiming he had been rescued by a dragon.

The whole situation would have gone smoothly if everyone had their minds relaxed and opened with a few pints. As it stood, he almost would have rather been falling toward the ground and certain death than deal with the scrutiny and glares.

Almost. The ground was hard, after all, and the ride on that dragon's back had been quite a thrill. Or was it her shoulders?

Her voice had been so beautiful.

"Captain Windkeeper! Are you listening?"

He blinked and sat up in the leather chair at the end of the long, polished table. "Yes. I am hearing every word."

General Markem raised his eyebrows behind the small, round spectacles perching on his nose. "See that you do. This is serious business. Grand Count Nul financed the majority of that vessel's production as a sign of good faith in the war effort. Your failure to protect *The Silver Streak* from harm is worse than careless."

"Sir, it was a routine sail of celebration that had been approved by port command." Shance leaned forward on the table, meeting the general's gaze head-on. "Its destruction was sabotage, pure and simple."

"So you say."

Next to Markem, General Brody cleared his throat. "The reports from the other surviving crew confirm Captain Windkeeper's statements. His liability in this situation is not under question, General Markem."

"Thank you, sir." A good man, Brody. Also a good card player, something that probably went a long way to explain the understanding twinkle in his green eyes. Unlike Markem, whose pasty skin hadn't seen shipboard sunlight in decades, Brody's face and hands were still leathery-brown from frequent trips to the sky—and trips on the water as well. A true sailor worth listening to.

Then Brody's expression hardened, his wrinkles drawn tight against his cheeks. "Still, that doesn't explain the sudden loss of your Talent or the appearance of the dragon. I agree with General Markem that both are highly disturbing."

"Trust me, I'm just as concerned as you are." Shance made a flicking motion with his hand, sending a stylus on the table flying toward his fingers with a gust of wind. He held out the writing tool. "As you see, my power has returned, fully intact. My guess is that its disappearance had something to do with the effects of the bomb."

Markem grunted. "Ah yes, the mysterious green smoke."

One of the captains, a sturdy middle-aged woman with a square face whose name he couldn't remember, cleared her throat. "We have reports in other Scepters of this smoke, as well as reports of large dead zones in the plains between them. All say that this smoke eradicates usage of Talents around it for a period of time."

"Dragon work?" Brody asked.

"They've never shown this capability before. Chemicals aren't their trademark." She shrugged, the action doing nothing for her small chest. That, and the ashen hair she kept tightly bound from her face, jogged Shance's memory.

Captain Annabel Tegan. Recently assigned to the Scepter of Commerce after her airship had crash-landed on its first attack in dragon airspace. No survivors except her, and no sign of the ship. Rumor was she'd been grounded for life. Her assignment as Markem's personal aide and liaison to the local police brigades was a formality. She'd kept quiet about her Talent, but it certainly hadn't helped her face down dragons or spare one life from her ship.

Markem nodded. "The dragons have shown great cunning. A weapon like this could be in their grasp."

"Yes, but it's dangerous." All eyes turned to Shance again. He continued. "Smoke blows in the wind. Dragons use the wind. Using that kind of weapon would risk dead zones in their own air space—and they rely on their Talents as much as we do."

Sour looks twisted the faces of many officers in the conference room. Ah yes, another slip-up, daring to suggest that dragons had anything in common with humans. It was much easier to kill them if they were simply big flying reptiles who liked setting things and people on fire.

Shance had taken down his share of the beasts. But he also remembered family stories of dragons taking human forms and walking on Windkeeper airships as friends. That friendship was a reason open-air ships were a trademark of Windkeeper vessels—and why, for the sake of tradition, Shance had insisted on an open-air deck instead of an enclosed model.

As it turned out, a dragon had saved his life. Maybe the old luck still held.

"It could also be the Lawless." That was Captain Cryor, a fresh-faced kid of nineteen rumored to be here because his Talent for memorization allowed him to pull out any historical battle strategy at a moment's notice. "In the Battle of Sunward Hills, between the southern tribes of Kowfin and Mittrin, rebels sabotaged both sides of the skirmish and set the enemies against each other in weakened states, and then finished off what was left. Only two units survived on one side and none on the other. The Lawless could be trying the same tactic."

"Also a possibility," Brody allowed.

"In any case, we must be extra vigilant." Markem coughed and adjusted his dark red command hat, the kind with the peaked brim that Shance would never be caught wearing unless forced to do so, and had conveniently forgotten for this meeting. "Captain Tegan, double the security around the dignitary quarters and public locations."

"Aye, sir." Tegan fisted her hand and touched her mouth with the bent fingers.

"Cryor, you and Heflersin patrol the Low Quarter for any sign of rebel activity or this mysterious smoke."

They both made the same salute as Tegan. "Aye, sir."

"Captain Windkeeper, these are your orders." Markem released the full force of his glare, looking rather like a wrinkled, peeled potato. "You will remain portside until *The Silver Streak* has been repaired. Consider yourself and your crew on furlough until further notice."

Surprise jolted Shance to his feet and forced a sudden blast of air into the room. "Sir, considering my abilities, this is—"

"These are your orders, Captain. Your crew need to recuperate from their experiences, and you need to allow the shipbuilders time to do their work. Do I make myself clear?"

Shance opened his mouth to speak, but Brody caught his eye. A tiny smile that twitched the general's lips hinted at another plan, one that Markem maybe didn't know about. Relief washed over Shance. At least one of his superiors wouldn't waste him on furlough.

The breeze died down, and Shance sat slowly in his seat, schooling his face to something close to respect and giving a salute. "Aye. Sir."

"Good." Markem stood, brushing off the dark red sleeves of his fitted dress coat. "You are dismissed."

Shance waited for the last of the other officers to leave the room before making his exit down the hallway. It was made of sculpted claymesh, like all buildings in this part of the land, and the cream-colored stone was inlaid with elaborate mosaics depicting various historical events, most of them economic treaties or significant business leaders. The entire city was ruled by an elected council chosen from the shrewdest business leaders and entrepreneurs. A Windkeeper had even served a few terms in the past, or so the story went.

Of course, all of that was changed in wartime. Now, the High Command had their own seat at the council table, and their word was law.

Shance shrugged his shoulders, trying to escape the feeling of being trapped. He didn't belong here. He belonged in the open sky, with the wind whispering in his ears and coming at his call with a great burst of power. Even when he managed to escape the lacquered prison of the Central Market and step into the late afternoon sunlight, towering buildings crowded him, forcing the airflow into unhappy tunnels along the paved streets. That the winds carried the taste of the Trebbian Seas was only a partial relief, because they also carried exhaust from the smooth-topped cars that crowded the streets. Blaring car horns rang in his ears, along with the din of licensed street-sellers that lined every corner.

Not as beautiful as the Scepter of Pleasure and lacking the vibrant creative energy of the Scepter of Knowledge. The Scepter of Commerce was more tolerable than the smoke-clogged Scepter of Industry, but if Shance were at the Scepter of Industry, his ship could have been repaired in half the time.

There was one perk to the Scepter of Commerce: almost anything was legally for sale, including drinks at all hours of the day and night.

He set off for a tavern down the street with some of the finest brew on this side of the Cloudpeaks.

"Could you use some company?"

Someone nudged him from behind. The voice was male. Not interesting.

"Not right now, thanks. Already got some." Shance turned away from the speaker for a moment in favor of the bright-faced young woman in his lap. Wylie wore trousers, like most people of the Scepter of Commerce and the surrounding villages, but hers hung low on her hips, and her tight tunic revealed a generous amount of sun-toned midriff and torso that felt very nice beneath his fingers.

He had every intention of investigating further. After all, he was on furlough, which was paid leave. Might as well make the most of the situation. Wylie's attentions were very welcome—and possibly, could lead to love. Certainly the feelings in his chest equaled something like that. Considering he could die in battle on any duty assignment, it would have to be enough.

Shance traced a finger just below Wylie's chest, along the hem of her tunic. "So, my dear, you were saying your Talent is skillful fingers?"

"Well, I suppose." She tossed her short, bleached chestnut hair and giggled, her lips quivering. "I'm good at strumming things and figuring out instruments. My fingertips are very sensitive to the needs of whatever I'm playing."

He flashed her a smile. "I'm sure they are. I would love to hear you play and admire your skills further. How are you not more famous?"

"Oh, the Music Quarter hires what sells." She leaned close to whisper in his ear. "But I always play from my passion."

Heat flared in Shance's body. He pulled her closer, burying his face in her neck and trailing kisses up to those incredible lips as she giggled and gasped.

A hand grabbed his shoulder. "Not this one, I'm afraid. He has a record."

"A what?" Wylie raised her eyebrows, uncertainty replacing her eagerness.

"I have nothing of the sort." Shance tilted his head back to take in the person behind him, his pleasure turning to anger. "Who are you—"

His voice trailed off as General Brody folded his arms. Even in civilian clothes, upside down, and softened by three pints of local beer, he was a formidable figure. Enough to quench the fire in Shance's loins like a bucket of ice.

Brody raised an eyebrow at Shance. "Captain Windkeeper. I believe we had a meeting."

The conference meeting. The hint.

"Yeah, what took you so long? Ah, I mean, yes, sir." Shance gave a quick salute and turned to Wylie, who had slipped off his lap and signaled for another drink. He gave her a knowing smile, grabbed her hands, and pulled her close, aided by a breeze from the open window of the small tavern. "Where are you performing next, lovely one? I must get a closer look at your skill."

She pressed her finger to his lips and trailed it down his chin, playing with the open buttons of the collar of his shirt. "Come and find me, sky-man, and you'll get all you need."

Shance watched Wylie turn and leave, her hips swaying beneath the trousers. He always remembered the women he'd bedded, at least for a little while. But they seldom remembered him. The captain insignia and charm were enough for ladies, never mind his desire for more. Who would take the risk of a relationship in wartime, especially with someone frequently sent into battle?

So Shance filled the hollow in his heart with something else. Like more alcohol. That usually worked.

"Captain." General Brody's tone cut through his hazy thoughts. "This way."

Another shot of cold, although this time, Shance would either need an actual shower or a tumble with Wylie to fully clear his mind. Even so, he automatically pushed back his chair and followed the general across the dimly lit room, around small tables crowded with card games, seashell turns, and other forms of gambling. True to form, Brody had opted for a booth tucked near the open window at the front, a square of sunlight hitting the worn wooden table. An airman never liked being shut up in the dark.

Brody sat down on the bench, leaned back, and took a slow swig from his stein. "Are you sober, Captain?"

"Enough." Shance leaned forward. Worry flickered in the other man's eyes as he glanced around the room. The loud room filled with people. "Do you want privacy?"

"Affirmative."

"Done." Shance made a flicking motion with his index finger, calling the breezes to his will. A moment later, they were enveloped in a gentle tunnel of wind that would prevent their conversation from being heard by anyone outside the booth.

The general nodded shortly. "I'll make this brief: your services are needed in the fleet."

"I already serve the Congruency with my life." Not that he had a choice. Conscription of those Talented with useful abilities was standard. "What else could I give?"

Brody smiled sourly, tugging at his collar. "Your freedom."

"Sir?"

"Grand Count Nul Thredsing has no male heir. Are you aware of that?"

Shance shrugged, rubbing his fingers in circles on the table. "No, but what does that matter? Women can inherit wealth and property in the Scepter of Commerce."

"Indeed. He strongly favors his daughter, Countess Nula. She is exceptionally Talented in ways that suit this city, and I believe he would give her anything she asked for. As it turns out—" Brody paused for another swig. Either the brew was exceptionally horrible, or this was the worst news since the loss at Edgefell Peaks. "—she wants you."

Shance stopped tracing circles on the table. For a moment, the wind tunnel ceased. Shance snapped his fingers absently to restart it. Then he asked, "Wants me as what?"

"This is in the strictest confidence, Captain Windkeeper. It is a very delicate arrangement for our fleet. The Grand Count is a key player in numerous aspects of politics, including the Curious Intrigue, and has been a generous supporter of the war effort. Unlike others in this money-grubbing city, he donates his funds instead of offering a loan with a high interest rate. He's a shrewd businessman in his own right and can afford to give money for good publicity. His only weakness is the happiness of his daughter. And she wants you."

Anger surged through Shance. This couldn't be happening. He slammed his palms on the table. "Sir, are you suggesting I bed this woman for the good of the fleet?"

"No. I am strongly urging you to marry her."

CHAPTER FIVE

ZEPHRYN'S BARE CHEST GLISTENED in the lamplit cavern, the residual gleam from his recent slatesheen application. Slatesheen enabled dragons in scale form to deflect nearly any projectile. In skin form, it shielded against some types of gunfire and resisted blades and other forms of torture.

For all that, the skin remained natural, enabling dragons to blend in with humans while bearing nearly undetectable shields—once the dose had absorbed. Until then, it was difficult to miss, setting off every inch of her fleetwing's smoothly muscled form, turning him polished bronze.

He was equally muscled beneath the fitted exercise pants and boots. Heat rose in Kesia's throat.

Zephryn met her eyes across the practice room. <Is something wrong, Rose-Wing?>

The heat in her throat spread to her cheeks. She gripped her short swords. <Oh! No, just carried away by a thought. It's nothing.>

<Good.> He flicked his longsword to the door carved out of the cavern wall, guarded by six dragons in skin form. Typical for Kesia and Zephryn's training sessions in the small cave. The reason

there were only six was that the floor of the cavern abruptly dropped off into a steep cliff on three sides. Get too close to the edge, and you fell. Not as frightening for dragons, who could shift into flight. But shifting without permission meant the end of the session. <Six guards today.>

Kesia smirked, trying to feel braver than her fluttering heartbeat. She could take out three, and Zephryn could take out three. <Observant as always, Midnight. You should receive an award.>

Their words could be heard by all six guards. Which meant trying to set them at ease with the usual banter and mocking of sparring matches, all the while choreographing their actions to have a far different outcome.

A brief meeting the night before had established the plan. But it had been *too* brief. Fear gnawed Kesia's gut as she thought of the ways they could fail. But she had returned to find answers. Zephryn insisted she make good. All they had to do was distract the guards, take them out, and then search for answers.

Get answers. Then escape.

<Wait until I take you to the ground, Rose-Wing.> His eyes swept over her form once, then lingered a second time with a steady, penetrating gaze and a faint smile that sped her heartbeat further. Kesia had also been coated with slatesheen and wore the same outfit he did, with a broad band of fabric that tightly secured her breasts. <Although, with your lips parted so, perhaps I should strike your face.>

She shut her mouth with a click and swallowed. <Not if I strike first.>

<We shall see.> Zephryn lunged forward, his sword swiping at her exposed skin.

Kesia blocked the weapon off to the side and danced a few steps back, making a few parrying defenses. Foolishness. She was letting herself be taken in by the appeal of this flesh. They were dragons. They didn't need flesh, except between their teeth. An oddly appealing thought where Zephryn was concerned.

He lunged forward again with another series of precise attacks that hemmed her in one way, then the other, meeting her blades at every angle. Kesia ducked into a crouch and rolled to the side, then jumped to her feet, blades up.

Irritation flowed through their mental link. Zephryn grimaced. <Impressive. Do you forget who you are, Kesia?>

Forget herself? He rarely reminded her of her criminal status.

Then, she remembered. She was supposed to fail in sparring. Fail badly and quickly in the fight, feigning enough injury to make the guards concerned. It had been her idea. Since, for some reason, the Pinnacle valued her, any potential damage to her would gain more attention.

Which meant Kesia had to stop trying to win, without looking like it. She breathed out a puff of smoke. Apparently, foolishness was one of her defining traits.

She snarled. <How could I, when you continue to remind me?>

One wild swing at Zephryn's neck, spinning around in a circle, strands of hair flying in her face. She stopped, blades at ready, just in time to block another lunge. Or try to. This time, instead of bringing her full momentum to bear with both short swords, she only raised one, withholding her full strength.

Allowing Zephryn's sword access to her side. He slashed at her skin, sending a streak of pain into her torso. Plenty to fuel her for another attack.

Only, she wouldn't be attacking anymore. Kesia gritted her teeth.

She fell to the hard stone, resisting the urge to break her fall but making sure her short swords fell conveniently near her body. Her head thudded against the ground, and her eyes shut. The smell of fire and ash flooded her nostrils as Zephryn stood over her, his blade at her throat.

<Yield.>

She silenced her thoughts, making them as still as her body.

Footsteps echoed toward her.

<Stand down, both of you!> One of the guards. Kesia didn't recognize which one by voice alone. It didn't matter. If it came down to it, she and Zephryn would have to kill all six.

Zephryn's voice seethed with anger. <She lives.>

<She doesn't move.>

A hand grabbed her wrist, checking for a pulse.

<She lives.> He dropped her wrist.

Kesia focused on the heat signatures of the guards. One was behind her as she lay curled up on her side. Two others stood on either side of Zephryn. Which meant three still guarded the exit.

Impatience burned in her veins. The situation wasn't ideal for their plan.

But it was good enough.

She twitched her smallest finger. The go-ahead signal.

<She will.>

Zephryn's confirmation.

She rolled to the side, smashing into the legs of the guard at her back. He cried out as he fell forward over her. Kesia finished her roll and leaped to her feet. The whistle of air by her ear foretold another attack. She ducked to avoid the blade and whirled around. The guards from the door had joined the fight. Kesia backed up, hoping Zephryn had cleared out the other two attackers. She grabbed one of her short swords off the ground and waved it in wild arcs, trying to keep her trio of attackers at bay.

The guards fell back, forming a line and blocking her path to the door. The one nearest to her spoke. <Kesia Ironfire. Stand down now, and you will only be removed from the training session instead of facing punishment.>

She ignored them. There were still too many to take on alone, especially since she and Zephryn had lost the advantage of surprise.

Kesia huffed, tightening her grip on her weapons. <Are you ready to end this, Midnight?>

<Entirely ready, Rose-Wing. Let's show them just how worthy we are together.> His words held undertones of wry humor and a dismissive attitude.

A smile tugged at her lips. <Join minds?>

She still wished she could touch his skin, just once.

<Agreed. Join minds.>

Even as Kesia continued to retreat across the floor, she reached out through their link and sought Zephryn's heartflame, the potent essence of his heart, mind, and spirit that was available to her alone. The maze of his strategic and calculating thoughts descended over hers, and her strong sense of creativity and outward focus gave shape to his drive.

Together, they were nearly unstoppable.

<Move.>

Kesia knew not who gave the order. It didn't matter. *They* reacted. Back to back, plying their weapons with breathless speed. Then side by side, blocking sword strokes and calling out commands.

Cold wind chilled her despite the warming effects of battle. Kesia stiffened. They were perilously close to the edge of the cliff. The alarm jolted her, separating the union of their bond.

Zephryn opened another secure mental link. <What thoughts, Rose-Wing?>

Her thoughts raced. <Manifest wings and fly over them.>

Manifesting wings required a half-shift between skin and scale forms. It wasn't dangerous, but it was certainly forbidden. Yet this entire scheme was forbidden. What did they have to lose?

She felt Zephryn's concern. <Is the ceiling high enough?>

<It will have to be. Unless you have other ideas?>

<...we'll do it.>

Kesia felt him tense, energy rushing to his back, anticipating the shift into wings. Complex plans and movements filled their minds as they again joined to plan the attack. It should work. But even that couldn't fill the pit in her stomach.

The three remaining dragons were nearly upon them. <Very well.>

<Step. NOW.>

Kesia was off the cliff, wind singing around her for a moment. Then her large, deep red wings pushed out from her back, catching her mid-air and propelling her up with smooth, swift strokes. Scales covered her skin in variegated patterns. She sailed over the dragons, low enough to aim kicks at their heads and necks.

Elation filled Kesia. She and Zephryn zipped around the dragons on the ground, attacking quickly and relentlessly to keep them from manifesting their own wings and taking the pursuit to the air.

At last, only one straggler remained upright.

<We did it!> Kesia blew out a stream of fire. "We did it!"

A bolt of fear arced through her, as intense as it was sudden. Not hers. Zephryn's. She turned to see dread in his eyes as the remaining guard pulled out a pistol.

He aimed it at Kesia.

An explosion echoed through the cavern.

Searing pain arced through her right wing. Kesia retracted it, spiralling to the ground in a haphazard circle, her ears ringing and mind filled with fog. Her head slammed into a rock, and blackness coated her vision.

The last thing she saw was her right wing, limp beside her, with a Pinnacle-made barb-hook shoved through the delicate inner scales.

Then darkness silenced the pain.

He wanted to kill them all.

Zephryn paced the length of the small room. It was little more than a rectangular box with rough-hewn corners and a cot in the center, where Kesia lay on her stomach, eyes closed in sleep. From her back sprang her wings, the hole made by the barb-hook coated with healing scale-screen.

It would heal in a few days, the caregivers assured him, but she wouldn't be able to shift for at least a week.

Fewmets to the Pinnacle! Fewmets to this whole situation. He and Kesia should have left after Kesia rescued the airship captain. Why had he let her ideas about finding answers in the Pinnacle sway him? She was clever, but she sometimes had the brains of a mountain grazer when it came to her own safety.

The Pinnacle could also be blamed for that, in part. They certainly didn't treat her as invaluable, except for choosing not to kill her. She had invisible scars from the flay-room, the evidence sealed over with the same scale-screen that was healing her wing.

But some of this dangerous absurdity was Kesia's own invention, her own stubborn insistence on trying to improvise solutions when following a clear plan would be far better.

Yet, Zephryn couldn't imagine life without her.

He strode to her side, sitting on the stool next to the head of the cot. At least the medicine they'd given her had removed the pain. A lock of hair had fallen over her face. Zephryn stroked the strands back behind her ear. Such fine, silky brown strands, threaded with red.

His fingers hovered over her face. Kesia was in her half-shifted form, rose-red scales patterning her forehead and cheekbones, the bare shoulders visible above the sheet, and presumably the rest of her body. Not that he'd ever seen it.

Zephryn gently stroked the scales behind her ears. Smooth, warm scales. She sighed and leaned into his touch, her contentment radiating through the fleetwing bond. Everything in him desired to slip into bed next to her and hold her close.

That, too, was forbidden. Right now, they had broken enough rules.

"Physical contact in skin form?" A new voice resonated. Zephryn stiffened as footsteps echoed behind him. The voice continued. "Now, Nightstalker, you know better. Even if you're above our leash, she certainly is not. I would have thought the consequences of your illegal maneuvers would have taught you that, but it appears I was wrong."

"You are wrong. Wrong about everything. She isn't yours to punish."

He stood and turned to face Highlord Garishton Razorclaw. The Pinnacle leader had taken skin form and wore a robe glimmering with green and gold dragon scales—those of the fallen as a memorial to their sacrifice. Or so the Pinnacle leadership claimed. In truth, the scale cloak was a subtle threat to the living; cross the Pinnacle and they would wear your pelt as well.

"That is not yours to decide, Zephryn Nightstalker. She is a criminal, and you both owe your allegiance to the Pinnacle."

Razorclaw's voice thickened with command, using his voice Talent to force obedience from others. His lined face wrinkled further with disdain, and his eyes flashed.

Zephryn stared back at him, ignoring the tugs on his will. Did Garishton really think that he could twist the mind of an heir? "You are the last person who should talk of allegiance, Razorclaw. She is the only reason I remain, yet still you choose to treat her poorly."

The highlord flashed sharp teeth. "Bold words for a boy whose careless actions caused his own fleetwing such pain."

"No. Your punishments against her did."

"She is a convict. She escaped from custody. Would you have her given more clemency? She must earn it, like all the others."

Zephryn's blood raced, and claws slid from his fingers. "I spoke with the caregivers. She cannot fly. She cannot even shift except to hide her wings, and only under great pain. Her abilities are what make her an asset to the Pinnacle, and you would squander them?"

Razorclaw's eyes flashed to slitted dragon pupils. "She is a convict. Do not forget that, Nightstalker, and outlast my patience. I know you broke her out of her cell and encouraged her foolish mission."

"Foolish? It yielded valuable intelligence." Zephryn's throat grew warm. "Or was that another lie? Was the explosion on the airship an attack by the Pinnacle after all? I never thought you would stoop to chemicals, but then, I shouldn't be surprised by anything you do."

"And yet, you still test me. As your parents did." Razorclaw breathed out smoke. "You are closer to their fate than you think. I thought your genes would be valuable to breed with hers, but this latest insolence is proving otherwise."

The statement chilled Zephryn's anger. Who else could they breed with Kesia? Fleetwings were partnered precisely because of ideal genetic compatibility, a compatibility detectable upon first meeting through their heartflames. Now that they were of maturation, the time had come.

Not that he looked forward to it. Rumor had it that the process wasn't enjoyable, especially when it had to occur in a large cavern in dragon form before a host of monitoring scientists. All to ensure optimal insemination, as if they truly were animals.

Razorclaw still stood there. Why was he here? Kesia was not his.

Zephryn stepped toward him. "You should leave now."

"And allow you a few last moments with the criminal?" The highlord spared him a withering glance. "Such a waste. Such valuable skills in a fragile shell. I only hope she produces good stock with her breeding partner. Who will not be you."

"We're bound. We're only compatible with each other."

"Not if the heartflame bond is broken. She could find another."

Zephryn swallowed. "You fool. That would kill both of us. You would lose both of our skills."

Razorclaw sniffed. "Well, at least it will kill you. A fortunate benefit."

He swept out of the room. Zephryn's mouth burned and his veins were a fury of fire. It took every ounce of his strength not to follow and exact vengeance.

But that wouldn't help Kesia. There was only one choice: flee and avoid all contact with humans and dragons. Kesia had expressed concern, but considering their Talents, slipping into obscurity wouldn't be that difficult.

What of your kingdom, Midnight? Kesia's optimism haunted him even when she was unconscious.

Her arguments were based on the belief that people still wanted to support the old kingdom. A kingdom whose name Zephryn couldn't even remember anymore. Then again, between the dragon Pinnacle, the human Congruency, and the bloodthirsty anarchists, it seemed no one remembered the old kingdom. Not enough to try and resurrect it.

Pinnacle deserters were killed on sight, but how was that any worse than lingering here and watching them attack his fleetwing behind the guise of enforcing their rules? Could he watch her be taken from him?

No. They would have to flee as soon as possible, which meant before Kesia was healed.

"Fewmets!"

Kesia flinched on the cot, silencing any further curses. Zephryn rushed to her side, but her eyelids hadn't opened. A single line wrinkled her forehead, and her hands clutched the blankets on either side of her. <Zephryn? What's wrong?>

<Many things, Rose-Wing.> Zephryn took a deep breath and released it slowly, descending into the chair. He closed his eyes, imagining the coldest snow and ice upon every part of his body, forcing his anger and frustration to a place where it wouldn't upset her vulnerable internal state. He drew a mental shield around their mindspeak to give them privacy for a few minutes. Shields would alert the caregivers, but with Kesia so disabled, they would assume

no further trouble could happen.

They didn't know his fleetwing.

<Tell me what happened.>

How many more dragons would suffer in this war? How could he consider leaving them entirely at the mercy of the Pinnacle?

One target at a time. That's what Kesia always told him when he projected too far into the future.

He sighed. <We need to leave. Now.>

<Why?>

<They're going to separate us.>

<I knew it.> She stayed very still on the cot, but he felt her worry through the fleetwing bond. <Zephryn, what about your kingdom?>

<We can deal with that later.>

<But if we could have just discovered the Pinnacle's plans, maybe we could have—>

<We didn't!>

<I know.> She didn't flinch that time, but her fingers gripped the edges of the cot. Zephryn sighed. <You're in danger. That's what matters. We can deal with the situation

of my kingdom and any possibilities therein later.>

He felt her stubbornness rise, then abate, her grip on the cot loosening. <Very well. I want to go to the Scepter of Commerce.>

<Why there? It will be filled with military officers. Besides, I suspect the Pinnacle might have had a part in the attack.>

He began stroking the scales on her forehead again. It seemed to make the entire situation easier.

<The Pinnacle denied it.>

<They deny a lot of things. But other than your audience, they have betrayed no outrage and demanded no further inquiry.>

She frowned. <I was on the ship, Zephryn. Something didn't feel right. It erupted from the inside. I can't imagine how the Pinnacle could have gotten any chemical bombs in there. I want to investigate. The ship came from the Scepter of Commerce, so the sabotage may have come from there.>

<Why is this important to you?>

Kesia breathed out slowly. <As I said before: something about it reminded me of when I was a child, when I killed—I want those answers. I need them. We couldn't get them here, so I need to find them somewhere else.>

Something in her quiet stubbornness stirred him. Despite her teasing, Kesia was rarely so assertive.

<Very well.> Zephryn moved on to the next task. <I know you shouldn't shift, but can you? It would make things far easier.>

<Yes. I won't cry out.>

He brushed her hair one last time, savoring the silkiness. <I know, Rose-Wing. We only have one chance at this. On my mark.>

Kesia reached out and grabbed his arm, squeezing it tightly, her skin warm on his. So strong, even in this state. Even when she shouldn't have to be.

<Mark.>

She gritted her teeth. Her wings collapsed, bones pushing against cartilage until they were doubled over behind her. But what should have been easy and painless took endless seconds.

Minutes.

A slick of blood coated her scales. There were only fragments and bits left of her wings, pressing hard against her back as she forced them to shift. Sweat beaded her brow. Her fingers sank into his arm, sending throbbing arcs of pain through his veins. Zephryn pushed the pain away.

<A little more, Kesia. A little more.>

She nodded, releasing a short breath.

The final bit of bone smashed into her flesh and vanished. Instead of wings, Kesia's back was swathed with blood stains, and she bore deep bruises and scars from the shift.

She released his arm. Zephryn's shoulders slumped, and he rubbed feeling back into the limb.

<All right, Zephryn. Let's go.>

His muscles tightened once more.

She truly was his equal. The ideal tactical partner.

By life or by death.

CHAPTER SIX

"IS THIS A HOUSE OR A PRISON?" Shance muttered to himself. Not quietly enough, from the look the butler gave him. He returned the stiff man's scowl with an apologetic smile and took another look around Grand Count Nul Thredsing's mansion.

The front hall was constructed with the same claymesh found in the rest of the Scepter of Commerce, with glittering shards of mirror and silver forming orderly mosaic patterns in the walls. Both sides of the hall were lined with square pillars painted pale gray and studded with silver and steel, both rare commodities this far south. The three-story pillars emphasized the wealth of the Nul lineage, as did the steel railings that fenced the second and third floors. Even the windows were barred with embossed steel.

The whole effect made his skin crawl and his chest constrict. No airflow was possible here—this box employed the finest industrial cooling technology instead of breezeways. It took everything Shance had not to run out of the house and camp in *The Silver Streak* throughout its repairs. Although, even his damaged airship was in the underground shipyard.

There was no escape.

He took out the small flask Brody had given to him at the end of their meeting. Something to take the edge off, he'd said, promising to send a full bottle to Shance's room.

Good man, Brody, even when delivering piss-poor news. Shance took a swig from the flask. It burned his throat as if he'd swallowed engine fuel.

"Captain Shance Windkeeper." The velvet-voiced figure stood at the far end of the hall at the top of a metal-edged staircase. "We finally meet. I'm glad to see you're willing to hear my proposal."

She was powerfully female. Her skin was a rich umber, accented by the deep gray-blue of her fitted pants and corseted coat that cinched her breasts up and framed them with the low neckline of her cream blouse. Silver jewelry gleamed in her ears and pierced the bridge of her elegant nose. Long, tiny black braids were tied neatly away from her strong-boned face, and pale gray eyes appraised him openly.

So this was what it felt like to be surveyed like product on the merchant dock. Shance didn't like it one bit. Even so, he opted not to step forward and chose instead to put the flask back into his waistcoat. He didn't want to venture farther into this elaborate jail cell.

"Countess Nula Thredsing. I was expecting—"

"My father?" She lifted her chin. "This venture is entirely my own, Captain Windkeeper. And I am considerably interested in what role you can play in it."

"Oh?"

The heels of her slim black boots clicked on the stairs as she descended. She never took her eyes from him, her full lips slightly parted, almost as if she was tasting him. In other situations, that might have been highly enticing.

But not when marriage was on the line, marriage to a woman

who held no interest in his heart.

"You like playing games, I've heard." Nula began to slowly circle him. "And you are one of the best captains in the Congruency war fleet."

Irritation smothered his wariness. "*The* best captain. The skies are my home."

"Indeed. A reason that you persist in keeping an open-air deck, despite its antiquated and potentially dangerous nature."

The annoyance heated his skin. Was she trying to bait him? "I need to feel the winds to use them. That is far more important and powerful than any modern technology."

"Hmmm. And your crew? What of their lives?"

"My crew trusts me with their lives. I haven't lost anyone yet. Even in the explosion, everyone made it to the parachute boats."

Nula had completed her circle and stepped close, her face inches from his. Her voice became even softer. "Admirable. It is for all these reasons and more that I requested you as my consort. You follow your own path and make your own way, Captain Windkeeper. I like that. Such strength is quite impressive. And with my influence, you would have no trouble reestablishing your family's mercantile ways after the war is over. I believe we would suit each other well."

By the time her last words reached his ear, the countess's tone had dropped to a whisper, sending pleasant rushes through his body despite the abhorrence of her words. Fiarston, she'd be attractive if she weren't the daughter of a money-hungry businessman trying to steal his freedom and coerce him into selling the family name.

"Tempting, Countess Nula. But part of the honor and pride of the Windkeeper line is our separation from cartels and industries. We offer fair prices to all, we chart our own courses, and we never sell out to large corporate interests, even those as well-built as your own."

"Hm. I see." She lingered. Gods, if her lips only moved a little closer—no. That would not happen. "Is there any way I can convince you?"

Shance finally stepped backward, putting distance between them. Pride be damned; he wouldn't last another minute if she kept up that game. "I can't think of a single one. Your father already donated to fix *The Silver Streak* within a month."

"I could make it two weeks."

"So I can return to the front lines? Wonderful. Thank you." Too much sarcasm and honesty. He switched topics, grasping for anything to keep her at bay. "In addition, I am already engaged."

What? Where had that come from?

Nula scrutinized him for a moment, then her rich laughter filled the vast expanse of the room. "I highly doubt that, Captain Windkeeper. You are not subtle, and information sells very well in this city."

There was no turning back now.

"Yes, but this is a very recent development and a far more advantageous offer. An ideal arrangement and an opportunity that I cannot possibly pass up."

Her face hardened and her gray eyes glittered like the silver adorning the pillars. "Please, do share the name of this individual, for I cannot think of a single woman who offers more worth than I."

Thoughts and faces spun through Shance's mind as he remembered and discarded a host of women, none of whom would fit his description. Blind Viorstan! He would follow this course regardless and hope things sorted out later. "She is rather shy but has intriguing connections. I will introduce her to society soon."

"Intriguing, hm? I enjoy a curious intrigue myself. I didn't realize you had become so connected." Nula sniffed. "You will introduce her at the Congruency gala that opens next week?"

A week? Maybe he could pay Wylie.

Shance nodded. "Yes. She will be overjoyed to finally declare our undying devotion. I look forward to introducing you to her. Until then, Countess Nula."

He spun on his heel and strode to the door. His pace increased as he reached the threshold until he was running, pushing past the mid-morning rush that filled the sidewalks, following the only thing that made sense in his life right now.

The wind was swirling, tugging Shance toward the sea and open air. Away from the disastrous meeting with a disturbingly attractive woman.

Engaged? Where in all the lands would he find a woman to be engaged to? In the Scepter of Commerce, one could pay someone for nearly any kind of service, but that wouldn't hold. The countess would know the truth in a heartbeat and expose him.

He needed a real answer to this situation. To all the situations. Gods above! In case anyone was listening, Shance sent out a plea for escape. Escape from the endless war and bloodshed. From the confines of a military uniform and a regimented schedule that allowed for little freedom and less compassion.

Fatigue burned Shance's lungs. He finally slowed his pace near the waterfront. A half-dozen ships were still docked, mostly ferries carrying people from one Trebbian Sea to another. Ilyon, the sea in front of him, was the busiest, as it received tributaries from the north. Daily cargo ships arrived bearing produce and product from the northern farmlands, as well as visitors coming to see the great Scepter of Commerce with a few coins in their pockets.

Most of them would go home much poorer.

Shance fell into a stroll, giving the ships a cursory glance. Something in the wind urged him to the ship anchored at the pier farthest from the city.

There. He should go *there*.

"Why?"

Another gust of wind pushed at his back. Never question the winds, his father had always said. Only prepare yourself for the flight.

Considering the morning Shance had endured, this urging could only improve matters.

Somehow.

The ship was a cage.

Kesia didn't voice the words or speak them loud enough within her mind for Zephryn to hear. He had been pacing the length and breadth of the vessel during their entire voyage.

Now he paced down one end of the open deck and back to the other, pushing through the other passengers on the ship. Meanwhile she stood still and tried to pretend that she wasn't trapped in skin form on a rocking vessel that she did not control.

In the end, she couldn't really complain. Neither of them could. They had made it this far.

After escaping from the Pinnacle, she'd woken up in an isolated cave with Zephryn reapplying a bandage to her wounds. Later she had ridden astride his back, around the shoulder blades. It had been Kesia's idea since she could not shift into scales and descend from the Cloudpeaks herself. She remembered how it felt to have Shance straddling her shoulders. While that had been dangerous for the airship captain, holding on to a simple leather harness fastened to a dragon she was mentally connected with was incredible, with the wind in her hair and the rush of free flying. It was as if she were experiencing her first Launch Day all over again. Zephryn had turned into a show-off, wheeling around tight turns and through narrow passages in the cliffs at breathtaking speed.

Her breath caught at the memory. Incredible.

Zephryn ceased his pacing of the vessel and gave her a smile, sensing the underlying direction of her thoughts and feelings. She returned it, her heart skipping for a moment and her cheeks warming. This skin form reacted to things in different ways than scales.

The boat shifted beneath her feet. Her stomach roiled.

Sometimes it reacted in horrible ways. The swaying vessel had turned her stomach ever since they had boarded the first ship, a river barge, in the small village of Burnside in the Southern Plains, ten miles from the foot of the Cloudpeaks. Kesia and Zephryn had switched to larger ships until they had boarded this metal beast with stiflingly small cabins beneath a long, narrow deck and a pointy front bow.

No, just bow, Zephryn had said. The bow was always in the front, so the phrase front bow was redundant. Always wonderful to have him around to correct her.

Kesia rolled her eyes and tilted her face toward the sun. One thing she did appreciate was the warmer weather. Even though the Southern Plains garb suffocated her in an ankle-length brown skirt, a loose white shirt with a wide neck, and a vest that laced up each side and constricted her breathing. The shoes were torture devices of brown leather and laces.

She twitched the neckline lower, now that there weren't humans nearby to disapprove. Apparently, revealing skin was considered a bad thing for humans to do, at least humans who lived in the Southern Plains. Which explained their clothing options.

Kesia faced Zephryn again. He wore black pants, loose shirt, a long coat, and boots, his short black hair tucked beneath a hat. He was fully immersed in his skin form, without cobalt scales peppering his skin or the dark blue strands in his hair. Another rush of heat warmed her, along with a sudden craving for him to be shirtless, as he had been earlier. And a desire to help the process of unclothing him.

He frowned. <Kesia, is something wrong with my clothing?>

<Um, no. Why?>

<You keep examining it. That was your third pass.>

Fewmets! What was wrong with her? She swallowed.

<I'm merely trying to distract myself from my own ridiculous clothing. It will make it difficult to fight.>

Zephryn grimaced. <Agreed. From what I've learned from the other passengers, the Scepter of Commerce is known for being more progressive and, apparently, shocking in terms of what it permits males and females to wear. We'll find you something suitable, Rose-Wing.>

Kesia nodded. She hadn't asked where Zephryn had gotten the money for all these items. Naturally, he'd stolen it from the Pinnacle. The thought reverberated guilt through her, but she'd gotten over it. Mostly. They had needed disguises, and she didn't want to die. Besides, as the only surviving prince, wasn't it technically still his?

Was it truly worth it, stopping in the Scepter of Commerce instead of trying to hide in a more isolated area? There was so much risk in a city.

Then she remembered the whiff of noxious smoke, the memories stirring from the dark places of her mind.

Yes. It was worth it.

A man dressed in rough browns and black garb blew a whistle.

"Final stop ahead! Grab your luggage and any other belongings and make your way to the dock."

She followed Zephryn across the deck and down the gangplank. They had no luggage, save for pouches with money and a few generic tools. They had been travelling under the pretense of being poor immigrants who had sold everything to reach the city in hopes of a new life. The reality was they hadn't been able to steal much dragon tech on their way out.

Except for their voicelators.

Kesia rubbed the pendant, shaped like a cloud lily, that hung on a silver chain just below her collarbone. Zephryn wore a similar pendant beneath his shirt, only his was an engraved metal disc. Both pendants were created of gelstin, an alloy of tepstone, slatesheen, and blonde copper that blunted the resonant effects of dragon voices. There could be no hint of dragon attributes while in the Scepter of Commerce. They needed to find the truth about the green smoke and move on to somewhere safer.

Now, if only the dock would stop moving beneath her feet. She had thought the ship was bad, but this rubber-legged feeling was worse.

<Zephryn?>

Nowhere.

He had lingered behind to speak to a few passengers he had acquainted himself with earlier. Should Kesia have stayed near him? Was that what first cousins did? Their current cover was a human idea. In Burnside, the locals had assumed they were married, and then had assumed they were related. Since "marriage" was a foreign word, related seemed to be the best choice. While it prevented them from staying in the same cabin, thanks to human notions of propriety, the feigned family status allowed them to travel together without incident.

Since they were taking turns sleeping to keep watch, the situation was ideal for their mission. If only she knew what it meant for them right now. What she was meant to do. All this effort, and she was still worthless. Except to the Pinnacle. But whatever value she had to them wasn't dependent on her being useful.

After all, what use was a murderer?

Her stomach lurched. The sun pressed onto her skull like a giant hand. Kesia needed to sit down before she soiled the dock with her most recent meal of meat strips and bread.

She glanced around the wharf. A few benches were tucked in the shade of awnings from dockside shops and cafes. Zephryn could find her. She stumbled toward the nearest bench.

Only a few more steps across the dock.

Kesia's fingers had just grabbed the back of the bench when a blast of wind hit her face, carrying a mixture of sea-brine, engine oil, and some kind of strong, alcoholic scent.

It was too much.

"Can I help you?"

Her mind instantly catalogued the voice. She looked up into the blue eyes of Captain Windkeeper.

And promptly threw up on his shoes.

CHAPTER SEVEN

KESIA WANTED TO DIE, stomach first. And she wasn't sure if it was due to the insidious seasickness, the wafts of stench from the human next to her, or the possibility of disappointing Zephryn.

It could easily be all of them.

"Are you all right?" Captain Windkeeper's voice had the same light-hearted cadence she remembered from the ship, only this time it was laced with concern. "Do you need help?"

"Mmm, fine," she grunted, slouching down on the bench. Not that there was any need to hide her face from Captain Windkeeper—he'd only seen her as a dove and dragon—but leaning back on anything hard was still torturous for her right shoulder blade.

Perhaps it was additional punishment that she deserved.

Worry filtered in her mind from Zephryn. <Are you well?>

<I'm fine. Continue your conversations. I can manage this.> Kesia made sure to put enough irritability in her thoughts to hopefully ease her fleetwing's tension. He was doing important reconnaissance. Surely she could manage an airship captain.

An airship captain who wasn't there anymore. Where had he gone? She lifted her head enough to see him at the water's edge, crouched down in his dress pants and waistcoat, splashing something in the water.

His shoes.

A moment later, Windkeeper returned, carrying his shoes and socks in one hand. He settled onto the bench next to her. "No harm done, fair lady. My boots were overdue for a polish. Now, what's troubling you?"

"The sea." The words escaped before Kesia could stop them. She swallowed the sick-sour taste in her mouth, and with it, a few choice words about whatever chemical the airship captain had doused himself with.

Breathe in. Breathe out. It was only a scent. Apart from the brine and engine oil, the fermented smell wasn't that bad. She could acclimate.

He chuckled knowingly. "I've heard many people have such a complaint with it. For myself, I prefer the sky."

She rolled her eyes. "Well yes, anyone would prefer the sky."

"Would they?" Increased interest glowed in his blue eyes. "Are you a friend of the air?"

Scale mites!

"Yes. I mean, no. Oh no. It makes me as sick as the sea waves." The lies only added to the bile in her throat. "Thank you, Captain Windkeeper. I'm feeling better."

She tried to move from the bench. Her legs faltered and slid out from beneath her as if the ground were coated in slush. Fear knotted her stomach as her heels skidded out from under her. Her hands reached out to brace her—and met a cushion of air. She gasped as a gentle wind encircled her and eased her back onto the bench, closer to Windkeeper than she had been before.

"Somehow, I doubt that, fair one. Although I admire your

fortitude." His arm lay loosely across the back of the bench. He must have wanted to stretch it.

Did Zephryn notice? Kesia spared a glance in his direction. No, he was deep in conversation with a few dockworkers, very likely getting important information.

Which meant handling Windkeeper was still her concern. Very well. She could try small talk.

"Why do you call me 'fair'? How can you deduce that my actions are just?"

Shance chuckled. "You make a good point. You seem familiar. Do I know you? You seem to know me."

Her mind raced for more words, flitting back through her memory of him on the airship. An impressive airship, Kesia recalled, and Windkeeper had worn a special insignia. "Why wouldn't I? Doesn't everyone know the great Captain Windkeeper?"

"Hm. True. Although I must say, I don't remember meeting you. I would never forget such a beautiful face."

"I tend to blend in." Beautiful? Fewmets! Why did he keep using words she didn't know? Her skin itched with the urge to shift and scurry away. A mouse would be just fine, or perhaps a sea gull. No one liked sea gulls. Everyone would leave her alone, including confusing airship captains who kept smiling at her in ways that made her feel uncomfortable.

Kesia grabbed the voicelator disc around her neck, trying to avoid the shuddering sensation in her skin and the sharp spasms from the wound in her right shoulder. Keep it together. She couldn't shift now. The caregivers had said no shifting for another few days. She'd already broken that rule once, resulting in excrutiating pain. She had to heal.

Shance's voice interrupted her thoughts. "That pendant is

beautiful. May I?"

Kesia tilted away quickly, sending more sharp pain through her back. She bent over. "Um, actually I'd prefer you didn't."

"…all right."

Why did he pause so? She looked up. Windkeeper was staring at her, his jaw slack and eyes blazing with a strange emotion. Shock? Was that shock? "Are you all right?"

He swallowed. "That's where I met you. I didn't recognize you without your wings, my lady dragon."

How did he—the pendant! When she hunched over, the metal cloud lily dangled freely. It couldn't leave contact with her skin for more than fifteen seconds, or else her dragon resonance would be heard clearly.

"Fewmets!"

<Kesia, I heard your dragon voice. What's going on?> Zephryn was already on his way over. Kesia needed to fix this.

She straightened, pain forgotten, and grabbed Windkeeper's arm. "Come with me. Now."

It wasn't the first time a woman had dragged Shance into a dark tavern. Usually those incidents turned out quite well.

But those times hadn't included a woman with a voice that set every bone in his body on edge with an inexplicably haunting resonance. Shance had dismissed the voice of his dragon savior as well as he could, especially since he never imagined seeing her again. He certainly hadn't expected her to take the form of a brunette, with amber eyes lit with the warmth of firelight and a softly curving figure that even a sack-like skirt and blouse couldn't completely disguise. Especially not with that neckline. From the arch of her brows to her deft fingertips, she was entirely exquisite.

Still, she was a dragon, and she was dragging him to a wooden booth barely lit by a few flickering lamps. She flung him into the corner with surprising strength. Behind her, a dark figure coalesced out of the shadows. The dragons took seats on either side of the booth, sequestering him inside.

Sharp reality slammed down on his musings.

Dragons in the Scepter of Commerce. How had they gotten past the guards?

They hadn't faced the guards yet. The clearance at the end of the dock specifically checked for the energy signatures of dragons with a mild electric pulse. A clever toy from the Scepter of Industry.

No need for clearances. Apparently, he had his own way of attracting the enemy. "Dragons?"

"Quiet." The command came from the male, calm and deep. The dim light vaguely outlined his brown, angular face and black hair. "Your words are not necessary."

He glanced at the pretty woman. A subtle interplay of emotions showed on her face, from sheepishness to anger to a stubborn pout that did wonders for her pale pink lips. Shance shoved the observation aside and glanced at the man. His expression didn't change much at all, except around the dark blue eyes, but it was enough to confirm Shance's suspicions.

Of course. Dragons used telepathy. It explained the tight, intricate formations they used in battle.

He cleared his throat. "For the non-mind reader here, can you at least tell me what you're doing?"

The male leveled his gaze at him. "Why should we?"

Shance didn't like the look in his eyes. "Fair enough."

The woman raised her eyebrows. "Again you speak of 'fair.' What do you mean by that word if not justice?"

"Have you never heard of it? Where are you from, lovely?"

"Why did you—none of your questions make sense. My name isn't lovely."

"Then what is it, may I ask?" Shance edged closer to her, aware of the male dragon's eyes on him. As fortune had it, his lady companion was more willing to share information that Shance could take straight to the Congruency. Although the idea settled uneasily in his stomach, making him feel like the seasick one.

A Windkeeper never doubted a dragon. But the old family code didn't apply to dragon spies in wartime. He studied the female's face as she communicated silently with her partner, and he could find no evidence of malice. Only an openness and a sun-kissed beauty that captivated him, from the freckles sprinkled across the bridge of her nose to the rose in her pale cheeks. Adorable. The exact opposite of what anyone would expect of a dragon in human form. Perhaps that was part of the reason she was sent.

She was utterly disarming. Enough to convince anyone … of anything. Hope replaced the tension in Shance's gut. It was a ridiculous idea. A stupid idea.

Which meant it might work, if only they'd cooperate.

"Nightstalker." The male dragon spoke again. "My name is Nightstalker, and my partner is Ironfire. We are here to investigate the explosion on your ship. Ironfire detected unusual features from the green smoke, including the scent, and we are trying to locate any production facilities or information."

Shance leaned forward on the table. "So that explosion wasn't you? We assumed it was." Well, the others had. A thrill flitted through Shance at being right.

The male dragon shook his head. "You must be aware that dragons loathe the use of mechanical or chemical devices in warfare."

"True. And you've never come so near a Scepter."

"We've also questioned why the Congruency would harm their own vessel on a maiden voyage," Ironfire added, playing with a loose lock of hair. "We suspected—"

"Rebels. The Lawless." Shance's voice turned grim. The anarchists held strongholds in every city. The Scepter of Knowledge even permitted their dissent in public debates over policy. "It seems we have a common enemy. Perhaps we can help each other."

He felt the weight of two sets of dragon eyes settle on him, slit-pupiled and focused. It chilled Shance, though not enough to back down on his plan.

Nightstalker spoke. "How so?"

Now came the stupid part. Incredibly fool-brained, even for him. But Shance's gut told him these two were trustworthy. The winds agreed. They'd been quietly circling the table this entire time.

Hopefully family lore was right. In any case, he'd have collateral if this plan went hull-up.

"Anyone with the clearance to get a bomb onto an airship like *The Silver Streak* would have to be high-level. Someone within High Command, which is currently located within the Central Market. As it happens, I hold quarters within High Command."

Nightstalker narrowed his eyes. "Are you suggesting you could get us inside to investigate?"

"Not both of you. Only her." Shance nodded toIronfire. "I can get her inside. The rest is up to you."

The dragons shared a glance, then the woman tilted her head to the side. "You would do this in exchange for what?"

Here came the pinch point. Shance cleared his throat. "I need an escort—a companion, if you would—for the next two weeks. Someone who could attend public functions with me and accompany me around the Scepter of Commerce. It would allow Ironfire additional access to others of high rank, and would extricate me from a rather troublesome social situation."

Nightstalker studied him carefully. Shance held his gaze, despite every inclination to look away from the cobalt stare. "In what capacity would she accompany you?"

"As my betrothed. A declaration of upcoming marriage, a human social custom of bonding between males and females. Do you have something similar?"

"Nightstalker and I are fleetwings. Lifelong tactical partners, separated only by death." Ironfire's delicate brows wrinkled. "Is it something to that effect?"

"Yes, something like that. Only different."

She leaned forward. "Different how? Are marriages not permanent?"

Shance shrugged. "They can be. It doesn't always work out that way. And marriage involves love. Hopefully."

"What is love?"

The rumors were true then. Dragons were as cold as their reptilian forms suggested. Shance searched for a definition. "It's when your heart beats for the other person. When, if you could choose to be around one person, it would be them. When you spend as much time as you can with them and take care of them above yourself."

"Oh, so it *is* like being tactical partners. Except that I can talk to Zephryn, and sometimes human women aren't allowed to talk."

Was it the same? His heart sank. It couldn't be. Such a lovely woman, out of reach. Shance shook his head. If Zephryn and Kesia were bound in some way, it would make this all the easier. Two weeks of pretense and then Shance could cut her loose without a single thought or regret. It was only a convenient arrangement. Nothing more.

"Are there any other conditions?" asked Nightstalker.

"No one kills anyone. You share any reconnaissance with me, and that includes recon that you do in the city. At the end of two weeks, we part ways. No one mentions this to the leadership of either side. As far as our superiors know, we both just happened to make very good espionage connections and used them well."

Ironfire nodded. "Nightstalker and I will want to reconvene on a regular basis to share our findings and assess the situation."

"Fair enough. Excuse me, I mean, a just and reasonable request."

Nightstalker smirked. All right, at least one of the dragons seemed to have a larger command of vocabulary. "Very well then, we agree."

"Swear on the stars?"

They looked at him blankly. Shance sighed. "You don't have those? Oaths?"

Ironfire paused, a curious look on her face. She shut her eyes for a moment, as if reading something deep in her memory. "By the All-Maker. My parents used to swear by an All-Maker."

Her fleetwing looked at her in obvious surprise, and they fell silent for several more minutes. More dragon mind-speech. Finally, Shance cleared his throat. "All-Maker sounds close enough. I usually swear by Fiarston and Viorstan myself. Sky god and wind god."

Ironfire tilted her head to the side. "Why are two gods needed for that job?"

Shance shrugged. "No idea. Okay, by Fiarston and Viorstan

and this—"

"All-Maker. All are his."

"That works." Shance held out his hand to Kesia. She stared at it curiously. "You are supposed to grab hold of it and move your arm up and down."

She pursed her lips. "If you say so."

Her hand was warm, and her grip almost broke his fingers. But the handshake was made. And she still looked beautiful.

Repeat the action with the fleetwing. Bones crushed a little more.

Shance rubbed his fingers. "It's a deal then. Let's get out of here before High Command puts us all in cells."

Chapter Eight

ZEPHRYN COULD BARELY BREATHE.

The Scepter of Commerce was a maze of claymesh buildings and populace-clogged sidewalks, mired with fumes from the squat ground-cars that scurried along the streets like gleaming silver beetles. The visual noise, combined with the thick, heavy air, made him wish for the open skies of the Cloudpeaks.

It was of no consequence. By some great chance, he and Kesia had managed to secure far more than he could have imagined. She would be able to infiltrate the highest ranks and discover the truth about the green smoke, and then they would escape. In the meantime, he could scout and research information in the city's underground to find the best place for them to hide, never to return to the Pinnacle.

The sentiments pulled at the loyalty born and nurtured deep in his heart by his parents, figures who were now but vague memories. He swatted at the nagging guilt as if it were one of the spraygnat clouds that had pestered him aboard the ship. Yes, Zephryn held a prized lineage, but what good was a title without power and support to claim it? And even if he found enough support for his own claim, Kesia would still be branded as a criminal. The other dragons had been conditioned for years to despise her. And she was more important than anything.

Even more reason to try and make new plans during their time here.

The human known as Shance Windkeeper halted in front of them, ducking into a side shop. A noxious mixture of odors assaulted Zephryn's nostrils, and next to him, Kesia covered her nose with her sleeve. He followed suit, only to find the raucous music filling the air to be just as bothersome. If that weren't enough, every shelf and display rack in the stuffy shop was filled with brightly colored fabrics, layered so it was impossible to discern direction easily.

Windkeeper waved them to a back corner, where the sounds and scents were strongest. Kesia gave Zephryn a wan smile, and he returned it. The overload made it difficult to think properly.

"I'm not sure if we've been followed, but most of the spies and street officers around here have some kind of sensory Talent. This shop should stifle most of their abilities—and for the future meetings, we should keep places like this in mind."

"Wise." Zephryn only managed that word before another cloud of scents numbed his olfactory senses. "Where are the exits?"

The airship captain nodded. "There are two out the back. One is for receiving shipments and the other is for the girls."

Kesia tilted her head up. "The girls?"

Windkeeper spared her a sly look, then shook his head. "It's not like that."

"Like what?"

"The owner here, Zilpath," he gestured toward an old woman barely visible behind a long wooden counter, "takes in girls from the neighboring jungleland tribes as boarders. They work as seamstresses or in other businesses in the area. One of them is how I first discovered this place. Windkeeper flushed. "Although, apparently Zilpath has strict rules on tenant behavior." He cleared his throat. "Besides, I couldn't stand the five perfumes the girl doused herself with. Some tradition from her tribe south of this Scepter."

Kesia snorted smoke. "But you soak yourself in one perfume. That's awful enough."

Shance's mouth fell open. "Is that why you threw up? I'm so sorry."

"Sorry? What does that mean? And I'm getting used to the scent."

Nightstalker rolled his eyes. "The exit?"

"Yes, of course. If you take the right exit and follow the alleys to the southwest part of the city, you'll come to the Low Quarter. There should be cheap lodgings, no questions asked."

Zephryn crossed his arms. "Law enforcement?"

"Not usually, but the possibility of rebel activity has made High Command nervous, so keep your head down. They'll have bioelectric scanners."

Why did humans place such faith in those devices? The ones at the dock clearance had been inconsequential. His cloaking Talent had helped significantly in that regard, as had Kesia's ability. Her shifting Talent allowed her skin form to be especially convincing.

And fascinating.

He stole a glance at her now; she was still clad in her peasant clothing. Truly, the garments hid her predator nature well, though she *had* drawn Windkeeper's attention. Then again, he had seemed to be fascinated by a number of women during the journey from the wharf to the shop.

Did he really think a dragon was the same as a human female? Was he truly that foolish? Kesia could more than care for herself—although she was still wounded. Less capable of defense.

The thought sent a bittersweet pulse through Zephryn, enough to evoke a concerned frown from Kesia.

<Are you well, Midnight?>

Zephryn's lips twitched into a half-smile. Hesitantly, he took her hand in his as he'd seen humans do. It felt necessary. <As well as I can be in this nest of deadly vapors. And you, Rose-Wing? Are you sufficiently prepared?>

<Yes. I only wish you could accompany me.> Her hand squeezed his more tightly, a curious softness accompanying her natural dragon strength. The thought of releasing her grip seemed unimaginable.

At that moment, he could have held her hand forever.

<I as well. But we will still be linked, remember? I will be with you regardless. Right here.> Zephryn stroked her forehead with his other hand, remembering the scales that had been there before. <And we will reunite regularly.>

<Yes, we will. Or I'll show the captain what a dragon is really made of.> Kesia snorted, but thankfully, no smoke spewed from her nostrils this time. <I will find answers.>

She would. She was clever and able, far more than she knew. It didn't mean Zephryn wanted her to work alone; she had faced too much alone already. But this was an opportunity that was logical to take. Just as it was only logical to assist her. <And I as well.>

<Then all is fleet and sure.> She released his hand and turned to Windkeeper. "We are ready to depart. Lead on, Captain Windkeeper."

He made a fist of his right hand and touched the bent knuckles to his lips. The Congruency salute. Unbidden, fire flared in Zephryn's throat, which he quickly swallowed down. At this point, Windkeeper was not their enemy. Everyone else was.

The airship captain made a few curious gestures toward the elderly woman whose gray knot of hair was nearly obscured by a mound of fabric. She returned the gestures with a scowl, adding a few others that made Windkeeper wince.

Perhaps he was not on good terms with her after all. Zephryn's muscles seized, and for a moment, he considered ending this entire plan.

<Worry not, Midnight.> Kesia swatted his shoulder the way she would have swatted at him with her tail in scale form. <I can handle one human male. If all else fails, I'll return to the form of a sun-dove. That seemed to please him well enough.>

<Indeed.> Zephryn grinned at her tease.

He had the strangest urge to take her in his arms. For what reason, Zephryn couldn't imagine. How would holding her improve any part of this situation? Somehow, it would; he was certain of that. Certain enough to start reaching for her hand—

"You'd better go, Nightstalker." Windkeeper nodded to the window. "The winds tell me the street officers will be here any moment. And I don't know what Talents they'll have—they might even be able to detect you through your invisibility."

Right. Too sensible. Zephryn nodded. "Until we meet again."

He pressed through the corridor that Windkeeper indicated, drawing anonymity around him like a cloak. The Talented humans were of little account.

But if he lingered too close to Kesia, he might never leave. And he had to.

For a little while longer.

She watched Zephryn be swallowed up in the layers of cloth and overpowering smells that filled the small hallway. She felt his mind go curiously blank, as it did when he used his cloaking Talent.

<Zephryn?>

<Yes, Kesia?>

She released a short breath.

<Just checking to make sure you were there. I couldn't sense you for a moment.>

<I'll always be here, but I need to focus. Contact me if you need to.>

<Of course.> She smiled.

She wasn't alone. Ordinarily, dragons needed line of sight or nearness for mindspeak, but Kesia's fleetwing bond with Zephryn overcame that limitation. Time and again he had proven that she would never be alone.

Not like the night she had killed her father.

For a brief moment, the image of a twisted half-skin, half-scale dragon floated before her eyes, stinking with death that was not his own. *The monster took one step toward her. Another and another, each one shuddering the cavern beneath her bare feet. Her fingers reached around for the small piles of metals on the nearby shelves, seeking out anything to defend herself.*

"Ironfire?"

A hand touched her shoulder. Kesia grabbed it, twisting the arm at the wrist and driving it toward the back of the neck. Her attacker was quick, forcing wind beneath her fingers to loosen them and pushing her back with another blast that pressed her against a pile of soft cloth and cleared the smells.

The smells. The clanging cymbals and drums. Her mind quickly spun into focus. She was in a shop in the Scepter of Commerce, and she had almost killed the human who was her pretended betrothed.

Windkeeper watched her warily, his blue eyes wide and calculating. She needed to set him at ease. Kesia pressed her lips together, summoning a regretful tone. "I'm sorry, Captain Windkeeper. Old memories sometimes refuse to stay in the past."

"Must have been a firestorm of a past." He ran a hand through his blond hair, causing the ends to stick up. "Just for future note: people who are betrothed do not fight with each other. Well, sometimes they do, but not physically."

She tilted her head up. "Then how do they know how to fight side by side if they lack knowledge of each other's capabilities?"

"Generally, betrothed couples don't fight side by side either." Windkeeper chuckled wearily, brushing off his waistcoat. "Another thing. Don't call me 'Captain Windkeeper.' Call me Shance. It's my first name. Not my family name—my personal name. Do dragons have those? If so, I'll need to know yours. Betrothed couples would use those names with each other."

Kesia opened her mouth to speak, then closed it, the words catching in her throat. She grabbed a handful of fabric on either side of her, staring down at it for a moment. Slick stuff, with intricate threads all over it. Nothing that a criminal would wear.

At least, here, no one knew about that.

Windkeeper—Shance—moved closer. Her muscles seized, still remembering that hideous odor from the dock.

Shance sighed. "Still bothered by the odd scents? Hold on, I can fix that."

A fresh breath of wind circled around her, clearing the air. Leaving only the scent of fermented tree branches. Somehow, it wasn't so bad when combined with his winds. Oddly … compelling.

Kesia inhaled, then exhaled. "You truly are skilled with breezes."

"Yeah, it makes me a popular guy." He blinked only one eye for some reason. "Besides the betrothal issue, Ironfire sounds too much like a dragon name."

"Kesia."

"Kesia." He spoke the word with a soft reverence, his body moving closer to hers. Her heartbeat skipped with the urge to attack and clear her space. At the same time, something warm, but not unpleasant, prickled her skin and sent tingles down to her fingers and toes. Shance continued speaking. "Now that is a beautiful name. What does it mean?"

She studied him. "It means 'earthbound.' Your name is Windkeeper. Why do you have a dragon surname?"

"It's part of the family inheritance. We used to be allies with dragons before the war. They gave us the name because of our abilities. What about your surname?"

"My family were metal-workers and mechanics."

"What happened to them?" Shance's face softened. So different from Zephryn, who rarely showed what he was feeling, except to her. To do so would invite attack from other dragons.

And she knew just how brutal dragons could be. A memory surfaced in her mind. *Her parents' workshop: the forge, the shelves filled with tools, the workbench carved from stone in their cave. All of it consumed in a sickening greenish haze as the monster crept toward her, one step after another.*

Kesia silenced the memory.

"My family died in the war. We were prime targets, for obvious reasons. Kill off the dragons who could repair structures and forge … things."

Yes, that was enough information to give him. Not entirely

true, but enough.

"Windkeepers were air merchants before all this sky-bilge started." Suddenly, Shance darted a look toward the doorway. Two figures stood there, clad in plain clothes like many other civilians in the Scepter of Commerce. But Kesia marked their fluid actions and sharp stares.

Military. She had to disappear, become a rodent or a cat. She closed her eyes to shift, but fierce pain shot up her back and through her shoulder blade. Scale mites! No shifting yet. "We should leave."

He shook his head. "No. They'd notice and give chase. Do you trust me?"

"That depends."

Shance's jaw worked. "Do you trust me when it comes to human social customs?"

"I think so."

"I need to kiss you."

Kesia raised her eyebrows. "What's that?"

"You don't know what a kiss is?" He sighed and rubbed his forehead. "We'll touch lips and sort of—taste each other? I'm better at demonstration than explanation. Listen, it's the only way they'll believe we're betrothed."

"Why?"

"Because I kiss women I'm not even betrothed to! And they've seen me take girls into this shop. For some reason, the scents are alluring."

The security agents were nearly at the back of the store. Kesia's pulse jumped. What harm could this custom do? "All right."

Shance leaned in close and covered her mouth with his in one of the most ineffective attempts at suffocation Kesia had ever experienced. Her chest tightened, ready to retaliate with a fist to his jaw. Only, the mouth contact was soft and explorative—what in all the stars was he doing with his tongue? What was there worth tasting on her lips?

The scent of fermented tree branches broke through her thoughts. Only it changed, becoming fresh and irresistible. Her muscles relaxed, and she leaned forward. Sweet and cool—

"Captain Windkeeper. Enjoying your furlough, I see."

Shance pulled away from her and turned to face the military figures, half-shielding her with his body. He addressed the nearest human, a honey-skinned woman of forty years or so, perhaps. It was hard to tell with humans. "Ah, Officer Fim. Always a pleasure. Yes, you've found me out. Can I help you with something?"

Kesia fisted her hands, then consciously released them. This wasn't the time to fight. She had to stay quiet, or she would endanger everything.

Fim gave a thin smile. "Merely checking on a suspicious sensor blip. After what happened to *The Silver Streak*, we must be extra cautious about dragon invaders. The flamers could be anywhere."

"Indeed. I heartily applaud your valiant service. Now, if you will excuse me, my betrothed has misplaced her luggage on her trip here for our wedding, and sadly, the only thing the ship's crew could give her were these rags." He stepped aside and drew Kesia forward, placing his other arm around her back. She clenched her jaw, then relaxed it, trying to pretend she didn't want to elbow him in the kidney. "May I introduce Kesia Ironsley from the Scepter of Industry."

"A pleasure, Miss Ironsley."

Kesia nodded with a smile, not trusting the voicelator to disguise her dragon resonance. Instead, she yawned, a gesture familiar to both dragons and humans.

Shance chuckled. "It seems the trip has been too much for her. We are only here so she can be fitted with a proper wardrobe for her stay."

Fim exchanged a look with her cohort. "It appears you have the matter in hand, Captain Windkeeper. We will leave you to your activities. Such as they are."

The other officer smirked. Both made the same salute Shance had made earlier, then left the store. Only then did Kesia let herself breathe, nearly panting with relief. She pressed the voicelator firmly into her skin before daring to speak. "New clothes?"

"Yes. As of now, you are Kesia Ironsley, a bright young mechanic from the Scepter of Industry." As Shance spoke, he signalled to the woman at the register, then began moving around the store, pointing to various fabrics. "We had an exceptionally fast courtship and, just recently, you forgave my regrettable indiscretions with another woman and agreed to marry me to keep me in check."

Her mind spun, trying to keep pace with all the lies. "If you and I are meant to be together, why would you need my presence to keep you from partnering with another?"

"Human frailty and the stress of wartime."

She rolled her eyes. "If you were a dra—a better man, you wouldn't fall prey to things like that. Wartime increases the bond between tactical partners. Wouldn't it be the same for betrothed people? Yet you were disloyal to me."

"We kissed. If tactical partners were the same as betrothed, that would make you disloyal to Nightstalker."

"*You* kissed *me*." Her faced heated. "And it's an act. A human tradition that has no relevance for dragons."

Or did it? She'd noticed Zephryn's lips before, along with other parts of him. Would it taste as pleasant? More?

None of that was important to their mission.

"Of course." Shance made another one of his odd, one-eyed blinks. "And thoughts like that, my dearest, are why I love you."

"You can't love me. You don't even know me." Kesia was about to ask what was wrong with his eye when something tugged hard on her arm. She pivoted, ready to fight—but it was only the gray-haired woman. She studied Kesia as if Kesia were a young recruit with no more sense than a dragonet.

The way she held out the thin tape with numbers and lines on it clearly indicated it was another weapon. Kesia cleared her throat. "Shance? What is she doing?"

"She's not here to hurt you. Just relax."

The sly smile he gave her made Kesia certain she would kill him when this was all over.

Chapter Nine

SHANCE LIKED ZILPATH'S STORE. The chaos of colors and incense added intrigue. Sure, the old woman didn't always look forward to seeing him, but the Windkeeper name still counted for something. No merchant who wanted to stay on good terms with cargo shipping would alienate a Windkeeper.

Well, the few Windkeepers who were left. Most of his family had been killed in the war or scattered across the fleet. He only remembered speaking to his parents over clipse-mirror.

Shance scattered the air in the shop, idly twirling the streamers of cloth that hung from the ceiling. It had been a few hours since Zilpath and Kesia had disappeared. Zilpath was an old-school seamstress who preferred working by hand, but he knew some of her girls used sewing machines. With enough training under her tutelage, they'd be released into independent work without a single debt, which was far better than the slave market she'd bought them from.

The sound of Zilpath's heavy footfalls broke through his thoughts. He turned toward the back room—and caught his breath.

Kesia Ironfire was beautiful. This was already a fact, but the tight black pants, knee-high boots, and fitted dark red corset-coat with short sleeves enhanced her radiance. The color set off her pale skin and rich brown hair, which had been brushed and pulled loosely away from her face in a smooth braid. The lines of her coat flattered nicely, although Zilpath had opted for a higher blouse neckline than Shance preferred.

After all, it got very warm in the Scepter of Commerce. Wouldn't want Kesia to overheat.

She flushed under his attention. "Is there something wrong?"

Even in human form, her voice was fire and sweet honey, sending a shiver of pleasure through him.

"Everything is just right. You look … right." More right than any other woman Shance had laid eyes on.

A hand grabbed his arm, and he looked down to see Zilpath standing there, holding out her hand, her blue eyes shrewd. "How much for everything?"

Her fingers began arcing through the air in graceful swoops. Like other jungleland slaves, Zilpath's tongue had been cut out to avoid making trouble for her owners. She made up for it by having the most colorful collection of hand gestures he'd ever encountered. Shance mentally sifted through them for the answer. ~Three suits like this, plus a dress, underclothing, and boots. Ten thousand dels.~

~Ten thousand? Too much.~ He ended his series of hand gestures with both palms pressed down. Most natives of the Scepter of Commerce knew some pidsyn, the universal sign language from the surrounding villages. He'd just taken care to learn a lot. ~Two thousand.~

Her wrinkled lips curled back and she curved her hand. ~Two thousand? First you bring dragons into my shop, and now you try to rob me of hard-earned dels? No. For this, I should turn my house and girls back into the slave trade. Nine thousand, five hundred.~

~The slave trade wouldn't take the lot of you. You're too free-minded. They'd sooner cast you into the Trebbian Seas. Five thousand.~

She spat into a small pot and popped a fresh sprig of some herb into her mouth. ~The Trebbian Seas? Your shiny new airship mucked them up when it fell out of the sky.~

He winced. ~It crashed on dry land.~

~Seven thousand. Final offer.~

He clasped his hands over her arms and bowed his head slightly in the traditional gesture of acceptance. Zilpath could have charged him twice as much, and she knew it. But she'd also known his parents, and he had actually made good on a situation with one of her girls. And the Congruency paid him more than enough; after all, killing the enemy was good for business. ~And another thousand for a formal dress.~

~Another?~ She palmed the coins and paper squares, counting them in a matter of seconds. ~What are you doing, bringing her and her partner here? They're highly trained warriors. I saw how she handled you—and she was holding back, never mind your pride. She could have killed you as easily as you snap the neck of a crenbird.~

~A hunch.~

Zilpath leaned back against the counter, resting her elbows on either side, her voluminous frock hanging on her thin form. ~What kind of hunch?~

Shance paused, glancing out of the corner of his eye. Kesia was watching both of them intently, but looked away under his gaze and began fingering the nearest swags of fabric. She couldn't understand their words, could she? Not when she seemed so ignorant of everything else.

It was worth the risk. He could use an ally, and Zilpath was the only option. He turned back to the old woman. ~She saved my life during the explosion. She's the reason I'm alive, and I still don't know why she did it. I'm not sure she does either. But she and her partner are here seeking information on the explosion.~

~It wasn't them?~ Zilapth's eyes glittered with hidden meaning.

Shance shook his head. ~They say it wasn't. And it wasn't us. We're seeking a rebel infiltration in the Scepter of Commerce.~

~The hunter of my hunt is an ally. Until we find the prey.~

~I'll deal with that when it comes. For now, she is my betrothed. Understood? None of this information is for sale. Not yet.~ He tapped both hands over his heart and then touched his chin.

Zilpath repeated the gesture. ~The wind and the dragons dance again. For destruction and resurrection. You do your family proud in this, and you may one day be worthy of your name.~

~As you say, as it goes.~ He shrugged off the portent in her words and in her circular gesture, a supplicating plea to the Four Corners. It was one thing to invoke Fiarston and Viorstan, but all of the higher prophecy stuff espoused by the Four Corners followers made him feel as trapped as being groundside.

Shance stepped away from the desk and signaled to Kesia. She gave him another curious look. Words. That's right. For once, he understood her flustered attitude toward them, especially if she was used to mind-speaking with her tactical partner. A partner—and something more? There had been a softness in her eyes when he'd left, a softness Nightstalker hadn't seemed to return. Although, the male dragon was far more difficult to read than Kesia.

Which meant they were going to have to work even harder on maintaining the charade of their engagement. Her inexperience had shown in the kiss, and much higher scrutiny would be on them during the next two weeks. At least the Scepter of Industry was known for being more reserved in matters of the heart. That should go a long way.

But it wouldn't be enough to convince Countess Nula. For that, Kesia and Shance would need every pretense of being deeply in love.

"It's time to go, my dear." He held out his arm. Kesia studied it curiously. "Relax; it is simply a way for couples to show their commitment in public."

"All right." She smiled hesitantly at Zilpath, who favored her with a big grin and a wave.

They stepped out onto the sidewalk. Shance opened his mouth to speak, then closed it. There were too many open ears and eyes on the street. And considering Kesia's tendency to speak her dragon-born thoughts, it would be better to establish a custom of silence starting now.

As they continued down the street to the Central Market, Shance's mind wandered to the feeling of Kesia's hand on his arm, warm even through his shirt sleeve. To how easily they fell into step. To the kiss they had shared. No matter how inexperienced, Kesia still tasted of smoke and fire and passion, trembling beneath her hard, careful surface. There was a softness and a kindness to her that didn't belong with dragonkind.

Where did it belong? With him? The wind and the dragons dance again, Zilpath had said. But she had said dragons. More than one. Wait—dancing! Kesia didn't know how to dance. He would have to teach her. Hold her close. Move as one together.

A shiver of anticipation shuddered through him. In response, wind rippled down the street, weaving and rushing around the passersby and teasing at Kesia's braided hair. She lifted her face into the breeze and breathed deeply, seeming to savor the freedom inherent in each current, in a way he'd never believed anyone else could understand.

The Central Market rose before them with row upon row of square windows framed by ornate claymesh and glimmering gold and silver tiles. The main building stood twenty stories high, with wings on either side outlining a broad courtyard with three fountains in the center patterned in bright mosaics. The entire edifice was a radiant beacon, dedicated to the great levelling power of money and the free market.

Kesia clutched his arm tightly, her amber eyes wide with wonder. Shance grinned and leaned close to her. "Throw a penny in each of the fountains, and your wealth is guaranteed to increase."

"Guaranteed by whom?" She raised her eyebrows.

He chuckled. "Whatever deity or force you believe in!"

"Convenient how all of them agreed to the same deal."

Shance laughed louder, and she joined in, her face lighting up. She was even more beautiful when she smiled. They continued up the steps to the crystalline front doors that rose two stories high in the center of the main building.

Finally he pushed open one of the doors. Kesia frowned. "I should let Zephryn know we made it."

Nightstalker. Yes. "Is he concerned?"

Her lips curved into a little smirk as they walked inside the main lobby. "He would never admit it, but yes. He's always been more concerned than—" The dragon's expression suddenly became wary. Her grip on his arm loosened.

"Kesia?"

"We have to go outside."

"What? Why?"

"We have to go back!" Her voice echoed in the pillared room, drawing a few concerned glances. She shook her head, her eyes darting around the room. "What kind of place is this?"

"Calm down. You've had a long journey." Shance made the words clear and comforting, hoping others would overhear and draw their own conclusions that didn't involve Kesia being a disoriented dragon spy. Then he guided her over to an alcove away from the traffic of the lobby. "Kesia! What's happening?"

Her fingers played with the cloud lily pendant around her neck. Shance covered her hand with his own before she negated whatever power the object had.

"Zephryn. He … he's…" She gulped a breath. "I can't sense him. He's gone."

<Zephryn! Zephryn, answer me. Answer me!>

A singing emptiness echoed back her thoughts. They ricocheted around her mind, haunting her, mocking her. She was dimly aware of Shance's words, of the clicking and tapping of shoes on the marble floor outside the darkness in her thoughts.

A darkness that had held the solid presence of her fleetwing. Even in Zephryn's silence, she had been able to sense his existence since the day their heartflames were bound.

Strong arms surrounded her, drawing her close. Shance. A part of Kesia was comforted by the support and knew that she would have fallen to the ground without him. The other part wanted to rip the pendant off her neck and keen an urgent cry, loud enough to drown all other noise, bold enough to silence all thought, deep enough to shake the foundations of this city, high enough to shatter every window.

Just like she had with the hideous monster in the cave. Her father. Reducing him to a pile of scales, his innards liquefied, pooling out his ears.

She'd never told them what she could do. She'd never tell.

But what had she done?

Shance pressed his hand firmly over hers, forcing the pendant to her collarbone. "Kesia. What's happening? Who is gone?"

"Zeph—Nightstalker. I can't hear him in my head. There's only nothing. Nothing. Nothing." The floor rocked beneath her feet.

A calloused hand raised her chin to face him. Shance's blue eyes were earnest and anxious. "Can you think of why?"

"No." The fear choked any rational thought.

"Well, we can't stay in this lobby. People are staring. Can you hold on to my arm and walk with me to my quarters? Then you can do whatever you need to find him."

No! She needed to find him now, not go deeper into this prison where everyone lived trapped in their own minds. Kesia was about to voice this, then shut her mouth. She was a dragon warrior. She was stronger than this.

"Yes. I can do this."

"Brave woman."

She took his arm. She wasn't brave; she was a weakling, a dead weight, only good for pulling worthy dragons out of the sky. Even now, she hung on to Shance's arm while his excuses to others swept past her ears.

"Oh, my lady is tired from her long journey. All the way from the Scepter of Industry! Yes, I'm sure you can imagine. We look forward to meeting you at the opening gala. Good day."

All she could focus on was the hard floor, a cream color with swirls of silver and gold, silver and gold circling and swirling. Suddenly the floor changed to a thick, plush material of dark blue. She'd never felt something so soft.

It didn't matter.

Nothing mattered, except that Kesia was alone, like she had been before she had bonded with Zephryn. When she was kept in the dark cell with the criss-cross lights from the ceiling grate.

"Here, sit down. Can I get you anything? Something to eat or drink?"

"No. Leave me alone." Kesia sank back into something even softer than the floor, but surprisingly firm. A chair. Her hands found arms on either side. Everyone sat so much in human cities. The Pinnacle forbade any useless loitering as such. Even during meetings, everyone stood. Or so she assumed. She had only been to judgment summonings.

Judgment summonings. The only other place where she couldn't hear her fleetwing because of the tepstone in the walls. But tepstone and slatesheen were highly controlled substances. No one could get them out of the Cloudpeaks. Certainly no humans.

There had to be another answer. Where were Zephryn and his logical responses, his vast array of knowledge? Together, they could have figured this out. His long-range vision, her practical application.

Kesia didn't know how much she could trust Shance. He'd shown her kindness, but he had his own agenda. An agenda that included requiring her to be his betrothed for reasons he had yet to reveal. Who would want a dragon as a betrothed, especially a murderer? Even Zephryn had no choice in their partnership. Humans had choices, it seemed. Would Zephryn have chosen her?

Did it matter? Zephryn had escaped with her when their bond had been threatened. That had to mean something.

They meant something to each other. She fingered her voicelator, warming the flower with her heartflame. The metal heated and tingled into her skin, and she felt the ridges of tiny wires in a delicate filigree. An extra touch, but why? Voicelators didn't need decoration. The cloud lily shape was more than enough.

More than necessary, perhaps.

<What were you thinking, Midnight?>

A presence, slightly crinkled with mental static but filled with pride, met her mind. <Clever woman. I knew you would activate it.>

Her breath caught, and a rush of joy filled her. Kesia leaned back in the chair, muscles limp with relief. <Activate? The voicelator. You altered it to match our heartflames. Why?>

<We're fleetwings. An unbreakable team. The Pinnacle separated us with tepstone when we were in the Cloudpeaks.> Zephryn's mental voice deepened with anger and other potent emotions that the voicelator connection blunted only a little. <I couldn't allow that to continue. The expression on your face as you went in to face them alone ... I never want to see that look again. One of the assistants in the technology cavern is loyal to the old kingdom. He created the voicelators for me, matched to our heartflames and dipped in our blood so that we would always be together.>

Kesia's face stretched into a grin. The flame of a hundred fires filled her with dizziness, and her fingers rubbed the voicelator, wishing she held Zephryn's hand instead. <Of course. Because you still want that? No matter if I'm a murderer?>

<You are Kesia Ironfire, and we carry the flames of each other's

hearts. Why dwell on anything else?>

She sighed, feeling the last bit of tension leave her. <Midnight, do you know what a kiss is?>

<No, but I can research it. Is it valuable information?>

Kesia touched her lips with her free hand, remembering the odd, refreshing taste of Shance Windkeeper. Only, the airship captain's face was quickly replaced by Zephryn's angular features, his dark blue eyes and firm mouth. <Yes. I recommend it.>

<I see. I will make it a priority to research. Also, your use of the voicelators—>

<Why didn't you explain their purpose earlier?>

His frustration filled their mental link. <As I was about to say, I would have in due time, but I didn't expect the Congruency to have telepathy-blocking material. The voicelators were an emergency precaution.>

<Yes, because you're smart like that.> She sent back a wave of teasing. <But this means the humans have tepstone.>

<Or another way of blocking our mind-speech.>

<Possible, but unlikely. Humans tend to go for the easiest solution. Which means there are traitors in the Pinnacle.>

<There could be. We would need more evidence. But don't let this distract you from pursuing inquiries about the green smoke.>

She rolled her eyes. <I won't.>

<Good. Is there anything else?>

She paused. <Not at this time.>

<Very well. The voicelator connection doesn't work without persistent heartflame. If you want to activate it, you'll need to repeat the same actions: channel your heartflame through the metal and reach out to me. I regret that it isn't more efficient, but we were short on time when we departed.>

97

<Hah. Indeed. And the cloud lily shape? How is that efficient?>

<They're your favorite flower.>

Her cheeks heated. <I see. Yes, they are. Until next, Midnight.>

<Until next, Rose-Wing.>

The connection broke. Kesia continued to trace the cloud lily, her lips curled in a smile. Savoring the clarity of speaking with Zephryn. Of course he noticed what she liked. He always did.

Kesia released the voicelator and set her jaw. Time to work. The main focus was the green smoke, but if she could get insight into the Pinnacle traitors who were smuggling out tepstone, so much the better.

If this didn't earn her redemption, nothing would. It didn't matter if the Pinnacle approved of her anymore. All that mattered was facing the memory of her parents without fear and finding peace by Zephryn's side.

Just then, her stomach growled. Violently. Kesia placed her hands over it, trying to still the writhing and pinching. In scales, she was used to eating a large meal and feeling sated for a few days. But skin form stomachs were far more limited, and with their disguise, she and Zephryn had to eat less than usual to avoid detection.

But now Kesia was away from prying eyes, in a half-circular room with another chair identical to hers, a longer seat across from the two chairs, and on the other side of the room, a table and six chairs. A lot of chairs for only one airship captain.

Should she ask about them? Another growl and razor sharp nails scraping her insides convinced her of more important needs.

"Shance?"

He emerged from another entry, his shirt off and hair damp, a long piece of fabric draped around his shoulders. Towel. The fabric was called a towel. As for his lack of shirt, she'd heard humans had their own cleaning rituals with water from metal pipes. In the Cloudpeaks, they'd given her a bucket of tepid water and a rag to clean herself in front of a fire.

For some reason, the picture of Shance Windkeeper washing his lean, muscled skin in such a way sent a warm rush through her, her skin prickling similar to how it had during kissing him. Kesia filed the observation away for later. Skin forms were very reactive to all kinds of stimuli.

"You're looking better. Good to see a little light in your gorgeous face." He did that gesture with his eyelid again. "Did you solve the issue with the mind-speak?"

"Yes, in a way." Kesia frowned. Shance didn't need to know about the voicelator solution right now. "What are you doing with your eye?"

"Winking. It's a sign of flirting."

"What's flirting?"

Shance chuckled. "Showing romantic interest in someone. Dragons really don't know about these things?"

"I guess not." Although Zephryn certainly caught her attention, and apparently she caught his. Was that flirting? Kesia paused. "What does 'gorgeous' mean? Is it the same as beautiful and pretty?"

"I would say so."

"Well then, what do *those* words mean?"

The airship captain raised his eyebrows. "Dragons don't have words for physical attractiveness either?"

"We are soldiers during wartime. Physical attractiveness is frivolous and unreliable. A mirage. Why would we learn about such things?"

"Viorstan's blindness! All of you are missing out on what makes life worth living." He sauntered closer to her. "If you and I are going to pretend to be engaged, I suppose I'll have to teach you that as well. Why did you call me out here?"

Before she could respond, her stomach growled again. "I need food."

"Sure, I can have a meal sent to this suite. What would you like?"

Kesia blinked. "There are choices?"

"I'm the head fleet captain." He flashed a smile and sprawled in the chair next to her. "There are a lot of choices."

"I don't know. I've only had bread and dried meat when eating in skin form."

"Really? Did you like them?"

"No. Too tough."

"Not surprising. And you will need to be a little more aware of food than a dragon is." Shance's grin widened. "So, we'll try everything."

CHAPTER TEN

SHE WAS GONE. That was a problem. It had been one for the last hour.

Zephryn lay on the narrow bed, mentally tracing the cracks in the claymesh ceiling. On either side of him were walls, almost within arm's reach. A slack cord strung from the ceiling functioned as a clothing rack, and a three-legged table meant to have four legs perched next to the bed. That was the extent of the amenities.

When he'd thought to purchase a room, he hadn't considered space to pace back and forth. He'd been mindful only of the need to preserve funds—and the need for security. This boarding house in the Low Quarter had been inexpensive, but it also had bars on the windows and highly armed guards.

All far better things. Despite his power and skill, he was only one dragon. And now, he lacked the assistance of his fleetwing because she was pretending to be the betrothed of a flippant airship captain with a name that seemed curiously familiar.

Windkeeper. Had his parents spoken of a Windkeeper?

Zephryn pinched the bridge of his nose to restrain smoke from leaving his mouth. He needed the other half of his mind on this task. His fingers found his voicelator pendant, and he activated the device with his heartflame. <Kesia.>

No answer.

His heart sped faster. The walls seemed to suffocate him. There were a few logical reasons for her mental absence. Perhaps she had been rendered unconscious—but he'd felt no pain through their fleetwing bond. Not even tepstone could block physical pain. She could have been subjected to a mind-altering substance—unlikely, considering the mental stamina of dragons.

Then again, she was within the boundaries of a building lined with tepstone, suggesting traitors within the ranks of both the Pinnacle and the Congruency. Windkeeper could be one of those traitors. Hadn't his family been merchants? Perhaps that was why Zephryn's family had known them. Many merchants had come to the Cloudpeaks when his parents were alive; Zephryn remembered that.

But Kesia would be able to defend herself against any attack. She could shapeshift into any animal and hide for quite a while. She was a trained soldier and very resourceful. Even if Windkeeper was a double agent, Kesia could handle him.

If necessary, Zephryn could draw his Cloak about him and infiltrate the Central Market personally.

He palmed the entire pendant and sent another pulse of heat into it.

<Ow! Midnight, what's wrong with this pendant?>

Kesia's voice was warm and calm but slightly annoyed. All was normal. He sighed, his heart returning to a steadier beat. <Apparently, nothing.>

<Are the voicelators supposed to burn when they're working?>

<I believe so, as a side effect to alert the person on the receiving end. The technician mentioned as much.>

Her irritation filtered through the link. He could almost picture her tail twitching back and forth, had she been in scale form. <You could have mentioned that to me.>

<Oh. Yes, I could have.>

<Didn't it burn you when I called?>

He shrugged. <I didn't notice.>

<Of course not.> Her amusement warmed him like a sunrise. <What's wrong?>

Zephryn stood, walked two steps forward—and was nose-to-plaster with a wall. He spun around to face the bed again. <I wanted to hear your thoughts about Captain Windkeeper.>

<Shance? What about him?>

Maybe if he closed his eyes he could imagine the room was larger and ignore his dragon need for open spaces. <Does his name sound familiar to you? It's irregular for a human to carry that kind of name.>

<Yes, I know. Other than his Talent with winds, I can't think of anything unusual. But if you think he has some connection to us besides being a merchant, I'll keep an eye out for it.>

<And...>

<And I won't let on. Although, I doubt he would notice if I did. He seems quite infatuated with me.>

<Infatuated?>

Another rush of a warm emotion with an undertone of something sweet and fiery. It reminded him of the first moment he had seen Kesia in skin form. And every time after that. Such feelings didn't matter right now.

Surely not.

<Yes. It's one of the many words humans use to speak about romance and love. Shance has given me a dictionary so I can study the role I'm supposed to play. 'Infatuated' means a feeling of deep,

consuming longing and desire toward a person. Infatuation can come upon you quite suddenly and take hold firmly. Shance keeps wondering if dragons have these feelings.> She paused. <I told him I didn't know.>

<A wise answer, as it is true; we don't know. Although, when we first met each other, we knew the heartflame bond between us.>

<Yes, but that's different.>

Zephryn tilted his head. <How so?>

<When I met you, it was almost as if I'd known you my entire life already. I trusted you more than anyone else.>

<Agreed. Perhaps 'infatuation' is just another human word for their aimless wanderings trying to find other humans to marry.>

<Hm. It could be.>

More puzzles. Zephryn sighed and rubbed his eyes, then looked through the barred window. The sun had finally set. Shadows beckoned him into the street. He brushed the latest dust-rain from the ceiling off his clothing. A sudden thud from above caused another shower of flakes to descend in eddies.

<Fewmets! Foul place.>

<Hm?> Her presence was distant. She was probably studying her dictionary again.

<Merely noting the low quality of these inexpensive lodgings. Filled with dust.>

He could picture Kesia's innocent judgment, amusement dancing in her eyes. <Such a wise decision, Midnight. You can use the money saved on rent to buy new clothing.>

<Yes, perhaps I could borrow some of your new items.>

<The dress in particular would suit you.>

He chuckled in the empty room. <I'm sure it would, Rose-Wing. Until next time.>

<Whenever you need me.>

It was time to seek answers. Preferably from an individual or two in this troublesome rebellion. The Lawless.

Zephryn exited the room, walking down two narrow flights of stairs and out onto the street. He had to step around a human crouched by the door, a handful of trinket rocks in one outstretched hand and a small bowl in the other.

"Mystery stones from the far north!" The old man licked his gap-toothed grin and increased his volume. "Come and buy a glimpse of your future! Mystery minerals from the base of the Cloudpeaks, where the heat of fierce dragon fire gives them special powers. Come buy the stones of power!"

Zephryn considered blowing a plume of flame on the stones just to prove the fool wrong. Then he pushed away the impulse and continued down the street, drawing his Cloak around himself. A useful Talent that had earned his lineage the name Nightstalker centuries ago.

And proved an excellent mask for other Nightstalker qualities. If the Pinnacle knew of those, they would have locked him up as tightly as Kesia.

He returned his attention to his surroundings, such as they were. The Low Quarter held little of interest. The lowest peddlars littered the streets. Apparently begging was illegal in the Scepter of Commerce. Only transactions were permitted, which meant even the poorest had to find some kind of object or service to sell, no matter how degrading or repulsive. The Pinnacle might be harsh and unyielding, but even the criminals were allotted rations and living quarters.

An image of Kesia's cell surfaced in his mind, from the day they had first met. Barely large enough to hold her young scale form, manacles around her neck and ankles, wings tightly bound to her body. Her eyes shrouded in pain and a weary certainty of her fate in the mines.

At only a year older, it had taken all his control not to rush in and rip the shackles from her. To free his destined tactical partner from her chains.

Zephryn stopped. Destined tactical partner. Such an odd phrase for the feelings that overtook his heartflame. What did the airship captain say was an equivalent? Betrothed? Engaged? Or was it one of Kesia's words? Romance? Love? He certainly needed to conduct his own study of the words.

A short shape swathed in a long robe brushed past him. From a long sleeve emerged a thin hand which made a variety of gestures, all while the figure rushed down the street.

Zephryn's nose registered the perfumes lingering in the figure's wake. They were identical to the ones from the hideous clothing shop. Was it the shop owner—or someone else? What was she doing in the street? Where was she going? Either way, she was the first lead he'd found.

Granted, she could be leading him into a social gathering or some other useless human situation. But he didn't have any other options.

He slipped through the streets behind her, careful to stay just outside of her view. It was easily done; the elderly woman seemed entirely focused on her destination. Either it wasn't a secret meeting or it was too important for her to show discretion.

After passing a number of streets, she made an abrupt turn and vanished. Zephryn raced after her, not caring who noticed. People in the Low Quarter seemed far too interested in hawking themselves or their pathetic wares, and his Cloak would protect him.

He skidded around the corner and came face to face with the open end of a berringer pistol. Zephryn huffed in annoyance. Human weaponry guidebooks were plentiful in the Pinnacle. Berringers were poor weapons, using compressed wood bullets and tin shells instead of proper ones. Against his slate-sheened skin, the projectiles would be no more harmful than globs of feathers.

The woman's eyes narrowed, and she made a few more hand gestures, pushing the barrel at his chest. Then she grabbed his arm and pulled him toward her. Did she think that would make him understand her signs any better?

No, she was shoving him through a doorway cut into the patched claymesh. Never mind that Zephryn could have quickly killed her, useless weapon or not. A lead was a lead. If all her compatriots were equally armed, escape would be a matter of swift movements and dispatching any corpses.

Five steps into the room, and the shopkeeper yanked his arm to stop. They stood in a square space with a single electric bulb dangling from the ceiling. It illuminated two other humans, also in long, shabby robes that obscured their faces. The smelly shopkeeper joined them, drawing her hands into her sleeves.

It was akin to a meeting with the Pinnacle, or at least the Pinnacle as Kesia had described them. Zephryn was on more personal terms with the dragon leaders, whether he wanted to be or not.

The center figure spoke in a quiet voice. Male, softened with a slight lilt. "We know what you are, dragon."

Zephryn opted to remain silent. Let the humans think themselves in control and speak themselves out. If these were rebels from the Lawless, the Pinnacle and the Congruency had less to worry about than they thought.

You presume their Talents are so innocuous, Midnight? Do you assume the same of mine? Even in memory, Kesia still covered his blind spots. She always challenged his narrow perspective with new ideas. Granted, some of them were absurd, but even those were refreshing in their lunacy. She was far too valuable to be merely the imagined escort of some careless airship captain.

The quiet male spoke again. "Zilpath has told us all she can about your mission here with your fellow dragon. Our goals and yours are not opposed."

"I disagree. You are anarchists. From the Lawless group."

"Yes, we are the Lawless. But we are not anarchists, though there are those among us who hold those views and would cause blame to fall upon all of us. In truth, we are only interested in the same thing you are: the end of this war. There has been too much discord and loss of life between the five Scepters."

At that, Zephryn stiffened. "Five Scepters? There are only four, and they all attack dragons. We are outnumbered six to one on all sides. Why would you want the war to end? You humans have the advantage."

"We are not all humans."

Then the shopkeeper, Zilpath, emerged from her robe, fingers flying in a variety of word-gestures. The middle figure turned to her and nodded. "She says there were five Scepters. The fifth was located in your own Cloudpeaks, the Scepter of Justice, which mediated disputes between the other Scepters with fairness and mercy."

"Ah, I see. According to this human history, were dragons the interlopers, as you have always seen us? Is that not what started the war—humans wanting the only piece of territory they had not yet claimed?"

Smoke spewed from Zephryn's mouth with the words. There was little point in hiding his nature from these humans. They already knew the truth of that, even if they spread lies about everything else. It only cemented his desire to escape with Kesia, away from this war. Never mind his royal lineage or her convict past. There would be no sanctuary for them on either side of this war. Or among these rebels.

The final figure, who had not yet spoken, stepped forward, her voice deepening with a touch of resonance. "The dragons were the adjudicators, aided by humans who were sworn to impartiality and who lived in harmony with dragons in the Scepter of Justice."

Her voice. It almost echoed as a dragon's, though it lacked the depth of a true dragon. And the place she spoke of, the Scepter of Justice. Although strange, true. Zephryn had heard it from his own parents' lips. Long ago, before they had been taken.

A place of peace, sanctuary, and justice. Where all of his family had ruled. Grief and longing squeezed his heart.

Zephryn swallowed the emotions. "How do you know this? Who are you beneath the robes?"

The male shifted from foot to foot. "It is enough that we support you, your highness. Even if you do not believe it."

"The Lawless has a very odd sense of support." Anger burned in Zephryn's throat, though he kept his tone level. He glared at Zilpath. "I have been captive in the Pinnacle for two decades. Such gallant support."

"We had no way of contacting you, your highness. Our resources are precious and limited."

"Yet you never even attempted? No, you prefer to hide in robes and spout mysterious elements of history with no proof."

Zilpath made a flicking motion that was certainly a curse, then her hands whirled in fresh words. This time, the other female translated.

"The proof is within the Congruency itself. Find your partner in the Central Market and seek it out. Was that not already your goal? We only wish to help you."

"Or lead me astray."

"That's always a risk, but you already trusted that—" the robed figure paused and cleared her throat "—that fool of an airship captain with no more sense than a dust-storm. At least we are actually helping you." She paused again as Zilpath swiped out more words. "You don't need to worry about meeting with Windkeeper and your partner. Zilpath can arrange everything at the proper time."

A bold promise, but one he needed. If the Central Market was lined with tepstone, there was no telling what other dragon minerals they had on hand. The possibility of weapons that could pierce slatesheen could be a very real threat. "I see. Trust me with those plans, and I'll remain in this room."

Zilpath sneered, and her hands made the same flicking gesture. The translator hesitated again. "Eager to get back to that filth-nest on Twentieth Street?"

"It's better than a shop drenched in five different barrels of vile toxins."

Snickers emerged from the two robed figures. Zilpath only brushed her hands off on her robe, turning her back to them. The male spoke. "Your terms are acceptable. Zilpath will contact you with further news."

Zephryn raised his eyebrows. "You won't tell me more yourself?"

"Like you, we have our own identities and secrets to protect. Finding answers within the Congruency will be a sign of good faith on your part. We will contact you when necessary."

"Does Captain Windkeeper know of your allegiance?" That was directed at Zilpath.

She shook her head and made another dismissive gesture with a half-smile.

"He doesn't need to yet," her translator spoke.

The two robed figures bowed and turned to leave.

The female figure paused and faced him again. "Your highness, we would recommend more appropriate lodgings. According to city inspectors, that boarding house is in danger of collapsing. The claymesh walls are too heavy for the foundations."

"Understood."

Zephryn stifled the flames in his throat, this time from embarrassment. *Kesia, after this mission is over, we are never parting ways again.*

In the meantime, he needed to learn if the Lawless were worth anything or just another distraction from their escape.

Chapter Eleven

STEP RIGHT. STEP LEFT. STEP LEFT.

Forward once. Back once.

Only instead of marble floor, Kesia's heel sank into something thicker and softer. A boot.

Shance's arms fell away from her shoulders.

"Fiarston's bilge-soaked—"

"I'm sorry. These shoes are hard to move in." 'Sorry' was the word Shance had taught her for when she made a mistake. Remembering to say it was harder, but it was better than punishment from the Pinnacle.

Kesia rolled her shoulders back, sighing with relief. The movement was nearly pain free, which mean she could try shifting and investigating as soon as she had a spare moment. But Shance was on something called furlough while his airship was being fixed, which meant he was around a lot, ensuring she was prepared for the opening gala tomorrow. Apparently, mastering dance was a key part of this gala.

Shance winced and let out a slow breath, walking back toward the center of the front room. They had rolled up the rug and moved around furniture to make space for dancing. "All right, I have some feeling in my toes. Let's try this again."

Kesia stepped back, crossing her arms over her chest. "Maybe we don't need to. I'm supposed to be a mechanic from the Scepter of Industry. Who says I was ever taught to dance? I can just remain wherever the non-dancers are."

"Countess Nula won't believe it. None of them will. I love dancing. No one in that room will believe I fell in love with a clumsy woman."

"I'm not clumsy! I've mastered three forms of martial arts, armed and unarmed."

He blotted sweat from his brow with one of his unbuttoned shirt sleeves. Both of them had abandoned most of the required human outerwear except for shirts and pants. She still refused the skirt until absolutely necessary. "Which is why I think you can dance—I *know* you can. We just have to synchronize our movements. I've never met a woman I couldn't dance with."

"What about a dragon?" Kesia flipped a loose lock of hair over her shoulder. As with sparring, strands always came free from the tie. "You tell me to float, but humans don't float! Or fly. You're anchored to the earth, day in and day out, whereas I have these."

At the word, her wings emerged from her shoulder blades and along her back, bursting through her shirt and forming long arcs of scale and bone. A sigh of relief escaped her as she fluttered them. Even in the small room with the walls pressing in on her, having her wings meant there was still the possibility of escape. Freedom. Into the sky, where nothing could hold her.

Except for the Pinnacle.

Shance stared at her, his jaw slack with wonder. "They're even more beautiful than I remember." He moved toward her. "Can I touch one?"

"No." Kesia pulled her wings in, curling them against her back and shifting them into nothingness. Pain still ripped through her, but it wasn't as bad as before. "I'm sorry. I shouldn't have done that."

"No, you shouldn't have," he said absently, eyes still fixed on where her wings had been. He shook his head as if to clear his thoughts. "But floating ... can we try one more time? After this, if it doesn't work out, we'll go with your idea of being clumsy. Even if I'll be teased from here to the horizon."

"All right." It was a mystery why the airship captain was concerned with something so frivolous. How could he be a war commander when he was so easily distracted? So unlike Zephryn, who never wavered from whatever purpose he had.

Even if he ignored her from time to time. Never on purpose, though.

Shance placed his arms around her, holding Kesia in a kind of box, with her arms around him and partially braced against his shoulder. It was awkward and confining, especially when he pulled her close and she had the perfect angle to dislocate or break his jaw. That fresh wind and tree scent only helped so much.

"I'm not going to count off this time. Just relax and do your best to follow me."

Kesia snorted out smoke. "Do you really expect this to work?"

"Pretend I'm someone you trust intimately. Someone you would give your life for. Remember, those are two parts of love."

"Yes."

Trust. Giving her life for. Someone like Zephryn; but that couldn't be the case. Zephryn would never hold her like this. Although, he had seemed partial to keeping her close in the noxious cloth shop. And they'd run away from the Pinnacle rather than be separated.

But that didn't mean he would dance with her, did it?

Kesia swallowed. She didn't want or need her fleetwing to dance with her or anything else so silly. They were tactical partners. They didn't need these human emotions.

Which meant, for now, all she had to do was act. Pretend. She didn't trust Shance to keep his word or protect her, and she wouldn't die for him, but maybe she could trust him enough for a dance.

"Are you ready?" He wore another one of those concerned looks, his blue eyes soft and open. That odd stubble was still on his chin. How did it never grow longer? His lips curved into a playful smile. "Afraid I'll finally win you over?"

"Go ahead and try."

No more thinking. Release herself. Follow Shance's movements, moment by moment.

Step right. Step left. Step left.

Forward once. Back once.

Only this time, instead of crushing his toe, Kesia spun fluidly toward him. Against his chest, stepping in time with the flow of his hips. As easy as gliding on air.

Spin out again. Step back.

Step left. Mind the invisible person to her left. Half spin.

Back to center, securely locked in his arms, not confining anymore because this wasn't a fight. There was no assertion of dominance, no fear of receiving injury. No violence.

There was only moving together as one on a floor as light as the wind itself.

"And stop," he whispered in her ear.

For so they had ended, their bodies close, arms loose by their sides but still entangled in each other. She hadn't known bodies could feel that way. Only minds.

"Was that ... an improvement?" For some reason, Kesia matched his whisper.

His fingers trailed up her arms to her shoulders until they cradled her jaw. "Perfection, my lovely lady. Absolute perfection."

For the first time, the words settled into some part of her like the sweetest food and warmest fire. As enticing as his mouth. Close enough for a kiss. One soft brush of their lips against each other.

She exhaled softly. "You actually mean that, don't you?"

"Yes. More than I have for anyone else."

And just like that, the flight sank down to the ground. She sighed. It had been sweet. Of course it wouldn't last.

"So you have said it to others." Kesia chuckled, pushing away from him and tossing more hair over her shoulder.

Shance blinked, straightening his collar and adjusting his shirt, which hung askew on his lean body. "Yes, but you're the only dragon I've said it to and, well, I've never danced with anyone like that. We weren't even touching the floor. I was lifting both of us in the air."

"Clever. You should keep that in mind for your future conquests. Isn't that what humans call love affairs sometimes? Conquests? I *have* been reading."

"Kesia, that isn't—"

A knock sounded on the door. "Captain Windkeeper? A special meeting request."

"Can it wait?" Shance and Kesia began quickly rolling out the carpet.

"It came directly from Generals Brody and Markem. Your presence is demanded immediately."

Kesia pressed the last part of the carpet in place then pointed to the door. *I'm sorry,* Shance mouthed. She shrugged and walked off to the wonderful human device known as a shower.

Hot water from a fountain-like spout in the ceiling. Now, this was perfection.

Yet as she stepped beneath the spray, an image filtered into her mind. Almost a wish. Zephryn. What would it be like to dance with him?

With his shirt off.

"Captain Windkeeper. You are out of uniform." General Markem's lips formed a frown so thin it could have cut mast-line. Beside him stood General Brody.

"You said to come immediately, sir," Shance said as he saluted.

They'd called him to Markem's office. It contained only a small wooden desk, a chair, and a single bookshelf filled with maps and charts. The desk held a shiny wireless commer and a suspension clipse-mirror. No holograms were currently displayed within the chrome circle.

"That we did." Brody's expression was as stern as Markem's.

"It seems it didn't take long for you to forget any sense of discipline," Markem added. "The soft life agrees with you."

Soft life? Shance's joints and muscles felt as if they'd been through an air assault. Contrary to Kesia's verbal jabs, he hadn't actually danced much in the last few years. An afternoon here, a night there with a woman, but hardly anything considered true romance. The military stole that from him as well. At least they hadn't stolen the very words, as the Pinnacle had from dragons.

Soldiers on both sides had been robbed of their lives to keep up this damn war.

And for what? Because dragons were some great threat? As Kesia had pointed out once, there were far more humans than dragons. Plus, the four Scepters surrounded the Pinnacle, giving them the geographical edge over the land-locked mountain territory. Who was bullying whom?

Brody sighed. "While your personal matters are entirely your concern, Captain Windkeeper, you are aware of protocol when bringing your personal life onto Congruency property. It was brought to the attention of High Command that you have an unauthorized guest in your quarters."

Shance kept his expression neutral, even though fear tightened his shoulders. "She isn't unauthorized, sir. Kesia Ironsley is from the Scepter of Industry. All of her paperwork and clearances have been turned in to the main desk. I regret that I didn't get her pre-approved, but her arrival was sudden."

He'd managed to contact Zilpath about the forged documents. As soon as he'd commed her, she'd sent them over to the Central Market.

"Apparently, quite sudden." Brody's voice turned gravelly. Ah. There was that little matter of turning down Countess Nula Thredsing. Word must have gotten around. Yet another reason why staying in his rooms and tutoring Kesia was a good idea.

Markem grunted, toggling a switch on his suspension mirror and studying the document that hovered in the blank space "Hm. No living family. Good work merits, especially in the field of airship mechanics."

"It was how we met, sir. We fell out of contact with the war, but I remembered her." It was partly true. Shance did remember

Kesia, only in a different shape. "When I met her again, we realized waiting any longer to marry was foolish, especially in wartime."

"Yes, so you've told officers Fim and Ugresh." Markem flicked off the screen. "Very well. I have no further questions, Captain Windkeeper. But in the future, remember that all non-essential personnel brought onto military floors must be cleared before they are permitted on the premises."

"Yes, sir!" Shance gave him the official salute with the additional toe-heel click. "Is there anything more?"

Brody gave him a sharp glance. "As it happens, the crew of *The Silver Streak* could use any available help to assist in the repair work. I'm sure, Captain Windkeeper, you are willing to do whatever is necessary to speed its progress."

"Of course, sir." Anything but marrying a wealthy countess he didn't love.

"Then I am certain your highly-skilled betrothed would be happy to offer her talents to the war effort, especially considering it is your beloved ship."

Firestorms!

Markem nodded. "An excellent idea, General Brody. It will turn this minor infraction into something redeemable for the cause."

"Agreed. I'm sure you see the logic in this, Captain Windkeeper?"

Dread chilled his veins. He was blasted clear out of the sky, headed directly groundward. Having actually experienced that, Shance knew the actual scenario was worse—but this came very, very close.

Fiarston's beard! He had never explained a screwdriver to Kesia. Did dragons even have screwdrivers? She said she knew about mechanic work, but she could have been lying. Tonight he would have to give her a crash course. "Yes, sir. I'm certain she will help after we have finished preparing for the gala."

"Why not today?" Brody's eyes gleamed. Damn. "I would like to see just what this young lady is capable of to steal your heart so thoroughly."

"Yes, sir. Today will be fine. We will meet you in the shipyard in two hours."

Markem reached for the headset attached to the brass and wood wireless commer. "I'll have Captain Tegan arrange for coveralls and other appropriate items to be sent to your room for your betrothed."

"I look forward to it."

Shance saluted a final time and left before the situation could get any worse.

Kesia had said her family were metal-workers. Hopefully she was too, and a bit more than that.

Otherwise, they were both heading groundward.

Chapter Twelve

"YOU HAVE THE ENTIRE CITY to explore, and we find you here?"

It was the voice from a few nights ago, the one with the curious, not-quite-dragon resonance. The voice of the woman who had translated for Zilpath.

Zephryn looked up from his book, one of many spread across the table in the Scepter of Commerce's library. There stood Zilpath in a sacklike dress. Next to her stood a middle-aged woman in one of the suits females wore around here. A collar covered her entire neck, and a scarf was wrapped tightly around her head all the way to her eyebrows. She also wore gloves. That wasn't typical. It was third sunmonth, the six month of the year and a warm one even in the Cloudpeaks. In the Scepter of Commerce, the humidity was stifling.

Curious.

"Where else would I be?" Zephryn directed the question to Zilpath as both women sat down across the table from him. Although the library lacked an extensive collection of books on weaponry and military tactics, it more than made up for that deficiency in cultural textbooks, economic policies, and other useful information.

He'd spent the morning studying the surrounding geography of the city-state. Escape into the junglelands would be a possiblity. There were predators, but together, two dragons could fend them off. The only problem was, too long in scale form that close to the equator could trigger the Warm Sleep, nearly as deadly as the Cold Sleep. But skin form would leave them vulnerable.

Kesia, I need your mind. He sighed. They'd spoken periodically over the last few days, but it was insufficient.

The women were staring at him. Zephryn sighed. "Zilpath, is there a reason you are here?"

Zilpath made one of those gestures her counterpart refused to translate, but then the other woman started speaking. "What is that pile of books for? The ones on maps and engineering and horticulture? Have you read them yet?"

"They aren't for me." He pushed the stack away from the shopkeeper's hands.

"Who, then?"

There was only one person he knew who was fascinated with cartography, plants, and mechanics. One dragon, specifically, who was denied access to almost all books in the Pinnacle, except for those he smuggled into her cell. It was hardly Zephryn's fault he kept finding books Kesia would enjoy. "That is none of your concern."

"They're for her, aren't they?" Zilpath's muddy brown eyes pierced him like a lance as her fingers moved and the other woman translated. "Your embermate. What do dragons call it now?"

"I don't know—"

The translator cleared her throat. "That question was for me, your highness."

"How would you know anything about dragons? Who are you?"

She glanced at Zilpath, who made an urging sort of gesture. The middle-aged woman sighed, and a whisper of blackish vapor came from her mouth and nose. Smoke? Not the smoke of a healthy dragon; it was too thin. "Pryenil Slightshadow. I'm … something like a dragon. I don't count, not like others. But I know enough."

"How do you know?" Zephryn leaned forward, books forgotten. "Can you shift?" <Can you hear me?>

She shook her head. "I cannot hear your words, only a buzzing in my mind. You see, I was an experiment by the Pinnacle. They were intrigued by my Talent and held me prisoner with other enemies of the state. It was from my fellow prisoners that I learned the truth about dragons."

"What truth?"

Pryenil winced. "Have you heard of the Scientific Protection Unit?"

Zephryn snorted smoke then quickly inhaled it. "All I know is that they modified slatesheen to protect dragon scales, and they bind fleetwings together. They're involved in other scientific and scholarly matters as well."

He pressed his hand to his chest, feeling his heartbeat. Not only his. The pride of many fleetwings was in sharing their heartflame with their partner.

"Oh? That's not supposed to be their job." She sighed. "The Pinnacle's Scientific Protection Unit took many things from me." Her voice turned bitter. "There was an accident that resulted in my capture by the SPU. There, they used me as … practice."

Zephryn hissed, the air hot with steam. Zilpath glared at him and put a finger to her lips. He nodded once and turned his focus back to the woman. "Continue. Why did the SPU take you?"

"I'm … I'm not sure I can." Pryenil glanced around cautiously, taking in their isolated section of the library, sheltered with tall bookshelves. She focused on Zilpath, her fingers moving quickly in conversation. Zilpath reached out and covered the other woman's hands with her own. A softness gentled the old woman's face.

Zephryn raised his eyebrows. "Is something wrong?"

Pryenil exhaled another breath with trickles of smoke. "Yes. This."

She slowly unwrapped the scarf from around her head, her blonde hair falling free. She rolled down her collar, inch by inch, until her neck was entirely exposed. The air around her shimmered like the air around a live flame, shifting away the middle-aged appearance to reveal a young woman with honey-gold skin, silver-threaded gray hair, and patches of glimmering silver scales. They pock-marked her narrow cheeks and wide forehead, and clung in puckered swaths down her throat. When she glanced up at Zephryn, her left eye was slitted with a dragon pupil.

Shock and intense curiosity twisted in his gut. "What happened to you? Why can't you assume full skin form?"

Pryenil gave a sharp, coughing laugh. When she spoke, her voice was harsh and guttural. "I don't have a skin form, Nightstalker. In fact, until the SPU got their hands on me, I was human. Of course, they couldn't leave it there."

She ran her finger down her throat. Zephryn looked more closely. Neat cuts slit the scales and skin in vertical and horizontal lines from her jawline down her neck and disappeared beneath her clothing. "They were curious about my Talent for casting illusions, your highness. Shape-changing, even false shape-changing, is a rare gift. After they … studied that, they decided to see what use they could make of my leftover flesh. I can use a little resonance. I can summon smoke. I'm aware of dragon mindspeak, although I can't hear it." Pryenil slipped off her gloves and traced more silver scales on her hands. "With these, I can touch fire. That is the extent of my additional 'Talents.'"

Zephryn's jaw worked. "How is this possible?"

She flinched. Had he said something wrong? No, it was the sharpness.

"Another captive. A dragonshifter." She had returned to a no-nonsense tone. "She was kept in the cell with me. She gave me the name Pryenil Slightshadow. She was a friend." Pryenil's voice wavered. "They were taking her wings to graft onto me, and ... she died. I heard her screams through the cavern walls. Shortly after, the Lawless raided the stronghold and rescued me."

Wetness dribbled from her eyes and streaked down her cheeks. Tears. Zephryn had heard about this phenomenon. For a moment, something in him stirred, and he remembered the night his family had disappeared. "I am sorry, Pryenil."

"I need no apologies, your highness. I did not tell you my story to gain your sympathy, but to show you what evil the Pinnacle is capable of. What I need to know is if you'll fight for us. Your people. As much as I am one." She wiped her face with the fabric of her coat sleeve. "I know why you haven't, or I can guess. You are trying to protect your embermate, and they've likely held that over you for years. But you can't abandon us. Not when Garishton Ironfire—"

"You mean Garishton Razorclaw?"

"No, that's his false name. I mean Garishton Ironfire. Traitor to the throne, as all Ironfires are."

Traitor? Was that Kesia's secret? Zephryn grimaced. It would explain her reluctance to share her past with him and Razorclaw's possessiveness of her. But then, why would she run away with him?

Why would Razorclaw treat her so poorly?

His fingers stroked the edge of his voicelator. No. Right now, he needed to get as much information as possible. He and Kesia could discuss all of this later.

"Tell me more."

"Garishton Ironfire controls the Pinnacle." Pryenil sighed. "Zilpath now wishes to speak."

He turned to Zilpath, whose hands began waving around in speech. "According to the prophecy, a coalition of Ironfire, Windkeeper, and Nightstalker will bring an end to the war." Pryenil paused. "Your highness, I don't necessarily believe this but—ouch! Zilpath, we discussed this. I'm your translator, not your religious emissary!"

Zilpath made a few irritable motions. Pryenil sighed. "Yes, I know Nightstalker has been raised without religion. I'll explain." The half-dragon rolled her eyes. "Adherents to the Four Corners religion believe that there is a divine destiny for everything and that good will ultimately triumph in the power of Bonilus the Beneficent, whom you know as the All-Maker, who created all of our world and the beings within it. I don't agree with this, but from what other dragonshifters have said, the Windkeepers, Nightstalkers, and Ironfires have been closely allied in the past, so if a prophecy confirms that, so be it."

Pryenil's pocket buzzed. She pulled out a small wireless disk studded with gears and nudged Zilpath. The older woman quickly began wrapping the scarves around Pryenil's neck and head. The half-dragon's face shifted until she once more resembled a middle-aged woman.

Pryenil pressed a combination of buttons into the gears, then she and Zilpath stood.

"We have to go."

"Now? But there's so much more I need to know."

The half-dragon woman shook her head. "It can wait until after the gala. Right now, I'm needed elsewhere for the Lawless. Besides, we don't want to have to explain everything to your embermate all over again."

Zephryn grabbed her arm before she could leave. "Tell me, what is an embermate?"

"Oh? Kesia Ironfire. The other dragon." She smiled sympathetically and pulled out of his grip. "You don't know. The others probably don't either. Embermates are everything to dragons. Partners in all aspects of life who share a bond until death. You know each other on sight. Something about the resonance of the heartflame. It's a fundamental part of your world."

"You mean tactical partners."

"No, much more."

Zilpath tugged her clothing. Pryenil nodded, and the two women strolled down the aisle between the tall bronze and wood shelves. Zephryn sat down hard in the chair, Pryenil's words shifting around his thoughts.

All this time, the Scientific Protection Unit had been abducting and experimenting on humans and dragons. Zephryn had traded his position and knowledge of the Pinnacle's inner dealings in order to protect Kesia. If he hadn't been there, would she have been subjected to the same treatment?

The thought of his fleetwing being treated like Pryenil's dragonshifter cellmate made him burn enough to set flame to every book in the library. How was Kesia related to Garishton Ironfire? If he would treat his own kindred like that, if he was overseeing the SPU's experimentation, he could not be allowed to rule. Nothing could excuse this. The anger within Zephryn cooled into something hard and implacable. Were there others out there, other dragons in the Lawless who would support him?

More than ever, he needed Kesia. She had always encouraged him to reclaim his title. His fingers rubbed the voicelator. <Rose-Wing. We need to talk.>

<I'm sorry, Midnight, I can't right now.> Desperation clouded her mental voice. <Shance's superior officers are expecting me to display my advanced knowledge of mechanics.>

<What advanced knowledge of mechanics?>

<I'll explain later. Shance said someone called Captain Tegan is going to show up any moment with supplies and something called coveralls.>

Zephryn reached out through their link, sending her a pulse of reassurance from his heartflame. <I will see you tomorrow.>

<Yes. Tomorrow.> She paused. <I really miss you.>

<And I you.>

No answer. Had the link cut off before his response? Zephryn's fingers gripped the wooden table. The new information made this situation far too serious for them to be parted, even for the sake of infiltration. After tomorrow's gala, the arrangement had to end.

But first, he would take Kesia in his arms. Zephryn had seen the gesture between other couples in the Scepter of Commerce and at that moment, it seemed the perfect way of greeting her.

She could do this. She could do this.

Kesia repeated the words over and over to herself as she dressed in the gray one-piece garment. The coveralls fastened up the front with something called a zipper, a device that continuously got stuck on its own metal teeth.

She gave the metal tag another tug. "Move!"

A fold of fabric caught her foot. Kesia sidestepped to avoid tripping over her makeshift bed on the floor. According to Shance, betrothed couples could share the same bedchambers unless they had moral or religious qualms.

She had no such qualms; she just didn't want to sleep next him.

Shance had offered to give her the bed, but thanks to Kesia's years in scale form, the mattress was too soft to be comfortable. Instead, she slept on the carpeted floor near the window, wrapped in an extra blanket.

For his part, Shance said it was odd to sleep in a bed when a woman slept on the ground, so he slept on the other side of the bed, with far more blankets and sheets. He said the room cleaners wouldn't think anything of the situation.

She couldn't imagine what they thought and didn't want to. Human rituals about sharing a bed were one area that she could read about on her own, especially after Shance spoke of the male and female taking off their clothes. She was fine with Shance's clothes staying right where they were.

But Zephryn? Her chest tightened. Sleeping next to him in skin form … He'd said they might explore that area of their fleetwing bond.

Skin on skin.

"Kesia?" Shance called. "We've got to go."

She sighed. One last tug mastered the zipper, and Kesia left the room to find Shance.

He was waiting for her near the door to the suite. Captain

Tegan had left quickly after dropping off the items and hearing Shance's comments about wanting to *personally* ensure Kesia was properly dressed. Whatever that meant.

Now the airship captain held out a leather belt with small bags and holsters attached to it. Each section was heavy with metal implements or bits of wiring. "Here, let me put this on you. I organized it."

"How did you know how to do that? Did you have a romantic relationship with another mechanic?"

"No." Shance shot her an exasperated look. "I'm actually a decent mechanic myself. My father always said any captain worth their ship could do every job aboard in a pinch and should be ready to do so at any time."

Kesia allowed him to clasp the belt around her waist, and for once, he made nothing of his close proximity to her. Even his expression was grave and thoughtful. "An admirable man."

"Yes."

He stayed close, but Kesia let him this time. Instead of the annoying heat and skin prickles, there was only a comfortable warmth and that beguiling scent.

Shance continued. "My parents and I were separated during wartime. The Windkeepers were the last merchants to hold out against conscription, but while family lineage could protect his position, it couldn't keep me from the draft at age eighteen. I haven't seen them in years, but we try to keep in contact over commers whenever we can."

She nodded, sympathy swelling for him. "I can imagine that would be hard."

"Can't be helped, right? Everything for this damn war." He looked down at her curiously. "What about your parents?"

The warmth seeped away. Her muscles seized. "They're dead."

"From the war?"

Unbidden, the cavern workshop surfaced in her mind. *Her parents, hunched over the workbench, fiddling with various devices. The scent of fire and smoke and engine oil. The smell turning noxious and greenish-black. A monster looming over her, his skin curdled and pockmarked. Reaching out through clouds of thick green smoke.*

Coming for her.

"Kesia? Are you all right?"

She jumped. Shance had moved even closer, worry flickering in his eyes.

Kesia shoved the memories down.

"Something like that." She backed away from him, suddenly eager to meet her doom in the shipyard. "So, get to work, check the wires, look for the broken switches."

"That's right." Shance led the way out of the room and down the hallway. "There's always been some faulty wiring near the portside engine. Go there first if you can. And if they expect you to fix it—"

"Pray to Fiarston and Viorstan that a giant rock drops from the sky and crushes the entire ship before I have to answer."

He grinned. "Exactly. It is going to have to be a huge rock in order to break through the ceiling of the shipyard."

Kesia's blood cooled further. If she'd been in scale form, she would have instantly gone into the Cold Sleep. "There's a ceiling to the shipyard?"

"Yes, the whole facility is underground, which is why we're taking the elevator." He pressed a button on the wall, and the wall parted to reveal an ornate metal cage suspended on thick cables. "It's actually beneath the Ilyon Sea. Since we're such good friends,

I'll let you in on a secret: the shipyard is coated with this mineral called slatesheen. I'm not sure what mine it came from, but it's wonderfully strong stuff. Even the pressure from the water above doesn't stand a chance against the slatesheen. The underground tunnel is also made of it."

"Slatesheen. That's ... amazing." It was settled: there had to be illegal smuggling from traitors within the Congruency and those within the Pinnacle. Kesia fingered her voicelator, but resisted activating it. No contact with Zephryn. Not when she had to focus. She very well might try praying to imaginary deities if her luck kept running this well.

The marvel of the elevator ride was lost on her. Shance's instructions about wire colors and electrical conductivity swirled in her head until they became meaningless gibberish.

The elevator doors opened, and Kesia numbly followed Shance down a long tunnel that reminded her all too much of the ascent up the Pinnacle incline. Too soon, they walked through another archway, only instead of the darkness of the Pinnacle chamber, they entered an enormous bay, brightly lit and tall enough to contain a fifteen-story building. At least ten ships in various shapes and states of repair were vaulted on platforms or suspended from the ceiling. The air rang with the sound of hammers and steam-drills, along with plenty of shouting.

"Keep your mouth open and you'll catch lube or engine oil in it." Shance grabbed her hand and pulled her along. "Or you'll tempt me to try and kiss you again."

"I'll crush your jaw if you try." Kesia shut her mouth with a click of her teeth. The smell of engines filled the air, just like in her parents' workshop. "Should I look less interested? You said the Scepter of Industry was quite impressive."

"Oh, it is. But you're fine. General Brody and General Markem will love the compliment from a highly-ranked mechanic such as yourself."

Kesia swallowed the heat and smoke that suddenly filled her mouth. She had to be calm. This was no time to break down. This was no different than facing the Pinnacle naked.

At least then she had known what was expected of her. Here, she had nothing but a handful of information, a secondhand tool-belt, and a strong desire to shift into a bird and fly away.

As well as memories that wouldn't leave her alone.

Shance took her hand and squeezed it. "There she is!"

The Silver Streak towered in front of them, propped up on massive concrete keel blocks as tall as Shance. Holes the size of dragon jaws still gaped in the middle where the ship had nearly broken in half. Wooden scaffolding rose up on either side of the hull, and workers scurried around the deck making repairs.

Something in Kesia's fingers itched to join them. It was an urge she hadn't felt in a long time. Not since the monster came and stole her life away.

"Isn't she beautiful?" Shance's voice deepened with pride and his face lit up. Then his eyes narrowed. "Oh, blast! Where is it?"

"Where is what?"

"The masthead. It has to be there, or we're all doomed."

He dragged her toward the gangplank at a fast run, right up the sloping wood to the main deck where two generals stood in quiet conversation. Kesia gave them a quick glance. Markem was taller and had spectacles; Brody was tanner and had grayish black hair. An insufficient sweep for a spy, but right now, she didn't need more details to crowd out the ones already in her head. Besides, she was spying for herself and Zephryn now. That, and trying to survive this test.

Shance made his salute, and they responded, then both extend-ed their hands to Kesia. She shook them as she'd been taught.

"First Mechanic Kesia Ironsley." That was the man with grayish black hair. General Brody. "It seems you have kept one of our top captains rather preoccupied."

Kesia managed a faint smile. "I'm sorry, General. It's been a while since we've been together."

"Indeed. Although it didn't take you long to become be-trothed." Was there an edge of anger in his voice?

Shance's grip on her hand tightened, and he said, "Nor did it take you long to deface my ship. Where is my masthead?"

Markem cut in. "Enough small talk. First Mechanic, this ship was the pride of the Congruency fleet until it met an untimely end. Your record did list you as Talented in mechanics, but this should be quite a challenge, even for you."

"Yes." Kesia pulled up the information she'd studied from the last few days. "In the Scepter of Industry, an individual's Talent always directs their career path."

"A sensible plan." And yet, a flash of regret in Markem's eyes, so quick that she doubted if anyone else caught it. "General Brody and I are eager to see a demonstration of your skills."

She nodded, grateful that mechanics were outside the military chain of command. Kesia would have forgotten the salute many times over. "I would be happy to oblige. Shance—Captain Wind-keeper—has spoken often of this ship. I'm happy to assist him in any way I can."

"Well, prove yourself in this effort, and you might find a place aboard it yourself." There again, another hint of softness. Shance had warned her that Markem was the harsh officer, but he only seemed overly concerned with protocol and duty.

Brody was the one who kept glaring at her.

"We will check on your status in one hour. Captain Wind-keeper? Come with us. The head shipbuilder is going to give us an update on the status of repairs."

"Aye, sir. I have some specific questions of my own. About my masthead." Shance gave her a supportive smile and released her hand before turning and walking down the gangplank. Markem followed, but Brody leveled Kesia with another glare.

"I hope you are worth the time, Miss Ironsley. For your sake, as well as for Captain Windkeeper's."

He may as well have said 'murderer.' His tone held the same derision and promise of destruction as the voices in the Pinnacle.

Kesia shuddered, hands shaking as she reached for her tool belt. She clasped them together to still them. Unless that huge rock could sink through the Ilyon Sea and break through the slatesheen ceiling, she was on her own.

She wouldn't waste her hour on fear.

CHAPTER THIRTEEN

KESIA STOOD VERY STILL. Maybe if she didn't move, she would become invisible, just for a moment. She closed her eyes, as if that would help.

Wiring. Shance had said something about wiring. And broken switches in the stern. No, the portside engines.

But which side was the portside?

She knew this. Kesia turned to the left side, taking in the skeleton of the partially deconstructed vessel. There must be an engine down there, below the deck and the half-finished planks, but she could barely make out the squat metal hulk from the rest of the lower decks.

Panic stole her breath and clamped her chest like the vises in her parents' workshop. They had had so many tools there, but even more, there had been … joy.

No. Dragons didn't need those emotions.

She rubbed her palms over her eyes, trying to block the memories. They only flooded her more strongly. *The scent of tilc-dust, a curative for metal and a fixative for slatesheen. The careful flames from her parents' mouths as they tempered steel and twisted blonde copper between their fingers. The feel of those same metals in her hands, turning from liquid to solid and back to liquid, rippling around wires and cords. It was effortless. Her favorite game, due to both the ease and the amazement on her parents' faces.* "She's catching on so quickly. She seems to know instinctively what devices need."

Kesia sank to her knees, barely aware of the deck beneath her knees. She wrung her hands and felt the scales emerging before the memory tore at her again.

Fear twisting her mother's happiness into worry. "Do you think she could challenge—"

"I don't know. And she should never have to find out."

"But times are desperate—"

"Hasn't your brother done enough to her?"

Flames shooting from her mother's throat. "He saved her life!"

"And who knows what else he's done to her."

"I won't have her living in fear."

"And I won't have her be bloodstained as we are."

No. She was stained with only one person's blood: her father's.

But the monster had been so scary. *Coming at her, toward her corner in the farthest part of the cave, light from the entrance flaring around his mangled figure, scales mixed with skin and clothing, metal sunk in around his neck and head. Claws reaching out for her.*

Dried brown caked her father's hideous figure. Dried brown and fresh, slick red that smelled familiar, though never in such quantities. Whose blood? Where was the monster? Where had the monster gone?

Why couldn't she remember?

This was it, then. Kesia would spend an hour consumed in memories before being called out as a fraud. Would the Congruency bother interrogating her, or would they kill her right there? Shance would be upset about blood on the deck of his ship, but tilc and water could clean up anything.

The memory took her again. This time, Kesia didn't fight it. Let the memories come. At least she would know the truth about herself.

Her father reached to her out of the greenish haze, his misshapen mouth croaking incoherently. Croaking like a raven. She had always liked ravens.

<Kesia. Kesia, listen to me.>

She was ten years old, just tall enough to reach the work table and wield her father's pipe cutter. <Who are you? Why do you smell like my mother? Why is her blood on you?>

Relief and deep sorrow relaxed the monster's features. <Good. This will make it easier.> His face formed a snarl, snaggled with a mixture of human and dragon teeth. He took another step toward her. <I killed your mother, young dragonet. Killed her and shredded her between my teeth. And your father. Now, it is your turn.>

<They're . . . they're dead?> Rage burned her throat. Her grip tightened painfully on the pipe cutter. <Why? All they did was serve the Pinnacle. They did everything they were asked!>

<And now, they're of no more use. They rebelled against their masters. Execution was the only fitting punishment.>

She tried to find a way around the monster. She wasn't a killer. She was a maker, just like her parents.

The rock face pressed against her back. There was no escape.

The monster had killed her parents. The last of the Ironfire line was extinguished, except for her. Her rage flamed higher, and a stream of fire exploded from her throat, hitting the creature's shoulder.

He sneered. <You think that will be strong enough to stop me, dragonet? You're no more fierce than a bellows.>

"Stay away from me!" *The ground shook beneath her with the resonance of her voice.*

Fear showed in his eyes, but he only made another croaking laugh. <Is that the best you can do? Your parents fought harder when they were half-dead. Dear Warys and Otunk Ironfire, pleading for the life of their daughter.>

Something dark rose within her, streaming out of her vocal cords in a maelstrom of fury and fear. The room quaked violently, her little cot and chair in a corner rattling against the floor.

Then suddenly, everything became still in her head. Her screams became their own song, weaving among the substances around her and reducing them to nothing. The chair melted to the ground and the ceiling dripped into living stalactites, sliding over her skin and leaving no mark. She was beyond them. Above them.

Before her, the monster shimmered, and she knew that he was solid no more. <Good girl. I'm sorry, dragonet. I'm so sorry, my star.>

And then, it happened. The melting. It started with his skin slithering and sliding off his form. The rest followed in nauseating waves, muscles and bones and everything else that composed a being. She wanted to look away, but she couldn't.

He'd called her his star. Only her parents called her that, from the earliest moment she could remember.

Tears spilled down her cheeks, and her chest shook with sobs.

She had killed him. She'd killed her father.

Why? He'd acted like a monster. Why had he tricked her?

She fell to her knees next to him, her hands shaking from grief.

It didn't matter. She was still guilty.

Smoke arose from the puddle on the ground, a hideous cloud of bilious green that filled the corners of the cavern. It silenced her voice, choking her. She fell over, the rocks cutting into her cheek.

Green smoke.

She gasped. *The Silver Streak* snapped into focus around her, the portside engine looming in front of her. How had she gotten to the engine room?

A glance at the planks above her revealed a human-sized hole melted in the ceiling. That couldn't be real. She couldn't have fallen through the deck. More knowledge filtered into her mind. Melting and shaping materials had been her mother's Talent.

But a dragon or human only inherited one Talent, or else their own, unique Talent emerged. She'd never heard of anyone receiving both Talents.

And where had the cavern-shaking scream come from? She'd melted her father by yelling at him? It was almost as if something had made her stronger. Some other force.

Before her, a greenish haze of smoke particles surrounded the portside engine. Impossible. Any smoke should have dissipated at this point, yet the poisonous fumes wreathed the tall column with its steam-furnace, brass coolant tubes, and auxiliary wind turbines.

The same smoke that had consumed her father during his final moments.

A shapeshifter. Her father had been an animal shifter like her. He had been between skin and scales and something else when she saw him, with clumps of fur and feathers. A monster. As if he couldn't properly stay in any one form. Or like something had stopped him from shifting, something that had frozen his Talent in an odd, in-between stage.

How long had she been locked in her memories? Did she have enough time to fix anything?

She had to try. Whatever had held her back before vanished. Her father had killed her mother, then tricked her into killing him, but something else had started the process long before he'd invaded her cave. The green smoke. It had been used on board *The Silver*

Streak and in the Pinnacle. Her parents had reported directly to a special part of the organization.

The SPU.

They had killed her father, mutilated him beyond recognition. Kesia had simply finished the job, putting him out of the misery of being trapped in that horrible mixture of forms. That's what he'd wanted.

She needed to talk to Zephryn. He could explain the rest. Together, their minds could solve anything.

Right now, she was under a deadline, and she realized she didn't need anything Shance had taught her about ships or tools. For her, mechanics didn't work like that. Fixing things didn't have to be cold and rigid. It could be warm and organic. Fluid. The wires and gears and bolts didn't have to stay in their shapes. They could be whatever she wanted them to be. Whatever was needed to fix the problem.

Kesia could almost see her mother's smile. *Never let what you know limit you, my star. Only let it guide you to find new solutions.*

First, she had to get rid of the smoke particles. They were so small that no one else could see them; too small, she assumed, to affect Talents. But they still bothered her, like a cloud of toxic gnats. She waved her hand at them, pulling them away from the engine and into her palm. Kesia squeezed her hand into a fist, condensing the particles into a small disc. She opened her hand. The particles heated. Melted. Vanished into invisible vapor, too small to ever hurt anyone again.

Now, she just had to fix the engine. The problem was, the outer shell was in the way. All of that troublesome metal.

Find a solution. The smoke particles had been visible to her when no one else had seen them. Her mother had always known where the smallest bits of metal were going.

As if she'd had special vision. Had Kesia inherited that too?

She squinted.

Nothing. Apparently there were limits to these Talents. Well, there was no point in being able to manipulate metals if she couldn't be sure of what she was doing.

"Come on, Kesia, remember!"

She closed her eyes and tried to picture her mother at work, hands shaping metal, bursts of fire coming from her mouth, goggles over her eyes … goggles. She had had goggles.

Kesia fumbled through the tool pouch at her waist, hoping Shance had included something like that. Screwdrivers, pliers, some kind of miniature torch, and—

"Goggles. Please work." She slipped them on.

Please. Another word Shance had taught her to show others kindness. Unfortunately, it didn't work on the goggles. She pressed her fingers over the sides and found a switch. Suddenly, the lights turned on. Everything inverted. Grayish shapes surrounded her, outlined in white, each composed of parts broken down to lines and points and tangents.

Kesia looked at the engine again and smiled.

"Hi there. Let's have fun."

Chapter Fourteen

THEY HAD MUTILATED HIS SHIP.

The repair status was bleak. *The Silver Streak* would be grounded six weeks, if not longer. The mechanics, carpenters, and electricians couldn't begin building new until they had broken down the old.

But more than that, they'd defaced the heart of Shance's ship. The beautiful masthead and stunning bronze plating with wings were gone. Anger tightened his chest. Doldrums! It had to be Brody's doing. Retribution for Shance spoiling his plans.

Shance forced himself to listen to the head shipbuilder. General Markem looked unsurprised at the news, merely making notes on a pad of paper. General Brody, however, looked ready to burn a hole through Shance's skull. Thankfully, his Talent was far more benign: he could perceive the color of anything by touching it.

As soon as Markem had stepped away to discuss other ships with the chief engineer and officer of repairs, Brody cornered Shance.

"What the flaming sky do you think you're doing?" He closed in, not quite touching him, but close enough for Shance to know he'd had smoked fish for breakfast. "When I told you about the

Grand Count's offer, you were supposed to accept, not go behind my back and pull out a fake betrothal! Where did you find this girl, anyway? How much are you paying her?"

Shance set his jaw. "I'm not paying her anything, sir. She is my betrothed. All of the papers on our engagement have been filed with the proper authorities."

"An engagement you neglected to mention when that music girl was sitting in your lap! This First Mechanic Kesia Ironsley shows up right after you turn down Countess Nula's proposal. Very convenient for you, Captain Windkeeper."

Shance set his jaw. "I believe I have answered all of these questions before. Sir."

Brody harrumphed. "You do understand that all of this has resulted in the Grand Count withdrawing the additional monies for the repair crew. We are behind schedule because of you."

"Well then, my betrothed has come at just the right time." Considering Kesia's hour was nearly up, Shance could only hope Fiarston and Viorstan had favored him in some way by granting her miraculous mechanical powers.

"One Talented mechanic in exchange for wealth, privilege, and security, not just for yourself, but for the Congruency fleet. And the Countess is easy on the eyes too. The Grand Count is a leading member of the Curious Intrigue! They have ties to every city in the Congruency. Gods, can't you see I was trying to do you a favor?"

"With all due respect, sir, I don't need your favors or the honor of entrance into some secret society of half-drunk men and gossipy women." And why should he care about the Curious Intrigue? What some shut-up scientists did in back rooms didn't matter. Anger flared in Shance, and he fought to keep from shouting. "I was conscripted into the war effort to serve the Congruency because I had no other choice. In the situation with the Countess, I had a choice, and I made it."

An odd urgency came into General Brody's eyes. "Yes, well, I only hope that choice doesn't get you killed."

Shance exhaled, trying to keep his tone level. "The only thing that will kill me, sir, is the removal of my masthead."

"That old thing? It's been taken off for repairs. The shipbuilder wants to make you a new model deserving of your standing within the fleet."

"I don't want any other." His heart sank. Had they really destroyed his inheritance? "What happened to my masthead, sir?"

Brody shrugged. "Off in storage with the rest of the old artifacts. And those dragon wings? You were lucky we overlooked them thus far." He clapped Shance on the shoulder. "Honestly, Windkeeper, take care. Some people would consider using a dragon masthead as a sign of treason."

Despite his anger, Shance fought the urge to smile. *As opposed to being in league with two dragons?* Never mind that it was temporary, and that they kept their own secrets. It still felt right to trust them more than the Congruency.

"General Brody! Captain Windkeeper! I insist you come here at once." It was General Markem standing aboard *The Silver Streak* next to Kesia.

Fear sank into Shance's heart. She'd failed. He hadn't prepared her enough. The challenge had been too difficult. His muscles seized, and he felt for his pistol. He didn't want to use it, but if it came down to it, Kesia would need cover fire to escape—and he would make sure she had it rather than see her and her lovely wings shut away in a Congruency prison.

Brody gave him one last glare and leaned in closer, his voice a fierce whisper. "You fool no one, Shance Windkeeper. Neither does she. And yet no one here is opposing your hoax. Why do you think that is?"

Shance's mouth went dry. "Sir?"

"Take this. A little extra kick, for old time's sake." Brody slipped a flask into his hand. "Since you insist on going along with your charade. Don't say I didn't warn you. There are fates worse than arranged marriage. Stay clear of the smoke, or you'll die in it."

Brody drew away and made for the *The Silver Streak*. Shance followed.

What could he mean? Shance's mind returned to the mysterious green smoke from the explosion, which had been curiously absent from the reports after the High Command meeting. Had it suddenly slipped their minds that this smoke suppressed Talents? Where was the talk of rebel involvement? And why was Brody so concerned with a marriage when there were anarchists to repress?

When this was over, he and Kesia needed to talk and share information. That was part of this arrangement, and now he was far more inclined to listen.

Plus, if she was keen on exploring, she might be able to help him find that masthead.

Shance and Brody ascended the gangplank. There stood General Markem—was that a *smile* on his lips? Shance wasn't aware the stiff old goat was capable of it. It looked odd, but the glint in his eyes was genuine. Next to him stood Kesia. Her hair was half out of its tie, and there were grease and oil stains all over her coveralls, arms, and face. What he noticed most was the brightness in her eyes, shining with a glee Shance had never seen in their short time together. She might be trying not to smile, but her amber eyes were glorious. When he had left her, she'd been ready to turn invisible and disappear forever. What had changed?

General Markem spoke. "The papers Captain Windkeeper turned in may have been late, but they are certainly accurate. First Mechanic Ironsley is one of the most Talented workers I have met. First Mechanic, state your accomplishments."

"I have completely repaired the portside engine."

Brody raised his eyebrows. "You mean you have diagnosed it and prepared a list of necessary repairs. That has already been done by our own mechanics."

"No, I mean I have repaired it. Sir."

Her voice was clear and certain, her stare level.

General Markem spoke up. "I have personally assessed the work, as has the engineer for this vessel. She called it 'well enough.' She even said that in the event she had to retire, First Mechanic Ironsley might be a mildly competent potential replacement."

"Virna? Chief Engineer Virna Conners? That's high praise from her." Shance studied Kesia anew. Everything in him wanted to sweep her off her feet and never let her go, even though she was a dragon. No, *because* she was a dragon. A beautiful dragon woman who was far more clever and kind and loyal than any other woman he had ever encountered.

General Brody was frowning. "Naturally, such a thing is impossible. It would be entirely disruptive to the chain of command."

"Nonetheless, First Mechanic Ironsley has volunteered to work on *The Silver Streak* for the remainder of its repairs in dry dock. And I shouldn't wonder if, with her on our side, we should be back on schedule." Markem gave another one of those odd smiles.

"Astonishing." Brody's eyes narrowed. "And just how did you accomplish this, First Mechanic Ironsley? What is your Talent?"

Kesia paused, pressing her lips together, then she bent down and picked up a piece of stray metal. Her fingers worked at it as if it were clay, shaping and molding it, rubbing the edges until at last, she held out a perfectly-hewn piece of copper pipe. "It's a little like this, sir. Metal, wiring, they all make sense to me. I understand them. The engine was bent out of shape, as were the exhaust pipes and the fuel conductors. Normally, you'd have to put in new ones, but I fixed the ones that were there."

"Brilliant." Shance grinned at her. Kesia returned his grin before looking away, her cheeks flushing pink. They definitely needed to talk later. About all of this. "Just as I always knew she could. Will that be all, sir? The First Mechanic and I have plans tonight in preparation for the gala tomorrow. If you wouldn't mind."

"Of course." Markem nodded. "Unless General Brody has any objections?"

Brody gave Kesia a final scrutiny. "No. It appears everything is in order. For now."

"Very good." General Markem nodded. "Captain Windkeeper. First Mechanic Ironsley. You are dismissed."

She'd done it. She'd fixed the engine.

Kesia stared down at her hands, smudged with black grease and dribbles of oil. It was as if another part of her had come alive after a long Cold Sleep. A part that could look at things and pull them apart, rework them in her head, and put them back together in her hands. A part that never gave up, even if the circuits burned out the first few times.

All she wanted to do was fix everything. Eat. Sleep. Sing. Dance.

Tell Zephryn—but would he understand? He had seemed interested in skin forms. Could he understand her rediscovered joy of working with her hands, of shaping and coaxing metals into their proper places? She found that she loved it, as much as she loved flying through the open air or shifting into animals or protecting people. All of those things were part of her. Would he accept that?

Somehow, they'd reached Shance's quarters again. As soon as he closed and locked the door, his laugh, loud and joyful, filled the room. Kesia turned toward the sound and saw his bright smile moment before he grabbed her in his arms and spun her in a circle.

Flying without wings. It wasn't the same, but that wasn't a bad thing according to the beating of her heart.

Kesia smiled. "You're stronger than you look."

"And you're more incredible than I could have imagined." Shance held her close, and she could see the light shining in his eyes. "Kesia, I can't believe you did that. All this time, that was your Talent?"

"Well, one of them." Scale mites! She wasn't supposed to say that.

"Oh yes? I guess I shouldn't be surprised. What's your other one? Or is that another spy secret?"

She wanted to tell him. Wanted to say everything. After so long in the dark, Kesia wanted one person without any secrets, even if it was a human airship captain that she might not see again once this mission ended.

What did she have to lose?

"I don't just shift between scales and skin." She stepped away from him and tucked a lock of hair behind her ear. "I can shift into any animal that I've seen."

"Really?" Shance tilted his head to the side. "Can I see? Oh, wait, do you need to go into the bedroom to take off your clothes?"

"Not for this form. But do open the door to the bedroom for when I shift back." Kesia rolled up the sleeves on her coveralls.

Shance cracked the door to the bedroom half-open. "Ready."

"Good. I think you might recognize this form." She closed her eyes and calmed her racing heart with a breath in. A breath out.

Breathe in. Breathe out.

Sun-dove.

As quick as her breaths, her skin form shrank, vanishing beneath the yellow and pale blue feathers of a sun dove. Her coveralls fell to the floor. A beak pushed out from where her lips were, her vision became monocular, and as she had before, she flapped her wings and flew straight to Shance's shoulder.

He stared at her in wonder. "That was you? On my shoulder that night?"

<Yes.> Of course, he couldn't hear her. He'd never be able to hear her. Not like Zephryn. A part of Kesia faltered. Spoken words did have their limits.

She gave a trill and pecked gently at his collar. Shance chuckled. "A little luck charm. My good omen. That's how you knew about the crash and the green smoke. You were there already."

She bobbed her head deliberately. He reached out and tickled the feathers near her neck, drawing another coo. "Is that how you knew to rescue me?"

Kesia flew away from him and through the open bedroom door.

Mountain grazer.

Clawed feet turned to cloven hooves, legs lengthened and covered with brown and white fur, and horns emerged from her head. She quickly head-butted the door shut.

Skin.

Fur melted into smooth, pale flesh. Her bones and muscles elongated and pushed out two arms and legs, and her face stretched into human shape. Kesia did a quick check to see that every part was in proper order, then threw on fresh clothes and walked out to the sitting area. She grabbed her voicelator from the ground and put it on again. "Yes, that's how I was there to catch you."

"Where does the rest of 'you' go when you shift?"

"Into the Nether. Somewhere else." She made a vague gesture. "When we need it, we pull it back to us. A shapeshifting scientist could explain it better."

Shance nodded. "Why were you on my ship that day?"

There was no point in keeping that a secret. "I had talked Zephryn into an illegal recon mission. I wanted to impress the Pinnacle so they would lift my conviction."

His expression sharpened. "Your conviction?"

"Yes." Kesia paused. Swallowed hard. She knew the truth now, but saying it was an entirely different matter. "I killed someone. Not in battle. Self-defense."

"And the Pinnacle still condemned you for it?"

"They believed differently." Kesia surged ahead. "I saw your ship and I saw you, and then when you stayed with your ship trying to save it, that was really brave. It was foolish, but brave, and—I don't know. I couldn't let you die."

Shance's face softened to a look of awe. "I understand. The day we met on on the wharf beside Ilyon Sea, I was following the winds. Well, and I was running away from someone, but it felt as if the winds were pushing me toward you."

"I see. Well, I'm not sure if it was the winds." Kesia shrugged. "I'm just glad I was there."

"As am I, lovely one." He sidled closer again, with that melting look in his eyes that made her skin prickle and her mind spin with uncertainty. "You are truly extraordinary." He took her hand in his, slowly and easily, rubbing his finger over the back of it. It felt nice, and he smelled nice—if only it wasn't him.

Zephryn's narrow face and dark, intense eyes flashed in her mind.

Kesia pulled her hand away. "You keep saying that, but you don't know me. You've done all of these things, you've trusted me, and we've only known each other a few days. You haven't even seen my other skin form."

"I haven't?" His voice was curious but held an edge of alertness and concern. Good. There was some sense in him.

Kesia shook her head and focused, releasing the aspect of her Talent that hid her scales. Her skin shifted, rosy scales arcing over the back of her hands, surfacing on her forehead and along her cheekbones, trailing down her neck. She turned her slit-pupiled eyes to Shance and said, "I'm always a dragon, Shance Windkeeper. Even when I seem like you, I am still a dragon."

To his credit, he didn't flinch. He studied her intently. "Are there any other differences?"

"Yes. And no. Well, a few other things." Kesia breathed flames into her palm, cradling them for a moment before closing her fist and extinguishing it. There was no point in sharing anything more with him. "You seem to be a good human. You're brave, and you care deeply about your ship and crew. But we are not the same. I appreciate the opportunity to play this game with you to gain information, but you don't need to maintain any kind of romantic act here. We're able to work together. That's enough."

At that, he laughed. Not a loud, joyous laugh like before, but a quiet chuckle that perfectly fit the amazed expression on his face.

"You're really not used to hearing it, are you?"

"Not used to hearing what?"

Passion and sympathy burned in his eyes as he gazed at her. "Anyone being honestly attracted to you. This isn't an act, Kesia. It's a simple observation of what I've seen over the past few days." His voice grew low and firm, and he stepped closer. "The fact that no one has thought to let you know how your presence makes the world a better place, how your hair rivals silk and your face is beautiful, scales, grease smudges and all, is a damn injustice. I have only one question for you, dearest."

Kesia fought for breath. "What?"

"Why is such a worthwhile woman holding fast to the hope that her tactical partner will recognize her as a woman instead of a soldier, when there is another man here, willing to give anything just to hold her in his arms and let her know, every moment, how much she means to him?"

Kesia's lungs were frozen, her head filled with cotton and steel, her thoughts mush. Her fingers fisted, ready to punch Shance for confusing her with so many ideas and emotions.

For daring to attack Zephryn.

For luring her into trusting him with her revelations.

For smelling so oddly irresistible.

Finally, she found words.

"Um, I should take a shower."

Kesia fled the room, fighting the urge to shift into a cat or a bird, into scale form, anything to stop the pain in her chest and the wetness leaking from her eyes. She sighed in relief when she turned on the shower and faced the spray, letting her tears melt into the hot water.

All she wanted was to find answers to the green smoke and

escape with Zephryn. Now, it looked like the Pinnacle had killed her parents by making her face a monster. And then there were the rebels that had found Zephryn—the Lawless. They were determined to use him for their own ends to reestablish the old kingdom. At this point, even if they were anarchists, Kesia's sympathies lay with them. Her stomach churned at the notion that the Pinnacle and Congruency had been in league.

And what of Shance's words? Implying that Zephryn somehow didn't care for her. What did he know? She was a dragon. She didn't need human niceties like compliments and overt adoration.

Even though that sounded nice. If only she could have heard it from someone else.

She needed Zephryn.

Kesia rubbed the voicelator around her neck, heating it with all the anger, frustration, and desire that enveloped her heartflame.

<Rose-Wing! Did you pass the test?>

<Yes, Midnight.> She sighed and leaned against the shower wall. <With excellence. They assigned me to permanent duty on Shance's ship for as long as I'm here.>

His relief and delight enfolded her in reassurance. Kesia grinned. Compared to that, Shance's words were hollow echoes. <As always, you are resourceful in the face of difficulty. What did you do?>

<I ... remembered.> She swallowed. <I remembered what my parents taught me.>

<Your parents?> Intense curiosity filled his voice. <What of them?>

Kesia pressed her palms again the shower wall on either side, imprinting the metal. Guilt sank her heart. She'd told Shance first, not Zephryn. Zephryn, her fleetwing who deserved to know all.

What had she been thinking?

<They were metal workers. All Ironfires were craftsmen of some kind. Builders. Fixers. Inventors, sometimes. My mother could shape any kind of solid surface with her hand. Wood, steel, bronze, stone. My father could shapeshift into any animal. He's where I got that Talent from.>

<That makes sense.>

<Yes, well, I inherited Talents from each of them.>

<Two Talents? How did you survive?>

Kesia tilted her head to one side. <Why wouldn't I?>

<Dragons with two Talents die in early childhood due to the strain on their bodies. Again, how did you survive?>

She closed her eyes and searched through her memories. It was much easier to do so now that she had opened the door to her past. <My uncle. My parents took me to my uncle. He was a scientist, and he—>

A memory seared her mind. *A hand striking her cheek, then holding her jaw still in an iron grip. Tears prickling the corners of her eyes. Sucking in her breath and gritting her teeth instead of crying out. She wouldn't tell. She couldn't tell, or he would stop helping her. He wanted to help her, but she couldn't speak a word, or she would ruin it. All her fault. Even as they strapped her to the table and the room filled with green smoke, it was all her fault...*

Green smoke? She began to shake. What had he done to her?

If you tell anyone, they will know you're a monster, and they will kill you. Only I will understand.

<Rose-Wing?> Zephryn's voice pushed through the memories. <What happened?>

She swallowed hard, shoving away the dark images and emotions. <My uncle fixed me. But it was wrong, somehow, so my

parents hid me from him.>

<Who was your uncle?>

Garishton Ironfire.

Fear knotted her stomach.

No. She couldn't tell anyone. Not even Zephryn. She needed to figure out what her uncle did to her first. Process it and make sure there were no horrible aspects to the experimentation. Then she could reveal all the knowledge to Zephryn in exactly the way she wanted.

It would be safer that way.

<I don't know. They never told me because they said I'd never meet him. They said if I even thought his name, it might increase his chances of finding me, because names and heartflames—>

<Are how we know each other. Yes.> His tone was sharp, demanding. Kesia could almost picture his dark blue eyes gleaming at her. <What happened to them?>

<They were killed.> Suddenly, the shower stall seemed too small. She wanted to be free with Zephryn, circling each other in the sky or curled up together in a cavern. <Midnight, I didn't kill my father. Not the way I thought. It was self-defense.>

<I know.>

So simple. <How can you know?>

<Because I know you, Kesia Ironfire. You're my fleetwing. You are strong, caring, and brave. I wondered at your reasons and secrecy, but I never doubted your innocence of murder.>

Bone-deep warmth and assurance flowed from him, as steady and sure as always. Her heart beat like a million wing-flaps, and even more steam filled the chamber.

The walls sagged behind her. Her fingers pressed through the metal. Her Talent! Kesia straightened and stood before she melted through the wall entirely. She winced at the concave wall showing the impressions of metal pipes.

<Rose-Wing? What happened?>

<It's nothing. Just something I'll have to fix.> She swallowed hard. <Midnight, I—I really want to see you tomorrow.>

<And I you. What is the plan of action?>

Kesia closed her eyes, recalling the discussion she'd had with Shance a day ago. <Your pretense is as a relative of some kind, someone who disapproves that I ran away from the Scepter of Industry and became betrothed to Shance.>

<Ah. Well, I do disapprove, so that won't be difficult.>

<Oh, do you?> Her heart sped up even faster. <And why is that?>

<We're fleetwings. Or, to use a new word from a Lawless representative, we're embermates. The more I learn of betrothal, the more I'm coming to the realization that it is very similar to what we have.> His mental voice deepened with rough certainty. <And I have no desire to share you in that way.>

An odd relief filled her. <Ah, that's good. Very good.>

She could almost see his raised eyebrows. <Rose-Wing? What aren't you telling me?>

<Only that the esteemed Captain Windkeeper saw fit to declare his feelings and passion for me.>

<He did what?>

<And he also said that you were unfit to have me as a companion.>

A growl filled their mental link, along with hot possessiveness. <Ah. So that explains the strong emotions when you contacted me.>

Kesia exhaled relieved laughter. <Yes, I couldn't believe it! Who says that they want to spend their life with someone after knowing

them a few days? I'm a spy. For all he knows, I'm going to kill him in his sleep.>

<Excellent point. Although you wouldn't. You already have a high regard for him, despite your frustration. He must sense that.>

Was that a hint of jealousy? She grinned. <Concerned, Midnight?>

<Only that your heart will split from containing so much amusement, Rose-Wing.>

She laughed again. <A fear you will have for the rest of your life, because I have no intention of seeking another.> The idea was absurd. She and Zephryn were bound. Even if Shance held that strange scent attraction, it was no match for her fleetwing. <Although ... there are aspects of human betrothal and marriage that we haven't partaken of. The Pinnacle forbade physical intimacy in skin form.>

Zephryn's voice deepened again. <We're not part of the Pinnacle anymore. We can explore each other however we wish.>

However they wished. Skin on skin. An image of Zephryn shirtless on the sparring field, his lean muscles gleaming with slatesheen, his movements swift and deadly. His eyes intense as they studied her.

Her blood heated, and steam filled the shower so that she couldn't see the walls. Kesia took a slow breath in then exhaled. If she wasn't careful, she'd melt the shower room another way.

Embermates. Kesia turned the word over in her mind. If she concentrated, she could almost remember her parents using it, though not very often, as if they were afraid of it.

<We'll need to find an isolated place at the gala tomorrow.>

<I envision needing to take you aside to argue with you about the foolishness of your decisions.> Humor threaded his voice. <It

should be quite easy.>

Kesia rolled her eyes. <As I recall, you were the one who chose rundown lodgings without enough room for you to properly pace.>

<Hmph. Granted.>

<And I would recommend we stay isolated for another reason: I am required to continue acting as Shance's betrothed.>

<Yes, I remember. Do what you need to keep yourself safe.>

<Agreed.>

<The Lawless are only telling me half-truths. We need definite information about the Congruency's involvement with the Pinnacle. Will you be able to investigate tonight?>

<Yes, I will.> She turned the metal knobs on the side of the stall and grabbed a towel, rubbing her dripping hair and grabbing the plush robe that Shance claimed had come with the room. The robe would be coming with her when she left.

<Will you tell Windkeeper?>

She paused. On one hand, Shance had been nothing but open and honest with her. On the other, the less he knew, the less he could reveal under coercion.

And Kesia didn't need anyone worrying about her.

<Not if I can help it.>

<Very well. I need to go. Zilpath insists on fitting me with appropriate clothing in that hideous shop of hers. She continues to ask me questions through her interpreter and poke me with pins when I don't respond. These humans; why don't we eat them?>

She laughed. <Because they're aiding our cause, and they're our friends.>

<Yes. That word 'friend' makes things inconvenient.>

She sent him a wave of sympathy. <Endure it. I had to. You'll survive.>

<I know I will. I'm just not sure she will.>

<Until tomorrow, Midnight.>

<I count the hours, Rose-Wing.>

Kesia rolled her shoulders back, allowing her muscles to relax. Her fleetwing had an impeccable way of clearing her thoughts to focus on what was important. On completing the task. On their security as fleetwings. As embermates, whatever that meant. They could discover it together, in all aspects.

Her face flushed, but she shrugged off the arousal. Right now, she needed to tell Shance the truth, or at least part of it. Enough that he would keep his distance and allow her to think properly.

A moment later, clad in pants and shirt, she emerged from the bedroom, walking into the overwhelming scent of food. The entire private dining table was covered in different kinds of dishes, some that she'd tried and liked, others that she'd never seen before.

Shance sat in one of the chairs, leaning back, his eyes closed. Sleeping?

"What is this?" Kesia swallowed, trying to remember what she had come to say.

His eyes snapped open, and the front legs of his chair clopped to the floor. "Oh, I figured you'd be hungry because you eat every few hours, so I just ordered. If that's all right."

"That's ... fine." She sighed. Shance was only being nice, and he was right; she needed food. Shape-shifting took a lot of energy. The odor of freshly-cooked crenbird with its mixture of herbs and savory spices consumed her senses. "I need to tell you something while we eat."

She reached for the crenbird leg and started eating, just to clear her thoughts.

"I thought so." Shance ran a hand through his hair, making it stick up on end. It looked cute. "That was a lot to throw at you, and I'm sorry."

Kesia nodded. "Yes, it was. I forgive you. But this has to stop, Shance. I know that we're pretending to be engaged, but I can't actually consider being in love with you."

"Yes. That's fair." He paused. "Do you at least care for me?"

"As much as I can, but not in a…" She searched for the word. "Romantic way."

He picked at a fried root vegetable. "But you are attracted to me. I know that."

"Does physical attraction necessitate love?"

"No, I suppose not. Although it can."

"Maybe for you." She finished off the crenbird leg and took another. "I'm focused on more important things right now, like trying to find the truth about the explosion. And Zephryn is my fleetwing. We're joined at the heart."

Shance's brow wrinkled. "Wait … not literally."

"Yes, literally. The heart of a dragon is composed of the heart-flame. When dragons are matched with their fleetwing, both are cut open in scale form and their hearts cut in half. The parts are then sewn into each other somehow. I'm not exactly sure of the details. Medicine isn't my specialty. But from that moment, Zephryn and I were joined forever."

"How old were you?"

"Eleven. Zephryn was thirteen. It can be older, but eleven is the youngest the surgery can be attempted."

Shance spluttered on his drink. "Eleven? You were only a child! You meet your destined other half—literally—as a child and you just *trust* that? Enough to undergo major surgery?"

"Why not?"

He waved the goblet around, spilling some of the contents onto the carpet. "What if you're not compatible? What if you like completely different things? What if the other person turns out evil?" Shance's eyes widened. "What if one of you dies?"

"Are humans truly that wayward? Our heartflames wouldn't have called to each other if we had been incompatible. That pull, that bond, is an alignment of mental and physical connection."

"So if one of you is evil, the other would be too."

"Yes, although that rarely happens, as far as I know." Kesia paused. "As for death—that would involve both of us as well. Whether by life or death, we are joined."

Shance took another drink of wine. "So, you don't have marriage or love or family, but you have fleetwings. Do you have bed?"

"Bed? Perhaps some do sleep in beds—"

"No, bed. Bedding." She blinked, and he sighed. "…sex."

"Ah sex. Breeding? Only in scale form."

"As dragons?"

Kesia rolled her eyes. "I'm *always* a dragon. And yes in scale form. I've heard it's not enjoyable, beyond the flying aspects." Should she say more? It didn't seem important, but the more useless information she offered, the easier it would be to earn Shance's trust and sneak out later. "That was one reason Zephryn and I left. Lord Garishton Razorclaw threatened to break our fleetwing bond and assign us new breeding partners. The attempt would have killed us."

Shance frowned, running his finger along the rim of his glass. "Are you and Zephryn … married?"

"I told you, dragons don't have that word—"

"Why not?" He tilted his chair forward. "Why are you missing all these words for love and romance?"

Would the man not let her eat? She swallowed quickly. "If I knew that, I'd tell you."

"Would you?"

"Maybe." She threw the crenbird bones on her plate and stared at them as if they might give a reason for the anger and uncertainty churning in her stomach. "The Pinnacle says excessive relations are an unnecessary distraction from the realities of war."

Shance's voice was quiet. "You left because they were going to separate you and your fleetwing."

"I know." Kesia glanced up at him. Consideration tinged with sadness softened Shance's face. She felt as if she should apologize. But she wasn't sorry Zephryn was her fleetwing. Shance had given away his affections of his own will.

Far too freely.

"Yes, well." He cleared his throat. "We still need to portray a betrothed couple for the remainder of this charade. That includes the gala tomorrow.

"Of course. That was always part of our agreement."

"Exactly." Shance scratched at his stubble, staring into the distance for a moment. "Tomorrow there will be some women at the gala that I've been with. Intimately."

She nodded with a snort of smoke. "You've mentioned this before. I still don't want details."

Shance played with his fork. Why was he nervous? "There's something else you need to know. There is a Countess Nula who proposed to me as part of a military deal. I marry her, and her father increases his already generous military support. Everyone wins. I turned her down, but she was being very … persuasive."

Kesia frowned. "With words? Or was she trying to arouse you?"

"Both. Also, about the open discussion, remember—"

"Human females don't discuss matters of sex and arousal openly because it offends them. For people who have such a high view of love and intercourse, you're curiously scared about acknowledging it."

"I'm not arguing with you. Just … don't do it."

"Very well. But you think she will be there tomorrow and try to arouse you again?"

"I don't know. At the very least, she has the ears of many influential people in the Scepter of Commerce, including those of the Curious Intrigue." Kesia tilted her head to the side at the unfamiliar name. Shance added, "Some ancient secret society of scientists and scholars. Very powerful, but mostly harmless, I've heard. Focused on arcane matters of science and philosophy, trying to test the limits of humans. Supporters of the war, but then again, who isn't?"

"I see." Kesia watched her plans to get Zephryn alone burn to ash. But a stubborn ember remained, fueling her next words. "I will do my best, but I will also speak with Zephryn tomorrow privately."

"Why? Haven't you been speaking with him this entire time? I need you at my side tomorrow as much as possible."

The ember flamed higher with her irritation. "I have repaired your ship and accepted all your other pretenses. I will spend time with Zephryn, regardless of what you think you need. If you wanted fewer complications in your life, maybe you should have had less sex with untrustworthy women."

"I didn't have sex with this one!"

Kesia blew out a stream of smoke. Taking another shower sounded really good right now. Or shifting and flying out of this place. "Why did you have sex with all of the others?"

He leaped up from the table. "Better than dwelling on this damn pointless war!"

Her hands shook, eager for a knife. Better to deal with this situation through sparring than with more words. But then she'd probably kill Shance. Her heart sank and she slouched back in her chair, jaw set. "The war is part of life. Hiding away in physical pleasures won't change that."

"You haven't tried it."

"Why does that matter?"

Shance flung his fork at his plate, his eyes blazing with anger. "It's bad enough that the blasted Congruency took my family away and forced me to fight for them. Bad enough that every one of my actions is under their orders, never mind that my instincts tell me something is wrong with all of this. At least with women I get something good out of it. Even if it doesn't mean anything in the end, it's better than being alone."

Kesia frowned, and her heart sank. "Shance … I'm sorry. No, that's not right. I didn't do anything wrong. But I don't want you to feel sad."

"Saying 'I'm sorry' still works, then." He sighed. "It's a human thing."

"All right." She paused, tempted to rub the voicelator for Zephryn's wisdom in her mind. But this situation would stump even him. "I'm sorry."

"And that almost sounded like you believed it. Good work."

"I do." Kesia focused on taking a sip from her cup. Strewsberry juice, tart and dark red. "Ever since I've been around you, I care. Well, I see that caring isn't a weakness."

He stared at her for a moment, then burst out laughing.

She shifted in her chair. "What?"

"You learn very quickly, Kesia Ironfire. You'll do just fine tomorrow." He paused. "And I won't push our betrothal appearance too far. I wouldn't want your fleetwing setting me on fire and eating my charred corpse."

"He wouldn't set you on fire and eat you. He would rip out your throat and leave you hanging from your own ship mast."

Shance's face paled. "Would he now?"

"Yes." Kesia grinned a little, reaching for another roasted meat, a jungle boar. She pulled off a chunk with her fingers and took a bite, savoring the gamey juices. "Zephryn enjoys joking, but he would never eat a human."

"Some civilization then in dragon kind?"

"No, you just aren't worth the effort. Too many bones, not enough flesh."

The airship captain leaned forward, his expression deadly serious. "Kesia, have you—?"

"Oh, no. It's not required. And my parents," her voice caught, but she pushed through it. "My parents said not to eat anything that could talk back to you."

"Good for them."

Kesia shrugged. "I suppose so."

She only half-listened as Shance launched into more conversation, enough to make sure he felt listened to. He seemed to appreciate that.

In the meantime, she began forming a plan to sneak around the Central Market after Shance was asleep to find the origin of the green smoke. She needed proof. Nothing against Shance, but if this went belly up, he could lose his entire cover, whereas she could slip away far easier. It would be better for him to learn everything afterward so he wouldn't put his honesty in jeopardy. Plausible deniability and all that.

She needed more food.

CHAPTER FIFTEEN

AS FAR AS KESIA HAD SEEN, the Central Market only had one pest: clayborer beetles that attacked the claymesh and loosened the mosaic tiles. If metal hadn't been requisitioned for use in the war effort, it was likely more of the buildings would be made of it instead of clay over wire frames.

She should be grateful the clayborer beetles were there. But as Kesia studied the small bug in her hand, she couldn't manage one appreciative feeling. From a mighty dragon to a tiny, squirmy bug with a greenish-brown back.

Augh. Why couldn't they have had a bird infestation? Or something cute and furry?

Enough. She closed her eyes and allowed her skin to absorb everything that made the clayborer unique. Every crevice of its carapace and pointy barb on its legs slipped into her. The bug itself disappeared, but she could feel it in the nether, waiting for her to shapechange. One instant, then another, and her body was shrinking and wrapping itself tighter and tighter to fit inside the small shape.

Wings fluttered at her back. Her tiny legs pushed her off the ground, and she let the buzzing wings move her forward. She flew a few hesitant circles around the room. This was far different from being a bird. The buzzing was louder, the shifting quick and jerky. Everything happened too fast and took too long at the same time.

Her heart thudded in her ears. A purely mental response, but it felt real. What if she couldn't control this form? It was too small.

Hold to your heartflame, Kesia. It isn't an evil: it is a Talent even more precious than your other Talents, my star. Let it guide them. Those Above gave us our heartflames so we would always remember who we were, no matter our form.

She remembered the words of her father and mother, holding her tight after an unexpected shapeshift had left her in tears, ready to never use her Talent again. She could almost hear the resonance in their voices calming her, reminding her of where she came from and that they loved her, even if she did something unforgiveable.

Kesia laughed silently. She was more than the beetle form that encased her or even her skin form that waited in the nether.

She was a dragon with a heartflame that burned clear and strong.

With those thoughts, she landed on the floor and crept under the door from the bedroom to the living area. Another quick flight and she scuttled beneath the door to Shance's suite. As long as she stayed near the top and bottom corners of the corridor, she should be fine. The last thing she wanted was to encounter other beetles. Trying to fake a form around creatures who naturally owned it always meant trouble. It usually involved them attacking her or trying to mate with her.

Kesia shuddered internally and zoomed through the hall. This late at night, the electric lights were at half-power, which was all the better for her. From the fear that beat her wings, it seemed that clayborers were adverse to light. It made sense, given their interest in burrowing.

She continued on. She had an hour, maximum, before she had to shift back. Shance might sleep like the dead, but being too long in a foreign creature's form had negative effects. She could start to lose her true mind, or she could simply pass out due to malnourishment. It was easier to shapeshift when she could eat the large quantities a dragon stomach could hold. In any case, she didn't want to chance too much in this new form. Her heartflame and memories might give her confidence, but without Zephryn's anchor in her mind, slipping into the instinctive urges of a clayborer would be far too easy.

Focus. Remember the maps she'd studied of the Central Market.

After a few trips down side hallways, she finally found people to follow. They wore long black coats, and goggles were strapped around their heads, the kind that had many lenses for looking at very small things. Those were only used by mechanics, technicians, and scientists. She would know quickly which one they were.

Kesia drifted closer, hoping to catch some of their conversation.

"...I'm telling you, taking the coats and goggles out of the lab is bad business. They're never meant to leave for a reason. All materials must maintain a high level of sterility." The man's voice was high and anxious, and his gloved hand nervously picked at the front pocket of his coat.

The other man snickered lazily and ran a hand through his thatch of red hair. "Do you even know what you just said?"

"Sterility?"

The redhead snickered again, his steps wavering to one side before switching to the other. He was drunk. Kesia remembered learning about that. Drunk people were easier to take down and kill. "And this is why you had no ladies in your life before I joined your lab team. Did you see how those women were all over us, asking questions? It's worth every possible fine. But no one will fine us because no one will know we took them out."

"Yes, well, I'm not sure name-dropping the Curious Intrigue was the best idea, Petre. What if those women tell the authorities?"

Petre slapped him on the back of the neck. "Horton, they were drunk too. What police would believe them? Eh?" He tapped his head. "Smarts here—ow!"

Smart enough to smack himself in the eyeball. Nevertheless, they were exactly who she needed. Kesia trailed them, hoping for more intel. Their conversation was mostly of exploits from their time that night and which woman had favored which man. More human mating rituals, including this idea of dating. Unlike dragons, humans didn't have a fleetwing bond to guarantee they would be equally matched. Instead, they had to fumble around like animals in the dark, hoping they would meet someone compatible.

It certainly seemed like Shance had done a lot of that. The defeat in his expression tugged at her heart. He needed to take time away from all women, and here she was, having to pretend to be in love with him. She definitely wasn't, not according to what she'd learned about love.

Although she did feel something for him. What was it about him that made her skin prickle and her heart beat just a little faster? If she was meant only for Zephryn, wouldn't that mean that no one else could tempt her?

Enough. Reconaissance missions were far easier to deal with.

After a trip in an elevator that left her reeling from the speed of travel, she and the two scientists entered a large room. The walls were made of glass held together with thick bands of steel overlaid with bronzework, and the ceiling was covered with a glass dome. It was almost like being outside, and her clayborer instincts wanted to fling her at the nearest pane and try for freedom.

Her dragon nature was tempted as well. When was the last time she'd flown? Felt the breeze beneath her scaled wings? Enjoyed the freedom of the heights, far above where humans trod the ground?

Kesia was halfway to a window before she caught herself. Instead of hurtling into the glass, she landed on it, the sticky bits on her legs clinging to the surface. Now, where had the scientists gone?

Fewmets! She should have been paying more attention. Carefully she zoomed down a little closer to a glass doorway. From what her multi-faceted eyes could make out, there was another laboratory there as well. The scientists were on the far end, examining some substance she couldn't see. It looked like the redhead, Petre, was flinging something at Horton and laughing.

Why on earth would humans get drunk? It only seemed to cause them harm.

Her beetle eyes would be useless for reading anything. As it was, she could only see the objects in the room as vague outlines filled with color. It was time to change into something more useful. Dare she hazard skin form? She probably shouldn't, but comprehending anything in other forms was much more difficult.

But she'd be naked. Perhaps there were more lab coats or even coveralls nearby. If nothing else, she could always shift back before someone showed up.

Might as well go for it.

Kesia landed in front of one of the corner cabinets and cast off the beetle form in exchange for her skin form. She pressed her fingers into the ground until the world came into focus, then she stood and took in the lab again.

Gray metal cabinets lined the room, reaching halfway up the

glass walls. One cabinet stood taller than the others, and Kesia went to it, twisting the lock and easing the door open. White lab coats and coveralls hung in a neat row. She grabbed a pair of coveralls and glared at the zippers.

Thankfully, this time they worked.

Thus clad, Kesia studied the half-height cabinets. They were topped with various kinds of containers–cylinders, round jars, square jars—with all manner of glass and blonde copper tubing threaded between them. There was a wooden device that held smaller tubes. She pushed at it. Yes, it was able to spin, with a contraption attached that could make the spinning continuous.

So many things to learn about. If Zephryn were here, his mind-speak would be firing with all manner of wild and enthusiastic conversation. He rarely verbalized it, but Kesia had listened to his intellectual excitement for years. It was one of the things she appreciated about him.

There was no sign of any green chemical in the vicinity, smoke or liquid. She sighed and turned her attention to the pair of long tables in the center of the room.

They were filled with more glass containers, only these were systemized. Less experimentation and more practical work, she guessed. She traced her fingers over a box of neatly-printed labels for various chemicals she couldn't decipher. There was an assembly line with a vat of some kind of softly simmering liquid at one end of the table that traveled down to the other end, the liquid undergoing various stages of processing: dripping, steaming, and finally coalescing and seeping into small vials.

Her breath caught in her throat. There was a greenish tinge to the liquid. Kesia crept over to the table and carefully picked up one of the vials, studying it closely. The green hue was barely there. But chemicals could change form and consistency, couldn't they? She had learned only a little about that. It wasn't a key part of metal-working, and it led to tasks too difficult and dangerous for a child.

She had already endured enough danger as a child.

"I'm feeling better, uncle."

She stepped forward, closer to the door. Maybe today she could leave and never come back.

"Ah, dragonet, you are far from done with your treatment." Garishton loomed over her, his brown eyes soft with concern. How could he be concerned for her when it was his treatments that hurt her? Did he really want to help?

Sometimes, he did. But then came the accusations. The beatings.

She couldn't tell anyone, or her parents would suffer.

"Are you sure? Maybe I'm a really strong dragon now."

"No, you aren't." He reached for a vial of green liquid on the table. "But I can make you strong."

He picked up a second vial.

"Two doses?"

"You are very ill…"

Footsteps at the door.

Fewmets!

Kesia started, the vial almost slipping from her sweat-slick hands. Lands, she was getting to be as bad as Zephryn when it came to situational awareness. She carefully set down the glass container and slipped behind the desk.

Clayborer beetle.

This time the shift was nearly instantaneous. She launched herself onto the counter and hid behind the box of labels so she could see when the two scientists left. Just in time too. The door swung open, and Horton's quavery voice clamored above her.

"I still don't think it's safe! And how dare you say the women were more interested in you? I'll have you know that three of them gave me their addresses."

Petre snorted, half falling over the counter nearest to Kesia. "Lemme see the paper."

"Here."

A loud braying laugh escaped Petre. "Viorstan's blindness! This is nothing more than the address to the bakery at the corner of Midshell and 7th street. You, my friend, have been had. Wonder if the others are shop addresses too."

Horton's puffy face turned red. "It is not! She said it was her house."

"She lied." The red-haired man drew out the word like molten metal. "Like all the ladies do. At least around you." He slapped his hand on the counter for emphasis, and his palm landed perilously close to where Kesia hid. It missed her and hit the vial of greenish liquid, pushing it toward the ground. She should shift to try to catch it!

It crashed to the ground and shattered, spewing thick clouds of sickening green smoke everywhere. Before she could flee, it descended upon her, filling her line of sight and squeezing every part of her body.

Her Talent. The green smoke canceled out Talents!

Unbidden, Kesia felt her consciousness violently thrust out of her beetle form and into skin form. She began coughing as soon as her lungs took over breathing.

"Eh! Horton, d'you hear that?"

Fewmets. She ducked below the counter, forcing herself to breath in the smoke and not cough. She'd survived countless treatments like this as a child. Kesia dug deep in her mind, calling on those memories, that strength. She allowed the smoke to sink deeply into her lungs, and then expelled it once more.

Her first thought was to rip the table off the ground and smash it against the wall, trapping the scientists in between. A regrettable loss of life, but this was war.

And risk giving your true nature away? Do you think human investigators that foolish? They will know. Ah, there was Zephryn's voice back in her head.

No. She had to make this look like a human did it. Or, even better, like the fools had done it to themselves, which meant no deaths. Kesia crept around the corner on her stomach as silently as possible, slipping past them.

Horton slapped his friend on the back of the head. "Petre, you numbskull! Now I won't be able to use my Talent for a day."

A day. She wouldn't be able to shift or use her object shaping powers for a whole day. Wonderful.

"Oh well. It's not like they're that helpful. Mine only lets me signal to dogs." Petre shoved himself up against the table, trying to gain his footing.

Just a little closer. Horton was almost in place as he stood with his back to her looming over Petre, his pasty face dark red with anger. "Don't you understand? I was hired for my Talent! Now I won't be able to scent-identify chemicals in solutions."

Just a little closer.

"Tomorrow is the gala, you fool. Everyone has the day off—"

Kesia leaped to her feet and lashed out. Two hard shoves. Petre smashed his head against the edge of the counter and went down. Horton wheeled around unsteadily. She landed a sloppy right hook against his jaw, just enough to knock him out. He hit the ground next to his coworker.

One more loose end. She pushed Horton aside and bent over Petre, giving the unconscious redhead another right hook. It wasn't perfect, but hopefully it was enough to convince others that there had been a drunken fight. She checked his pulse. He seemed to be breathing. She didn't know anything else to do for them. Healing wasn't her Talent.

She grabbed their keys and a vial of greenish liquid, slipped them into a small bag at the end of the assembly table, and headed for the door. It wasn't a perfect break-in, but it gave her one valuable thing: proof of an alliance between the two sides of the war. The green liquid she had found made the smoke that had erupted from her father upon his death, and it was the same smoke that had exploded on *The Silver Streak*.

Which meant it wasn't a fair fight. There was a conspiracy between the Congruency and the Pinnacle. Soldiers like her, Zephryn, and Shance were dying for nothing.

Her stomach knotted and anger flared within her, enough to make her want to smash the walls of the elevator.

Kesia studied herself in the bronze metal and frowned. The coveralls covered her bare arms and legs, but walking around like this would still attract attention. Especially without any shoes on her feet. So much for fitting in. If only she hadn't taken in that green smoke!

She glared at the reflection, willing herself to shift back into clayborer beetle form. Her skin rippled, her body shrank, and an instant later, she buzzed through the open elevator door with clayborer wings.

Kesia's nonexistent human heart hammered in her mind. How had she done this? The green smoke cancelled out Talents. She had breathed it in successfully but that had been discipline from the childhood experiments, when her uncle had forced her to inhale. Exhale.

A wall loomed precariously close. Kesia darted away, mentally gasping.

She had to stay calm or she'd splat herself onto the nearest flat surface. She could consider the ramifications of her uncle's experiments later.

But one thought persisted in the corner of her mind.

Had her uncle turned her into another monster like her father?

Chapter Sixteen

HE WAS A WALKING STINK BOMB.

The odors of a hundred different perfumes clung to the clothing Zephryn had to wear to the gala. The entire process of fitting him with the black coat, high-collared white shirt, silk neck-cloth, and trousers had worsened when he'd realized Zilpath had no translator earlier that morning in the shop.

There was no reason why, other than a scribbled note saying Pryenil was otherwise occupied, as well as instructions for how to infiltrate the gala. A pity. He had wanted to ask her more questions. He'd searched for information on embermates and the Ironfire family, but as expected, the city library held limited information on dragons. Most of the material he found was of the "flying scaled beasts of death and doom who seek to devour all mankind" variety. Charming.

Zephryn tugged at the silk strip around his throat and glanced toward the front entrance. A line of guests stood there, arrayed in similar clothing. The outfits were surprisingly light and cool, despite the layers. Something to do with the fabric weave, according to his research.

The clothing was still constricting. Zephryn couldn't imagine

Kesia enjoying such discomfort. No dragon enjoyed tight restraints.

He glanced at his newly-acquired timepiece. Two hours past noon. That was the other information on the note; sneak in at two hours past noon through the side entrance. When he'd inquired as to why, Zilpath had rolled her eyes and glanced above her head, making one of her rude gestures. Perhaps one of her tenants? Why would they need to sneak to and from the Central Market?

Whatever the case, the gala celebration was to be held inside and outside, which meant for part of it the tepstone structure shouldn't interfere. He and Kesia would be able to mind-speak like proper fleetwings, without the need to activate their pendants.

No. They were embermates. The next time Zephryn saw Pryenil, she would have to explain herself more clearly, just as he would need to share with Kesia the truth about her uncle. He should have spoken of it earlier, but the outpouring of fear and pain from her, the way she had disappeared from contact for a moment then avoided the topic—all of it suggested she hadn't been in a logical frame of mind.

The knowledge she had conveyed still astonished him. Garishton Ironfire, the head of the Pinnacle, had helped her condition her body and mind to use two Talents. It should have killed her. Knowing what had happened to Pryenil and the agony she had endured at the hands of the S.P.U., Zephryn could only imagine the torment of Kesia's childhood. But those imaginings were futile, for they only made him want to kill Garishton in the most painful way possible.

Redundant, really. Killing the dragon leader was already on his list.

Another glance at the timepiece. Two o' clock.

Time to move.

He pushed open the door hidden in the steel and bronze wall that surrounded the gardens of the Central Market. It gave easily and smoothly, just as Pryenil's note had indicated. He stepped into a large rectangular court twice as large as the sparring cavern. Trees and bursts of colorful flowers were contained by marble pavement threaded with gold and dark blue.

"Good afternoon, dear sir." The rich, cultured alto came from his left. A woman stood there with deep brown skin and a glittering gold dress that draped the curves of her figure. She toyed with a tiny black braid hanging over her shoulder. "Countess Nula Thredsing. What is your name?"

Walking away was tempting. This woman was not on Zephryn's agenda. But he needed to try to blend in. His Cloak could disguise his scales and nature, but using full invisibility wouldn't be wise. There would be too many people to evade; individuals tended to become suspicious when they knocked into something they couldn't see, especially in broad daylight. Instead, he took a step forward. "Count Zephryn Nighten."

She parted her full lips. "Ah, quite a distinctive name."

"It was none of my doing, I assure you." It sounded ridiculous, but better a foolish surname than a dragon surname that could evoke suspicion.

"You could have bought it for a pretty price. But you aren't the sort to do that, are you?" Countess Nula cocked her head to one side, her grey eyes calculating. "No, you are far too valuable for that. Although you haven't accrued nearly as much worth as you will. If you survive."

Zephryn's jaw tightened. He recalled the place of every single weapon hidden beneath his coat. Where were Kesia and Windkeeper? "Is my survival under threat?"

"No more than anyone else who sneaks into this gala through a side entrance." She chuckled at his glare. "Oh, don't worry, Count

Zephryn. No one else saw you, and I wouldn't dream of exposing you. Yet. I am much more interested in why someone of your value is so concerned with hiding their presence. You see, I am a *curious* woman like that."

A curious woman? As in the Curious Intrigue? Why would that matter? Something in Countess Nula's eyes mocked him, daring him to reconsider using his weapons.

No killing. No killing.

"My business here is none of your concern." Now was the time to leave. He began walking toward a staircase on the other side of the courtyard.

She kept pace with him easily. "Oh, but it is. I've already heard *curious* things about the new mechanic from the Scepter of Industry who has so quickly stolen Captain Windkeeper's heart. Your presence here only intensifies the *intrigue*."

"Countess, if you continue—"

Countess Nula placed her hand over where his had unconsciously reached for his hidden dagger. "Two options if you pull out that weapon. I could scream and expose you, or I could retaliate with my own Starven 300 pistol. I think it would be far more pleasant if we kept company, yes?"

The human was infuriating, but the set of her eyes revealed she was willing to do exactly as she said.

Fewmets.

She squeezed his arm. "I'm glad to see you are as wise as you are wealthy. Now, I think the happy couple is about to make their grand entrance, and only two hours late."

Kesia.

Zephryn followed the Countess's gaze toward the top of the staircase. There she stood. Kesia Ironfire, her soft brown hair pulled loosely away from her face and falling over her shoulder in waves. She wore a white dress that strapped around her neck, leaving her back and shoulders bare. A vine of green leaves and deep red flowers flowed around the edge of her corset and flowed down to the edge of her skirt. Like the other women here, she had favored a long, flowing skirt that was cut high in the front and draped, revealing her upper legs clad in a much shorter underskirt.

Countess's Nula's dress was similarly cut, but it was not nearly as distracting. Odd, since gold should be more distracting than white. It made as little sense as the flame that suddenly burned his throat when he saw Captain Windkeeper next to Kesia, clad in a dark blue and black uniform, leaning down to whisper in her ear. Something made her laugh—a genuine laugh that reflected in her amber eyes.

Kesia so rarely laughed. Each time was always a treasure, and not one Zephryn wanted to share in that way.

She surveyed the crowd, her eyes turning sharp and careful for a moment. Not enough for anyone else to perceive, but he knew his fleetwing. She was as clever as she was ... distracting?

No, not distracting.

Beautiful.

Looking at his fleetwing, his embermate, his Kesia, he finally understood the meaning of the word.

"Aha. Well, that explains everything, now doesn't it?" Countess Nula murmured next to him. "Not only is she attractive, but she is even more valuable than I. And just as much as you, Count, if not more. How very interesting, for a mere mechanic."

"Why do you keep speaking of value?" She didn't have to answer, but Zephryn had to ask, especially considering her level of confidence.

She turned to him and flashed a bright smile. "Oh, everyone has their worth, Count Zephryn. I'm just far more accurate at seeing it than anyone else. It has little to do with what's in their bank account and a lot more to do with what's in their heart, their mind, and occasionally," Countess Nula reached up and gave his chin a pat, "their future. And while the fair lady mechanic is worth enough matched with Shance Windkeeper, the possibility of her with you is exponentially more."

Zephryn stared at her, too focused on her words to mind the disrespectful gesture. So she had a Talent. "How do you mean?"

"I think I'll let you figure that out. After all, I have my own affairs to mind. You take care of yours." She tapped his chest. "Now, let me introduce you to Captain Windkeeper and this charming mystery woman."

"I can't do this."

"You're not doing it. *We* are. And it looks like we both get to face our fears." Shance chuckled quietly in her ear, sending a small, pleasant shudder through her veins. It was one of the subtle ways they'd decided to convey their fake intimacy without requiring kissing or other more affectionate gestures. "For that, my dear, is Countess Nula Thredsing, and it looks like she's latched on to your fleetwing. She has always had a knack for singling out key figures, or so the rumors go."

Kesia turned to him, raising her eyebrows. "Is she Talented in it?"

"She's never declared it, but I wouldn't be surprised. Her sense is uncanny."

They walked down the stairs, their movements smooth and effortless. One thing she was grateful for was the attunement to his body. Having never stayed in skin form this long, there was no way Kesia would have appeared so natural without his training.

In a way, she was grateful for the Countess's appearance. It was easier to focus on her than to think about Zephryn, standing next to her with the Countess's hand on his arm. Entirely unwillingly. That was obvious from the rigid way he stood.

She smirked. Good. He didn't need to enjoy the human woman's attentions.

Suddenly, the attractions she felt for Shance were like dust and ashes, paling in comparison to the dragon before her. Zephryn walked with the grace of a snow panther. His deep bronze skin set off by the sleek black clothing, his cobalt eyes rich and intent. Kesia's breath quickened, and her cheeks burned. She couldn't be thinking this yet. Not while she was still acting as Shance's betrothed.

She had to ignore the fire building within her for a little longer.

Kesia searched for other thoughts to distract her. Well, the necktie looked foolish on Zephryn. And the suit would hinder close combat. If only she could meet him on the sparring field, like normal. It would be so much easier focusing in sparring clothes than in this dress that stifled her. Shance said she was pretty, but that didn't help the tightness around her rib cage. Nor did it quell the throbbing in her heels from the shoes.

Shance had already started the conversation. "I'm pleased you could attend, Countess Nula."

She gave him a bright smile. "How could I miss the opening gala for the Congruency annual war conference? It's one of the high society events of the year. And my father and I have been such generous supporters of the war effort."

"Which High Command is quite grateful for." Shance caught Kesia's elbow gently and nudged her closer to him. "Have you met my betrothed, First Mechanic Kesia Ironsley?"

Countess Nula smiled even wider. "I haven't had the pleasure. What a delight to meet the famous woman who has caught the heart of the infamous Captain Windkeeper."

"The winds carry someone where they will. I just happened to be on their wings." She smiled back, stifling a giggle. It was one of the lines she had come up with late last night as she tossed and turned after her mission, still feeling the beetle form instead of her own skin.

Zephryn's eyes bored into hers with the same intensity she'd received walking down the stairs. It was not helping her focus. "Clever, my lady."

A shiver trickled down her spine. His voice was deep and attractive, even without the resonance.

"Indeed, aren't they the gem of the gala?" Countess Nula waved toward Zephryn. "May I present Count Zephryn Nighten, a recent member of the economic peerage that, I must confess, I have never met before. Isn't it lovely, being able to meet new members of your own social class, just like that?"

Kesia shared a brief look with Shance and felt his agreement. Somehow, the Countess knew something was amiss. Kesia needed to meet with Zephryn soon and decide their next move.

<Pretend you recognize me.>

<What?> His eyes flicked to hers for a second, then he resumed his detached expression.

<Like we decided before. I'll say you're an old family friend who

knew my parents in the Scepter of Industry. Pretend that's the reason you're here. Maybe you've been out of town or something. That should give us enough of a reason to have a private conversation.>

<Agreed.>

"Is that the best you can do, Zephryn?" Finding the tone of amused outrage wasn't difficult. Countess Nula's presence already annoyed Kesia sufficiently. She put her hands on her hips, as she had seen human women do. "I would think after all these years you'd at least give me a hug."

Zephryn gave a slow half-smile, and Kesia's heart beat faster. Fewmets, that smile stirred the deep, blazing part of her that remembered she was a dragon.

Zephryn nodded. "I didn't know if you would recognize me. It has been a while."

"Not that long." She stepped forward and let him enclose her in a hug that she returned fiercely. Perhaps a bit too fiercely, but she didn't have to worry about breaking his bones. She felt an answering sigh from him, a hint of relief and peace. <Too long, Rose-Wing.>

<Yes, too long. Midnight. Any thoughts on how to break away from them? I could say something has gone wrong in the Scepter of Industry. Perhaps with my parents?>

Sorrow pinched her heart at the last phrase. Kesia pushed it down as she pulled away from him. Not now. Not yet.

<Yes, I can manage something like that. Can Windkeeper manage the Countess?>

<Yes. He won't like it, but he can. She's the main reason he wanted to pretend I was his betrothed. Apparently she tried to coerce him into marriage.>

Kesia smiled at Zephryn. "What brings you to the Scepter of Commerce?"

"You." Zephryn paused, managing to summon a decent expression of consternation. "There is an urgent matter I need to discuss with you. It was too sensitive to convey over clipse-mirrors."

Shance leaned over, feigning concern. "Is something wrong? Can I be of assistance?"

"No." Zephryn leveled a stare at him. "I think you've done quite enough. Our entire family was upset when Kesia defied her family to travel here and reunite with you. If Kesia chooses to share this knowledge with you, that is her business."

Countess Nula glanced between the two men, her gray eyes bright and a half-smile on her lips. "Pardon me? The Thredsings are proficient at financial mediation. If this involves such things, I would be happy to—"

"No." Her fleetwing did have a way with thorough shutdowns. Kesia fought the urge to smile and caught Shance's eye, leaning close again to whisper in his ear. "It won't take long. Distract her. Please."

Shance sighed and whispered back. "As my lady wishes. I'll stir something up between her and Count Frenck. They've always been competing for … everything."

"Thank you."

She paused, then brushed a kiss on his cheek. He tasted fresh, of wind and freedom, that irresistible hint of fermented trees—but then nothing more.

Nothing at all.

Whereas Zephryn suddenly smelled of peak pine and hot coals. Far more tantalizing.

Where was this scent coming from?

She swallowed, placing a hand over her chest and pressing the voicelator beneath the dress fabric. "I need to—excuse me, but the sun is rather hot. Can we meet inside?"

"Yes."

Kesia released Shance's arm and turned, the back of her skirt whirling around her as she walked back up the stairs. Zephryn followed—she couldn't hear his footfalls, but she could feel his heart-flame all too clearly.

Shance had mentioned a side room that he sometimes used to spend time with a woman. Hardly bigger than a closet, he had said, but as private as one could find in the Central Market. Fortunately, there was no one passing that way. The Congruency gala was one of the top business functions of the year, and the weather was fine. Everyone would be in the courtyard networking, securing merger contracts, or trying to listen to others doing so and exploiting that knowledge.

Leaving her and Zephryn alone. Another rush of heat filled her.

The mosaics glinted off the claymesh as she strode down the hallway. Zephryn fell into step with her. "Kesia, your throat."

"My throat?" She pressed her hand to her neck and felt the flames within. "No! No no no no no!"

There was the door. She fumbled for the engraved skeleton key that Shance had slipped to her and shoved it into the lock. A soft click and the door was open, revealing a small room with a waist-high metal cabinet on one side and a few brooms on the other.

"Fewmets, I'm sorry. I don't know why I lost control like that." Kesia huffed out a cloud of smoke and turned. Zephryn's body blocked the door frame, filling the small space. "And here you are. All right. Well and good."

"Yes, here I am." His put-upon scowl had been replaced by a look she had rarely seen. Uncertainty and an odd, fierce need glinted in his eyes.

"Well, some things need to be spoken aloud. I like speaking aloud, sometimes. Shance assured me no one would hear us in this room." She paused, trying to settle the chaos of her thoughts. "And speaking will help me, and you, focus. On what we need to say to each other."

He shrugged. "Very well. As far as what I have discovered, it appears the rebels might not all be anarchists."

"You've had contact with them?" Focus on his words. Get through this part first.

"The shopkeeper, Zilpath, is a leader in the underground network. She led me to others, including a dragon."

Alarm lit within her. "A dragon?"

"A kind of dragon."

"We were told that all deserters were killed on sight. No survivors."

"She wasn't a deserter. She was experimented on, like you." Zephryn stepped closer to her.

Someone like Kesia. Relief and sadness filled her. She wasn't the only one. But no one should have to endure experimentation. "Can I meet with this dragon sometime?"

"Yes. Although she is quite reserved. And the Lawless refused to tell me much, but they did imply there were some higher figures in league regarding the war."

"Yes, there are."

"What do you know?"

She closed her eyes, recalling her reverie on the airship. "When I was repairing Shance's vessel, I found traces of the green smoke there. Then later that night, I sneaked into a secret laboratory." Kesia pulled the pouch out of the front of her corset and withdrew the vial. "It's the same, Zephryn. The same effects."

He took the vial of green-tinged liquid from her and studied it closely. "How can you be sure?"

"One of the scientists I followed was drunk and broke a bottle. It neutralized everyone's Talents."

"I see. That's inconvenient."

"Except for mine."

Zephryn's eyes narrowed. "You're immune?"

"Apparently so."

"How?"

Tell anyone, and they will be dead. Family never reveals secrets.

She and Zephryn had run away. They were already dead.

Kesia shut her eyes, pressing her lips together to focus and get the words out. "My uncle. He … injected and immersed me in the green smoke as part of my treatment for having two Talents. So he said." She clenched her hands. "The smoke is the same, Zephryn. And it's the same as … as the night I killed my father."

Her voice broke. She didn't know voices could do that—crack along the edges and split with shuddery breaths that left her weak. Dragons weren't weak. The weak were killed.

She felt his heartflame and knew he was only inches away now, listening so intently her skin prickled. "My father wanted me to do it, Zephryn. He baited me to do it because he'd become a monster. Somehow, the Pinnacle had disrupted his Talent. He had turned into a hideous, unrecognizable monster, and … he had my mother's blood on him, all over him."

"He killed her."

"Yes, at least I think so. And for some reason…" Kesia paused. "They made him into that monster. After he died he spewed green smoke. They were doing something with it beyond taking away his Talent."

"They were experimenting on him."

"Just as they were experimenting on me." Her voice was a whisper. She took deep breaths to calm herself, inhaling more of that irresistible peak pine and hot coal scent.

She should ask about it. Sometime.

"The dragon woman, Pryenil. She was experimented on by the Pinnacle. By a medical division called the SPU."

Kesia swallowed. "My parents always told me to stay away from them, but they never explained why."

"Considering what was done to the two of you, I can understand entirely. This is much worse than we anticipated, Kesia." His fingers tilted her chin up, sending a thrill through her. She opened her eyes, her breathing shallow. Zephryn's face was inches from hers. "The Lawless continue to pressure me to side with them. To pressure us."

"Us?"

His fingers traveled down her throat. Carefully. Lightly. "You are my fleetwing. My embermate. I will never abandon you."

Her heartbeat resounded in her ears. She drew nearer to Zephryn, pressing against him. "Embermate. My parents used that word. My father ... I think that hurt him most of all. Killing my mother." She remembered the haunted look in his eyes. "It was as if part of himself had vanished. I'd never seen him so lost. I couldn't imagine what that felt like until I walked into the Central Market and—"

"You lost a part of yourself that you didn't realize how much you needed until it was missing." Zephryn reached up and brushed a few strands of hair behind her ear. "And then you understood that you could never truly live without it."

Flames licked around his throat, and his cobalt eyes were slits lit with red and orange. Kesia felt her fire answer, her attention drawn to his perfect lips. "Zephryn ... can we kiss now?"

"Yes." His breath was warm on her cheek. "You may start, if you wish. Since you have the experience."

Kesia stood on her tiptoes and brushed her lips against his. Soft and careful. She pulled away for a moment, her heart threatening to burst from her chest. Zephryn's eyes gazed into hers, unfathomable without mindspeak. It was a mistake. It was foolish.

"More."

He leaned down and pressed his mouth to hers again, harder and more urgent. Kesia clung to his biceps, pulling him close, feeling the heat of his fire fill her mouth even as his hands traveled farther down her dress.

So much better than Shance.

Perfect.

Heat raged through her body, through her veins, her skin. She needed to breathe.

They parted and she gasped for air, ribs pressing against her corset.

"I ... I liked that."

Zephryn's hair stuck out wildly, his face flushed darker. "I agree. We should ... investigate further."

Kesia inhaled sharply at the thought—and coughed on the taste of bitter fog.

Not fog.

Green smoke.

She grabbed Zephryn's jacket. "We need to leave. Someone's going to set off another—"

The building exploded.

Chapter Seventeen

"ALL FORCES MOBILIZE! We're under attack! They're inside the building!"

Shance was already halfway up the stairs and down the corridor, using the wind to boost his speed. The explosion had come from the left side of the building. He knew of one particular room in that part of the building: his transformed utility closet with the pillows and blankets in the cabinet. Nothing flammable or explosive in there, which could only mean one thing.

Something had happened with Kesia and Zephryn.

Had soldiers found the room? Had Kesia been attacked?

His steps skated over the ground, flying on the currents like ice. A cloud of green smoke spilled down the hallway.

Green smoke. The Talent-stealer!

Shance came to a sudden stop and flung out his hands, forming a wall of wind around the cloud and forcing it back toward the door. "Kesia! If you're in there, you need to get somewhere else, fast!"

"Trying!" Flames burst from inside the doorway, sending fingers of red-orange flame flickering through the cloud.

His jaw dropped. The flames were eating up the green smoke as if it were the driest paper. Kesia, in that incredible white dress, emerged from the doorway in her dragon skin form, human shaped but with rosy scales across her arms and face and coiling down her legs.

All he saw was her delicate beauty combined with a look of fierce concentration as she spewed heat from her mouth and palms. Kesia attacked the remaining green smoke particles, obliterating them before they could reach him or any of the other guests in the building.

Shance looked around for Zephryn, but the other dragon was nowhere to be seen. Kesia swallowed her fire enough to say, "He's behind you, slipping back into the party. His Talent is cloaking. I had to protect him from the green smoke so he would be able to use it."

She did that to protect Zephryn's Talent? His heart sank as if with a sudden downdraft. "Right. That makes sense." And it did. Zephryn was her fleetwing. One reason she had taken him aside was to try and understand their bond. How had that led to this explosion? Had they been ambushed?

Footsteps echoed behind him. Kesia's eyes widened at the sound, and she quickly closed her eyes, concentrating on making her scales vanish. Shance watched them disappear with a twinge of regret. "Is there any way you can disappear or shift into something else and fly away?"

"And how would you explain my sudden disappearance?"

"How can you explain what happened to the smoke? You were obliterating it!"

She pressed her lips together, expression closed. "I'll tell you later."

"I'll hold you to that." His mind raced. "For now, you need to faint."

"What?"

Shance held out his arms. "Fall into my arms and act like you're weak and unconscious. Faint. Like when you're really tired and you have to take a break. You already look exhausted. Just pretend the attackers knocked you out, and I'm here to take care of you."

Kesia set her jaw, and her back, which had been bowed over from fatigue, straightened. "A dragon is never weak."

"Then maybe you're strongly attracted to the floor. It's pretend." Shance strode toward her, holding out his arms. "Trust me, it will work. They can't learn who you really are."

If they did find out, it would be the interrogation and execution chamber for her, and permanent grounding for him. The thought of Kesia being crushed within the Removal Vise was a far worse prospect than being grounded. His heart sank further. She couldn't die.

"All right. I trust you." Kesia suddenly slumped to the ground. Shance caught her with a breeze and guided her toward him, cradling her close in his arms and supporting her beneath her back and knees. Entirely limp weight.

He was right. She was ready to give out anyway. And yet, Kesia had been willing to try and fight through all of the exhaustion, no matter the cost to her. He stroked the edge of her cheek. "What a strong dragon you are. Do you know how extraordinary you are?"

"Captain Windkeeper." He turned to see Captain Tegan standing there in full dress uniform, her hair pulled back in its usual tight bun. "What's the report? Bystanders said your betrothed and an unknown Count had been seen passing this way."

"Uncertain. Kesia told me she wasn't on good terms with her relatives from the Scepter of Industry. She didn't travel here with their blessing." Words flew out of his mouth quickly, forming a story to satisfy Tegan's suspicions. "Perhaps this was some kind of vengeance from her family? All I know is when I found her, she had fallen on the ground. Count Nighten was nowhere to be found."

Tegan gave Kesia a quick look. "Is she harmed?"

"I checked her vitals. I don't believe she is hurt." At least that was a believable lie. Shance had taken a few field medic courses in case any of his crew needed medical attention. Another Windkeeper tradition. "I haven't had a chance to check the room."

"Understandable." The other captain drew her standard issue Heotzler pistol and walked cautiously toward the room, her eyes darting back and forth to search every inch. Her nose wrinkled. "Captain Windkeeper, did you see any traces of green smoke in the explosion?"

Shance shook his head. "No, I was too busy with Kesia. Although she muttered something about 'it's missing' before she lost consciousness. I don't know what she meant."

"Fiarston." Captain Tegan's face tightened. "Her Talent. The new, rising mechanic in High Command, and she's targeted for an attack to weaken her Talent. Or perhaps, it was this Count Zephryn Nighten. Did he show any signs of being a rebel?"

"I'd just met him."

"Hm. Right." She pinched the bridge of her nose. "My patrol is doing damage control outside. We will be sure to interrogate Count Nighten once we find him."

Shance nodded, hoping Kesia was right about Nightstalker's Talent. "I will get Kesia to our quarters and make a full report to High Command."

Tegan raised her eyebrows and she gave a short laugh. "You do actually love this one, don't you, Windkeeper?"

"How do you mean?"

"'Our quarters'? The next thing you know, you'll be giving her half your ship as well." Tegan smirked. "Be careful. The fiery ones will break your heart. I'll see you at the High Command debrief."

Shance watched her leave, feeling joy knot with despair in his stomach. As he walked through the Central Market, part of him was eager to see Kesia safely resting and recuperating. The other part was desperately trying to reclaim the heart she'd managed to steal from him in only three days. As he entered the elevator, Kesia stirred in his arms.

"I can let you down now, if you wish."

She shook her head, and moved closer to him, adjusting herself to curl more tightly in his arms. "You ... you were right. Doing that is tiring."

"How did you learn to do that?"

"In the ship. I burned up the leftover smoke in your ship." Kesia seemed to grow heavier each moment. His muscles burned in protest. Dragons must have greater density than humans. He swept a handful of breezes beneath his arms, supporting her weight and taking the strain off him. "Tell you more ... when you get back. Tell you more of everything. Shance?"

"Yes, Kesia?" He opened the door to their—his—quarters and walked through to the bedroom. He carefully laid her on the blankets near the window.

She sighed, breathing out a whisper of gray smoke, her eyes blinking to dragon slits for a moment. It didn't matter. It was still Kesia who stared out from them. "When I was burning away the smoke, I saw Countess Nula Thredsing."

Countess Nula? "Was she running away from the smoke?"

"Yes, but ... she didn't look scared. She looked..." Kesia winced. "I don't know how to describe it. Maybe ... pleased. Satisfied."

Her words were a punch to the gut. Anger burned within

Shance. "She did, hm? Well, I will have to see to that later. I can't have anyone trying to bomb my betrothed."

Kesia rolled her eyes. "Even if the betrothal isn't real?"

"It feels real to me." Shance resisted the urge to take her hand, choosing instead to give her space. Because he could. Because she was worth it. "You're different."

Kesia reached out and took his hand in hers, the pale skin on the back of her hand pebbled with scales again. It was as beautiful as the rest of her. "Thank you. I like knowing how you feel about me without having to guess or needing to mind-speak. Even if I don't share your feelings." She flopped back on the pillow, her hand slipping out of his. "I like ... you..."

She closed her eyes. It took everything Shance had not to sit beside her and watch her sleep. But that would be a little disturbing. Or a lot disturbing.

She cracked her eyes open, and a smile tugged at her lips. "Go to your meeting, Captain. I can take care of myself."

"I know, lovely. But sometimes, you shouldn't have to." He dared to press a kiss to her hand, then stood and left the bedroom. He was already guessing how High Command would interpret the attack and trying to consider fresh ways to deflect attention from Kesia.

Just before the door closed, his silver mirror pinged. Shance walked over to the desk and pressed his hand to the surface, allowing the subtle ridges within the metal to read his palm print. He pulled his hand away and an image emerged, slightly rippled by those same ridges. A wrinkled face and piercing eyes stared out at him, the graying hair pulled back in a bun. Shance sighed. "Zilpath, I don't have time right now."

~To the void of Ucurit with time! I heard about the explosion.

You're in dangerous winds, Shance.~

How good was dragon hearing? It didn't matter. He didn't want to chance disturbing Kesia. Before, he might have been worried about her being a dangerous spy and using any overheard information against him. Now Shance just wanted to make sure the dragon could rest.

~At least I'm flying.~ Considering Kesia's words, he was surprised his feet touched the ground at all. ~Did the Nightstalker get away?~

Zilpath nodded with a dismissive gesture. ~Yes, he is here. Although from what my source tells me, it's going to get complicated. It already is. We need an emergency meeting *now*.~

~I already have a meeting *now*. And Kesia is resting.~

~In your bed?~

"No!" Shance glanced nervously at the door. When it seemed like no one was stirring in the bedroom, he continued with his fingers. ~No. She would never. She's far too careful and thoughtful and responsible.~

Zilpath shook her head. ~You've fallen for her? I suspected as much. Don't fall any harder until the meeting, Shance.~

~What do you know, Zilpath?~

She only scratched her head. ~It's not her fault. But it might make things easier—and harder. Meet at my shop, upstairs, just after dusk. Keep your pants on.~

Shance sighed and palmed the mirror again, irritation flooding him, along with the same uneasy feeling that surfaced the night before when Kesia had spoken about the heartflame bond.

Cutting open two hearts and sewing them to each other was madness.

But it also sounded a lot like marriage.

<Midnight, have I ruined everything?>

Zephryn's voice cut clear through her insecurities. <No. You protected everyone from that green smoke bomb. How did you do that?>

A tug from Shance. She blinked, and the streets of the Scepter of Commerce came into focus around her. It was evening, yet the sidewalks were still crowded with people out for entertainment or sales.

<I just ... did. I'm not sure how. It must be related to my uncle's treatment somehow.>

"Kesia? Mind the curb."

The toe of her boot stubbed the concrete. "Fewmets!"

She careened into Shance, who deftly caught her by the elbow. He chuckled. "Careful. Are you still tired?"

"A little." It was true. Even after resting for six hours, she still felt weak. "I'm checking in with Zephryn."

"Ah, I see." Shance's jaw tightened. She'd learned to identify that as jealousy. "I forget that you two can do that even when you're not in the same place."

Kesia nodded. Pushing ahead seemed to be the best way to deal with jealousy. "Only between tactical partners and close family."

"Anything related to the accident?"

"Yes."

She focused back on Zephryn's voice in her head.

<A reasonable assumption, Rose-Wing. But your uncle treated you long ago. Why have these memories only come to the fore now? Why not before?>

200

Kesia frowned. <My uncle threatened my parents with death if I ever revealed the treatments. I think … one day, I must have, and that's why they hid me.> Her breath caught. <That's why they were captured and mutilated. It was because of me.>

<No. Your parents' deaths were due to the mistreatment and foul designs of your uncle. He is responsible for their deaths as well as the deaths of many others.>

As usual, he cleared through the muddle of her guilt. She nodded. <Very likely. He must have experimented on more than just my family.>

<Indeed. He would have.> Zephryn's voice was edged with bitterness. <And now, if you can obliterate this smoke, you'll be a threat to whatever powers are in league. Even the rebels might be suspicious. Be careful who you tell, Kesia. Even at the meeting tonight. Don't say anything unless there seems to be no other choice.>

<Are you truly so paranoid, Midnight?>

<I've only known the Lawless for a few days.>

<I've known Shance for the same amount of time. He saw what I did.>

She felt Zephryn's resignation. <Well then, yes. Windkeeper can be told.>

<Good, because I already told him. And I will keep it a secret from the rest for as long as it makes sense.>

Shance's hand squeezed hers, jarring Kesia back to her senses again. They had left the busy, downtown area and were now walking through streets that assaulted her nose with scents of food, sweat, and refuse. "Where are we?"

Shance chuckled. "The Low Quarter. Are you always this lacking in observation?"

She rubbed her forehead with her free hand. "No, not usually. But I'm tired."

"You haven't been tired before?"

"Not quite like this."

"True, you did burn off all that green smoke." He eased them around an open-air grill cooking some kind of meat. Rat? It could have been rat. "By the way, how the doldrums did you do that?"

"I don't know. Did anyone see me?"

"The only possible witness would be Captain Tegan, and she didn't say anything about it at the meeting. I think we're safe."

Kesia sighed. "Good."

"A useful skill, though."

She nodded, saved from having to make more conversation by raucous music spewing from an amalgamation of people in brightly colored clothing. The array of instruments was a combination of tins, barrels, and stringed wooden boxes.

Shance winced and whispered in her ear, "Rejects from the Music Quarter."

"I see." His scent was still irresistible. Oddly similar to Zephryn's scent during their kissing in the utility room. Another puzzle to sort out, one that she felt strangely reticent to share with Zephryn.

Surely she could solve some things on her own. In the end, kissing Zephryn was far more pleasurable. If only it had been allowed to go on longer.

Her heart raced. <Zephryn, the kiss. Did you enjoy it?>

<Entirely.>

A grin stretched her lips. <Me too.>

<In truth, I've had difficulty thinking of anything else today. Perhaps this was why the Pinnacle forbade physical contact in skin

form. The distraction is undoubtedly immense.>

<Indeed.> A pang of guilt chilled the heat in her body. <So, you believe we shouldn't indulge any more?>

His uncertainty flickered over their mental bond. <I believe we should make careful choices and research thoroughly the effects this contact has on dragons.>

<You didn't answer my question.>

The overwhelming odor of perfumes and musty shelving jolted her from her reverie. Zilpath's shop. Kesia shook her head to clear it. She needed to focus. Just speaking about kissing with Zephryn distracted her, as did every mental conversation they had. Craving his presence made other things less important. Maybe he was right: kissing was too dangerous right now.

"Come on." Shance tugged her hand again, leading her through the store. Bolts of fabric brushed her arms and face as they crept through the shadowy displays of colorful wares, their hues now rendered muted in the low light.

There was the spot where Shance had kissed her. His kiss hadn't been at all like Zephryn's. Her fleetwing's touch had been hot and fierce. Shance's kiss had been cool and refreshing, once she'd gotten past the general oddness of touching mouths with someone else.

Fascinating. But not as satisfying.

Why couldn't she stop thinking about this?

"Fewmets!"

The word was only a whisper, but as she entered the room, everyone else fell silent, making the epithet resound like cannon fire. Heat rushed to her face and forehead.

"We're glad you could make it." The words emerged from under the hood of a cloaked figure standing in the corner of the tiny room. In fact, everyone there was cloaked and hooded in gray, robes she'd seen in passing while walking around the Scepter of Commerce. Even Zephryn had donned a matching garment.

She fidgeted, worry raising the hair on her arms. What was wrong? Was this ordinary secrecy or something more?

The same cloaked figure spoke in a quiet male voice. "I regret the need for these cloaks, but we must do this for our own protection. Zilpath might not worry about her status, but the other cloaked individual and myself hold positions that we cannot risk. Particularly since dragons can search the minds of other dragons. Zephryn has stated he can cloak his own mind, but you, Ironfire, are still a risk."

Kesia nodded. "I understand."

As usual, she was a liability. Although if the Pinnacle did capture her and try to search her mind, she wouldn't make it easy for them. She'd somehow managed to protect her own memories from herself.

"What kind of robes are those?"

"The garb of Four Corners clerics," Shance said. He stood at her side, his expression dismissive.

"What?"

He glanced at her incredulously. "Four Corners. One of the oldest religions in all Sekastra? Keepers of destiny, followers of truth, devoted to Bonilus the All-Seer and his apostles, Allandra and Olosael."

Kesia raised her eyebrows. A small gust of smoke came from under Zephryn's hood, and he pulled it off, revealing his face. <Zilpath tried to explain it to me. It might be related to the All-Maker and Those Above, but I would need to do more research.>

<Of course.> Fewmets, he looked handsome. Heat stirred in her veins again. She would enjoy burning the person who had

interrupted their kiss with that green smoke bomb.

No! Focus on what he was saying. The All-Maker and Those Above were the makers and protectors of dragonkind, opposed by their foe, the Destroyer. Myths, considered foolish by the Pinnacle. Belief in them was banned, but that didn't stop dragons from crying out for their help during a mission.

Another figure pushed back her hood, revealing the gray hair of the shopkeeper, Zilpath. Her fingers began moving furiously, and Shance snorted. "She says you should remember there are humans in the room, so be careful with the mindspeak."

"Oh, I'm sorry. It wasn't anything significant." Kesia walked over to the wooden table and chairs that dominated the small space and sat down. "Can we start, then?"

The others took seats around her, Zephryn on her right side and Shance on her left, the other robed figures across the table from them. Kesia kept her hands clasped in her lap. She would be listening only. No revelations of her strange ability unless she had to.

Except that Shance knew. Would he tell them?

The tallest robed figure spoke, his voice level. "Nightstalker has told us what happened this afternoon, at least in part. Captain Windkeeper, were you able to make excuses to High Command?"

"Yes," Shance tapped at the table. "Although not without having to smear Nightstalker's name through the bilge. He'll need to steer clear of all military and political areas from now on, but Kesia is clear. They're very protective of her Talent and consider her to be an asset to the Congruency fleet."

Zilpath's fingers moved again. This time, a robed female translated. "She wants to know more about your Talents and what you told Nightstalker about the green smoke. As do we all."

Everyone stared at Kesia. Silently judging, protected by their hoods, as anonymous as the dragons in the top tower of the Pinnacle. As if she was still a criminal. A deep, intense sense of falling filled her, as if she had no wings to catch herself. Curious how the feeling of falling made everything she'd eaten want to come back up.

A hand, warm and pebbled with dragon scales, took hers. She looked into Zephryn's calm face. <You're safe, Rose-Wing. And I suppose we must reveal a few things after all.>

<Indeed.>

Kesia took a deep breath and began to speak. "I inherited the Talents of both my mother and my father."

Everything marched out of her mouth in slow, even statements. She pretended she was giving a field report before the Pinnacle, only no one here wanted to kill her for failure. That was one positive. Zephryn's presence next to her was another, reminding her that she wasn't alone.

She did not, however, speak about the treatments she had recived from Garishton as a child. From Shance's reaction, it seemed that humans could inherit two Talents without any adverse effects. Let them think dragons were the same.

Kesia continued on, relaying what had happened the night her parents died and how her own grief and confusion had skewed her memories. Each word was bland, although her grip tightened on Zephryn's hand. The story of her parents finished, she described her night mission to the laboratory. Kesia studied the knotted wood of the rough-hewn table. She was tempted to shape it into something beautiful, like the cloud lily voicelator she wore around her neck.

"The next day, Shance and I went to the opening gala, where we met with Zephryn. From there, Zephryn and I spoke, and the explosion occurred."

"Yes, the explosion with the green smoke bomb." That was the male again. "What alerted you to its presence?"

Zephryn cleared his throat with a puff of smoke. "Kesia scented it a few seconds before it exploded."

"She scented it? Ah yes, because she had smelled it previously on Captain Windkeeper's airship. Why didn't you act sooner? Was your conversation in the utility closet so interesting?"

Zephryn's face stayed impassive. "Yes. Very."

"And somehow all of the green smoke disappeared?"

"It can do that."

The cloaked man shifted toward Shance. "Is this true, Captain Windkeeper?"

Shance's jaw set. "As far as I know, yes."

Kesia's cheeks heated. This wasn't right. She couldn't return Shance's feelings, but that didn't mean he had to lie for her. <Midnight, we should tell them.>

<We'll give away valuable leverage.>

<This is a lot bigger than you and me. We've trusted the Lawless this far. Have you considered that this could be a test? Do you think they had no other spies at the gala?>

<Do you want them to see you as a potential threat?>

<I saved lives!>

<Suspicion alters many truths.>

<You trust me.> She fought to keep her expression neutral.

<Yes, but I am yours.>

<Is that the only reason?>

No answer. Just the odd pulse of Zephryn's intensely thoughtful mind, layered with assurance, concern, and a twinge of hurt at her question.

<I'm sorry.> It was turning out to be a very useful phrase. The truth needed to be told. She'd had enough of secrets.

Kesia spoke, "There is one other thing you should be aware of."
"Yes?"

"The green smoke. I was able to burn it away using my flames."
Silence.

"A fascinating addition to your array of skills," the male voice said. "Able to detect the green smoke and eliminate it? How?"

"I was ... treated, by my uncle. Garishton Ironfire." She explained the details of dragons born with two Talents as well as the green smoke that had been present at every treatment session. "I believe he was experimenting on me. Zephryn has told me many have been used for experimentation."

"Yes." The cloaked female spoke. "Although not in that way. Garishton seems to have attempted to militarize her, the same way he mutilated her father. Using the green smoke to turn Talents into weapons."

Zephryn leaned forward, voice low. "She was a child. She had no choice."

"Understood, your highness." It was the cloaked male who spoke. "And that will be taken under advisement."

"Under advisement by who? Who among the Lawless leadership?"

"We have dragons and humans among our leadership."

"Not the two other shifter races? No wolves or seals?"

"No. They have hidden themselves and refused to ally." The flat tone allowed for no further questions. "And we must consider your position as a compromised ally as well."

"What position?" Zephryn's voice grew even lower and quieter. Kesia knew that tone. Anyone who mistook it for gentle would be sorely mistaken.

Zilpath's hands flew in complicated gestures. The other female spoke, hesitantly. "Because Kesia is an Ironfire."

Kesia cleared her throat. "I don't understand. Ironfires are metal-workers."

"Do you know of the leader of the Pinnacle?"

"Yes, Garishton Razorclaw. Garishton is a common enough name among dragons."

The cloaked male cut in. "Not that common."

Kesia's mind spun with memories. Garishton's possessiveness over her treatments. Her parents' worry. Numbness spread through Kesia's body. But she had been so poorly treated by the Pinnacle. They believed her a criminal!

And yet, they'd never killed her, not even for escaping. The threatened separation of her and Zephryn had been to bond her with someone else.

Because she had value.

"Fewmets. This can't be true."

The male sighed. "The dragon you know as Garishton Razorclaw is actually Garishton Ironfire, head of the Pinnacle and the scientific mastermind behind the Curious Intrigue."

"But why treat me as worthless?" Her stomach lurched as if she was back on the ship at the docks. She swallowed hard and clung to Zephryn's hand. "How do you know that Garishton Ironfire is the head of the Pinnacle? Has he made an appearance? The Pinnacle keep their own counsel and are rarely seen by most dragons, much less humans."

<I've seen them.> Zephryn didn't meet her eyes this time. He'd held her gaze steadily throughout her discourse, encouraging her every time she'd looked to him for reassurance. But not this time.

Now, he stared straight ahead. Ashamed of keeping information from her? Or trying to avoid what he deemed foolish anger? Kesia released his hand and pressed her palms into the table, trying to slow the thoughts spinning through her mind. She recalled how Zephryn had never been called before the Pinnacle to answer for his actions with her. How he had been able to deflect punishments for her.

Because he was royalty.

Anger stirred within her. <You've met him? You've met my uncle?>

<I didn't know he was your uncle. He was the one who personally insisted you be bred with another fleetwing. He acted as though he owned you.> Zephryn snorted ruefully. <It all makes sense now.>

Shance cleared his throat. "Would you two please speak aloud again? I feel as if I'm missing some very important details in this matter."

Zephryn breathed out smoke. "I am Prince Zephryn Nightstalker, the last heir to the throne of the old dragon kingdom, the Scepter of Justice. My family was taken captive when the Pinnacle overthrew our rule twenty years ago, and over the course of my childhood, they disappeared. As far as I know, I am the only Nightstalker who remains alive."

Shance gave an incredulous laugh. "Blind Viorstan's beard. A dragon prince? I struck a deal with the dragon crown prince."

Something gnawed at Kesia. Why did the cloaked man keep focusing on her position? "If my uncle is the head of the Pinnacle," she asked "what does that mean for me?"

Zilpath's fingers moved far more slowly than normal. The cloaked female's translation was also weighted with reluctance. "It means you're a target."

"A target?"

The cloaked male spoke up. "Either you are a threat to Garishton because you can counter his green smoke, or you are a threat to us and aren't even aware of it."

"A threat to you?"

"Do you remember what Garishton Ironfire did to you in those treatments?"

Green smoke. Straps. Searing pain through every vein.

Screams.

A dragon voice thick with command.

"Tell. No. One."

Kesia grimaced. Revealing that wouldn't look suspicious at all. "No."

"And you're bound to the last prince of the old kingdom. Who knows what your uncle could have brainwashed into your mind? For all you know, you could be the very thing that brings about Prince Nightstalker's downfall."

Chapter Eighteen

ZEPHRYN HAD SEEN Kesia beaten and bruised, left unconscious from pain and fatigue. But he'd never seen her so betrayed. Her face bore the same shocked expression it had when she'd taken the barb-hook to the wing.

Had that only been last week? It seemed like a century ago.

He wanted to hold her, to reassure her that he would stand beside her. That he wasn't going to leave, no matter what her lineage was or what strange powers she had.

But the Lawless needed answers. Answers that neither he nor Kesia had.

He couldn't believe Lord Garishton would have put his own niece through that much pain, but now his interest in breeding her made sense. Did he know, even then, that Kesia was special? Unique? Was he simply waiting for the chance for her mother's Talent or her ability to dissolve the green smoke to manifest? Was that the reason for placing her under such harsh treatment?

<You're quiet, Midnight. Afraid they might be right?> Her mental voice was as flat as her face. <It's all too logical.>

<That doesn't mean it's true.>

<You're a prince of the old kingdom. And apparently I'm the

niece of the dictator that overthrew the kingdom.> Kesia's words were cold and simple, her eyes blank with disbelief. <Did you know this before?>

Zephryn hesitated. <Pryenil told me.>

<Why didn't you say anything to me?>

Her question stabbed at his heart.

<I needed to think about it. I didn't want to worry you. There was so much I didn't know, that *we* didn't know. We still don't know the whole truth.>

She sighed, her lips pinched tight. <And before we left the Cloudpeaks? You'd spoken to him, known him this entire time?>

<Rose-Wing, you knew that. I wanted to keep you away from the horrible machinations of the Pinnacle. You also know that I wasn't privy to everything.> He drummed his fingers on the table. How could he explain this? <At first, Lord Garishton kept my family in a comfortable prison. One by one they disappeared, and I never saw them again. By the time I was nine, I was the only one left. I planned my own escape, but when I met you, everything changed. I couldn't leave you. I knew then I would never leave without you.>

He didn't think it was possible for her face to grow sadder. He was wrong. Her stricken expression tore at his heart.

She exhaled shakily. "You did that because of me? A worthless murderer. Now it's even worse: I'm the heir of the dragon who made your family disappear. You're the hope of the kingdom, Zephryn. I'm nothing more than the daughter of metalworkers and the niece of a despot."

Pryenil cut in. "You are more than that, Kesia. Far more. You may be our only way to stop Garishton. You can use whatever he did to you against the Pinnacle. You already did so at the gala today."

"That may be, but you don't trust me. You wear robes to conceal yourselves." Kesia paused. "As you should. I'm not to be trusted. I understand. I can counteract the green smoke. I suppose that is a useful benefit from all of this. Do you want to keep me in a cage? A cell? I've grown used to them over the years."

The bitterness soaked her voice. Zephryn's throat heated. <You are far more than that, Rose-Wing.>

"Kesia, you know that isn't true." Shance's words followed his. How could this human have such confidence in Kesia after only a few days? Had Shance fought for reprieves for Kesia? Had he slept beside her on missions? Had he celebrated launch days with her? "You're worth far more than a fool airship captain like me."

The robed male spoke. "All of you are critical. Windkeeper, you too belong to a legacy."

The human, important? This merited further attention. Zephryn pushed his thoughts aside and pressed his emotions into a place where they couldn't interfere with his judgement.

From the surprised look on Shance's face, the news had startled him as well. "Me? I mean, Windkeepers used to work with dragons. We don't talk about it much, though. The High Command doesn't like that stuff."

"Not all of High Command is against you," the male continued. "You might be surprised at your allies, but we have to keep our identities very secret."

Shance gave him a sharp, speculative look.

Pryenil added. "In the days of the old kingdom, the Cloudpeaks were the home of the Scepter of Justice, the place of law and order, history and tradition. A place of refuge where any accused could receive a fair trial, as well as a home for officers who monitored the other Scepters for any trouble or injustice. There was a dragon monarchy as well as a dragon-human council that allowed dragons to fill elected seats but was always ruled by a human Chief of Council. By a Windkeeper, as long as the council confirmed it."

Shance shook his head, and breezes swirled in the room. "Windkeepers? No, we're simply merchant sailors. Very good ones. We don't rule anyone."

"It isn't a matter of ruling. It is a matter of keeping peace and ensuring that all are making wise judgements." Pryenil sighed out a faint stream of smoke. "It is a bit much to absorb, but I assure you, this is the truth."

Zilpath's fingers began moving furiously. After several days, Zephryn could interpret many of her basic gestures—mostly vulgar words she used as accents or for emphasis—but this was far too complex. He turned to Pryenil, who sighed. "Very well, Zilpath. I will speak your piece as well. Zilpath wants to inform you this was ordained for decades, and there are those among the Four Corners who have foreseen such a day as this. She warns all of you to hold fast to your vows and stand strong in the days ahead. She also says that many among the devout will give you aid, and if they don't— ah, something like they can go to Ucurit, the endless void, and Zilpath, no, I don't care if your holy scrit says that, I won't repeat it. It's disgusting."

Shance laughed shortly. "Apparently, the great Bonilus and his emissaries didn't mince words. She's right, though; the Four Corners clerics are trustworthy—and I had thought, neutral about the war."

Pryenil put in, "Keeping silent about a matter isn't the same as agreement. Many have supported the Lawless for years. The clerics who don't are identified quickly and avoided."

Zilpath's fingers were still moving, and Shance was frowning and replying to her in equally quick gestures. The male figure sighed. "Enough! Zilpath, you and Shance can debate matters of religious significance and calling later. Right now, we need to decide our next step. You have succeeded in proving something the Lawless have suspected for years. There is a conspiracy maintaining this war, one that likely sparked the war itself."

Zephryn seized the opportunity to turn the conversation. "Specifically, it was Kesia who risked herself to find the proof you needed. Why would she aid in revealing a conspiracy if she were a part of it? Wouldn't she turn us away from it?"

"Good point," Windkeeper added.

"Indeed." The cloaked male figure sighed. "At this point, we can only make assumptions. But it is a mark in her favor, as were her swift repairs to Windkeeper's vessel."

Shance raised his eyebrows. "How do you know about that?"

"I know many things, Captain Windkeeper."

Kesia finally spoke up, her expression neutral. "You mentioned a conspiracy. Why?" She tilted her head to the side. "Garishton benefits because he has control of the Pinnacle, but how does humanity benefit from this?"

Pryenil answered. "The Scepter had made poor judgements from time to time, so Garishton and the other members of the Curious Intrigue stirred up the discontent of anyone who felt victimized. We believe that in addition to scientists, scholars, and malcontents, their numbers include existing criminal elements who had been waiting for their moment to strike. It was a masterful plan—and one no one saw coming until it was too late." Pryenil paused. "But there is one thing he didn't count on: all of you. Especially you, Kesia. We need to get you out of the Scepter of Commerce and away from High Command before anyone realizes who, and what, you are."

Kesia raised her eyebrows. "Why? Because I can destroy the green smoke? Because I have unfortunate relatives?"

"Because even if you weren't brainwashed, Garishton clearly had plans for you. The Lawless need to discover that purpose first."

Anger filled Zephryn. "So you can decide her fate instead?"

"We only wish to assist her."

"And use what she can do," Zephryn growled. "But I agree. Kesia and I must leave this city. Unless there is need of us here?"

Pryenil shrugged. "Due to the open trade acts, despite the military presence the Scepter of Commerce is one of the safest and strongest places for the Lawless. The other Scepters jave individuals who are trying to oppose the war, but they face far more difficulties. They could use assistance and would be emboldened by your presence."

Kesia rolled her eyes. "Even the presence of a worthless experiment?"

The cloaked woman sighed. "You are not worthless."

Zephryn winced. If anyone could understand Kesia's plight, it would be Pryenil. If only the Lawless would trust enough for the half-dragon to remove her hood.

The cloaked male cleared his throat. "All the Scepters came together to end the Scepter of Justice. It will take all Scepters to rebuild it. Our strength is in unity for peace around the crown prince. Many are tired of the war. And despite their front of unity, the Curious Intrigue, the Pinnacle, and the rest are made of disparate individuals who seek selfish ends. They can be turned against in each other."

Shance cut in. "If escape is the plan, you'll need a fast ship. *The Silver Streak* is the fastest and most powerful airship in the fleet, if it weren't in for repairs."

"I can fix it." Kesia's voice was quiet but sure.

"Out of the question." The male's voice hardened. "We just discussed your departure. And your abilities are still unpredictable."

"I'm also the best mechanic you have right now. Could anyone else have fixed that engine in less than two days?"

Shance nodded. "Virna said it would have taken her a day and a half."

"I did it in one hour."

Zephryn shook his head. "But you don't know the ship specifications."

"I can learn them." She placed her hands on the table. "I can fix *The Silver Streak* if you can get me into the shipyard as much as possible. I know it's a risk, but if you want to use that ship, what other choice do you have?"

Zephryn smirked, torn between the urge to argue further with Kesia and the urge to kiss her. Strange, considering Kesia's emotions were still upset and twisted from the suspicions and surprises of that night.

But she was very attractive when she was proving her point logically.

"General Markem practically worships your work. I wouldn't be surprised if he gives you a personal entry code." Shance smiled wryly. "That way, you won't have to break in as a beetle."

She swatted at him, her fingers lingering on his shoulder. "I did what I had to do. And beetles aren't all that bad. I still had more brain power as a beetle than those scientists had as humans."

Shance gave her a mock-aggrieved look. "Next time, you should include me in your spy trip."

"Why? You can't shift."

"And clayborer beetles can't push elevator buttons."

"I sense a challenge." She grinned at him, then glanced at Zephryn. Her smile faded, and she tensed.

Fewmets. Irritation and concern clawed his heart. <We need to talk, Rose-Wing. Privately.>

Her shoulders slumped, but she nodded. <I agree.>

The cloaked male spoke. "Very well. You will work on the airship. But you must work quickly. Captain Windkeeper will pull you out at the first sign of trouble."

Zilpath's fingers started moving. Pryenil spoke. "Then it is settled. Shance and Kesia will return to High Command and maintain their charade until Kesia can repair *The Silver Streak*. Shance will communicate with the Lawless about finding a suitably trustworthy crew. Nightstalker will continue to work within the Lawless establishing connections in his status as prince and heir to the dragon throne. His presence could draw far more to serve the cause who were only sympathizers before. When *The Silver Streak* is ready—" Pryenil paused. "A week, Kesia?"

She hesitated, pressing her lips together. Zephryn knew that look. The look of practicality warring with desperation. "Yes. Maybe less, if I can direct the rest of the repair crew. And if I don't sleep much."

Shanced smiled. "Don't strain yourself."

Kesia set her jaw, and her spine went rigid. Zephryn chuckled inwardly. He knew that look as well. "I'm a soldier, Captain Windkeeper. I've gone weeks on minimal sleep under far worse conditions. This is what is necessary."

"Yes, but it shouldn't have to be." The airship captain's expression held the same softness always apparent when he looked at Kesia, but this time, it was touched with protectiveness.

She raised her head, fixing him with a glare. "Sometimes, it just is."

Shance held her gaze. "You won't do it alone, in any case. I know everything about *The Silver Streak*. Well, perhaps not as much as Virna, but more than enough for us to work together."

She turned to Pryenil. "We can do it. And Shance will ask General Markem for additional help and assign them to areas that don't require my special skills."

Pryenil nodded, and when she spoke, a trace of resonance—respect—vibrated in her voice. "Very well. Once all is in order, we will organize an escape."

The cloaked male figure added, "Between now and then, we need to consider ways to break *The Silver Streak* out of the shipyard. Pryenil, can your resources help?"

"Yes, we can count on them."

"Good. I believe mine will as well." The male sighed, and his hands emerged from the sleeves of his robe, only to disappear under his hood. To pinch the bridge of his nose? Zephryn had seen humans use this gesture before. "I call for an official dismissal. Discuss other matters among yourselves. For myself, I would enjoy a rest. I understand why night meetings are necessary, but they are not pleasant for those of us with greater years."

Zilpath patted his shoulder and swiped at the air. He chuckled dryly. "I'll die soon anyway? That is hardly comforting, Zilpath."

Zephryn's lips curved. The shopkeeper was annoying, but once in a while her words hit just right.

A hand touched his. Kesia's. Her amber eyes were filled with trepidation, laced with anger and self-doubt. <Should we speak now, Midnight?>

On the other side, Zephryn spied Zilpath ushering Shance over to a corner of the tiny room. Pryenil and the cloaked man were both gathering themselves in their robes and conferring quickly in pidsyn gestures on their way to the door.

<Yes. Now is the time.>

Curiously, his stomach seized and twisted, as though he'd eaten a kind of sick animal. Zephryn clenched his hand, trying to stabilize his feelings. One of the individuals in this conversation needed to maintain objectivity.

She had to understand his reasons. He was protecting her.

A rush of Kesia's disappointment and grief overtook his musings. <I understand. You couldn't tell me the details of the Pinnacle because I was a convict. I am a convict still, only fit for a soldier's life. And now, I'm worse than that.>

How could she think such a thing? Zephryn felt a flame tickle his tongue. He swallowed it, along with his anger. <Kesia, I never saw you as less than a worthy dragon. It was shame that made me hide Garishton's identity from you. Shame and disgust at what has become of the Cloudpeaks.>

<*Your* shame. *Your* disgust. *Your* desire to protect me—yes, I can sense that too! Never mind what I was feeling or going through. Never mind that I was searching for answers. *You* knew best, right?>

<You were already coping with so many difficulties. More knowledge would have distracted you.>

Anger blazed in her eyes. <So me learning the truth in a more public meeting where my trustworthiness is questioned is far better. Especially when they imply that I'm going to harm you.>

<I didn't want that to happen either.>

<Of course not. It still hurts. I knew you kept secrets occasionally, but I didn't think they were that ... personal.>

What could he say? He would do whatever necessary to protect her, even from herself. Even now, there were still matters ... that she could know later. Soon, but not yet. Zephryn sighed. What was the word humans used for regret? <I'm sorry. I never meant to hurt you.>

<...I forgive you.> Kesia swiped at her eyes. Tears? From the irritation she was projecting, she didn't want attention drawn to them.

Zephryn sent her a pulse of reassurance and compassion, then changed the subject for one of his own questions. <You weren't honest with the Lawless, were you? I felt your confusion over the issue of brainwashing.>

She winced. <I think I remember my parents telling me that Garishton had the Talent of vocal command. It is possible he invaded my mind to make me harm you, but if he could do that, then why not coerce me into joining him at the start? Why keep me in a cell?>

<Good reasons. Why didn't you refute the Lawless's arguments in the moment?>

She shrugged. <I couldn't think clearly. And I'm used to others having low expectations of me. Better to surprise people than promise something I'm unsure about.>

Still so little faith in herself. Zephryn placed his hand lightly over hers. <He does have that Talent. He's tried to use it on me, but Nightstalkers are difficult to manipulate. Although, sometimes I suspect he's the reason I remember so little of my parents.>

<You were only nine when the last of them vanished.>

He shook his head. <That's no excuse. A worthy ruler would remember more.>

<Ah, you *do* care for your kingdom.> She traced the top of his hand with a fingertip, a faint smile ghosting her face. <And yet, you

were willing to run away with me.>

He took her hands in his. <Until recently, I had no hope of restoring any part of the kingdom, so it didn't matter. Then you encountered Shance Windkeeper, and all of this happened.>

Zephryn glowered at the captain, who was currently turning his back on Zilpath in an effort to ignore her sign language.

Kesia gave a little laugh. <You're mad because he ruined your precious getaway plan, hm? Still the same old Midnight, always assuming you have every angle figured out.>

<I thought I did.> He grumbled. <But recent events have showed me otherwise.>

<Ah well, some of the developments haven't been so bad.> She breathed out a cloud of smoke. <Such as our time in that closet.>

A smile twitched her lips. He brushed an errant strand of hair from her face, his touch lingering around her ear. <Yes, there was that. Such a shame.> Kesia looked up sharply, and he laughed. <That it ended so quickly. You are remarkable, Rose-Wing.>

<I wonder...>

<Hm?>

<I was the one who wanted to spy on the ship. My seasickness made us interact with Shance. I kissed you, which distracted us.> Kesia paused. <It seems I too have a talent for ruining your plans.>

<What sort of talk is this?> Zephryn's brow wrinkled. <Have I said anything to make you think I blame you?>

<No,> she grumbled. <But *I* blame me.>

<Don't.> He flicked her nose with his finger, and her eyes flashed. <You are my fleetwing. Embermate. *We* will have a future.> He pulled her close until she was half in his lap. He didn't care what anyone else thought. <I've been in contact with another dragon in the city. Well, a sort of dragon.>

<Ah yes. The sort-of dragon. Can I meet them?>

<It's complicated. The individual prefers to remain anonymous for now. But there are more dragons in the Lawless. They are resisting the Pinnacle. We aren't alone in this, Rose-Wing. They want me to fight back, to face the Pinnacle and take back leadership.>

<To rule again?> Her shoulders slumped. <Yes, now I understand. They, too, will see me as a murderer. Everyone will know that I killed my father.>

<You said it was out of self-preservation and that he baited you to do it.>

<Yes. But I'm also Garishton Ironfire's niece. You saw how the Lawless treated me, and they were trying to be kind. I can't keep that connection a secret and use my power over the green smoke to help people.>

<These are outcasts as well, Kesia. They may not judge you as those in the Pinnacle do. I will stand by you, no matter what. We will find a way, I promise. We are together.> He traced his fingers over his heart, and then over hers. <And I do not regret that for one moment.>

<Nor do I.> Kesia's face flushed a darker pink that echoed the delicate undersides of her wings. Her gaze drifted to his lips. <And what of our kissing?>

Zephryn breathed slowly. Suddenly, an intoxicating mixture of cloud lilies and iron filled the air. The same scent from the utility closet, that came only from Kesia. They should discuss it. Sometime. <Well, a kiss is a human bonding ritual. We don't know how it affects dragons or what place it has in our lives.> His fingers played with the ends of her hair. <I would want to make additional study, although I wouldn't count it as high of a priority as our current mission.>

Kesia pulled away a little, her eyes glinting. <Oh, you wouldn't? Are you sure? I would say perhaps sex—>

<That...> He struggled to find the words in his mind. It was difficult to think with her fingers trailing up his chest, fingering the edge of his hood. <...would not be wise right now.>

Each word was calm and collected, exactly as it should be. The same could not be said for his pulse, the prickles in his skin, and the heat building in his throat from where Kesia gently stroked it with the tip of her index finger.

<Oh, I agree. As always, Midnight, you show great practical thought and purpose.> She smiled innocently. Only, he could sense the fire within her.

<And you, Rose-Wing, show strength of conviction.> Especially when she trailed her fingers along his scales and through his hair, her every touch a beckoning flame. <The human doesn't know what you are truly capable of, does he?>

She pursed her lips, serious for a moment. <I don't think anyone does. Not even me.> Then she smirked. <It will make for many interesting discoveries. But I always did like those with you. Speaking of discoveries, I do have an intriguing use for kissing, if you will hear me out.>

<Oh?>

<I was able to absorb the remaining smoke particles from *The Silver Streak*'s engine room. It caused no harm to me. I could very likely do the same for you.>

<I thought you kept me from the smoke particles.>

Kesia shrugged. <You can't be too careful. I wouldn't mind absorbing any that might have made their way to you.>

<Ah, I see. Through a kiss?>

<Or more than one. I'm fully committed to making sure you

can use your Talent again.>

She grinned, breaking down the last of his resistance. She truly was a dangerous dragon.

And she was his.

Kesia tilted her head to the side. <So, is kissing still off-limits? Because I think I've made quite a good case for it.>

Zephryn pulled her entirely into his lap.

<As you wish.>

CHAPTER NINETEEN

ZILPATH WAS A MADWOMAN. Yes, she was wise and cunning, and could set any trader in their place with a few words of pidsyn, but that didn't make her present words believable.

She was tapping Shance's shoulder again, her fingers jabbing his flesh like a knife. The old woman had learned pressure point manipulation in her earlier life and used it very unfairly.

Meanwhile, Nightstalker and Kesia's little interlude at the table continued. Their mouths were closed as they used dragon mind speak, but their body language gave away their emotions and perhaps explained what had happened in the closet earlier. Kesia's expression turned from hope to desire.

Before the two dragons started kissing passionately.

His stomach twisted with disappointment. Well, that settled *that*.

Zilpath's dagger-like fingers found a key point between the muscles of his shoulder blades, sending a fire of agony through him. Shance grimaced and turned to face her. ⁓What did you mean?⁓

⁓About what? The prophecy? The clerics?⁓

⁓No, about Kesia. You were the one who indicated she was special. That the wind would dance with the dragons. What did

227

that mean?~

She shrugged. ~I assume you have danced with her, so that was truth. And I did see the two of you kissing. She was surprised, but there was definitely something there.~

Shance coughed. ~Clearly not as much as you thought.~

Zilpath glanced over at Zephryn and Kesia, and her eyes widened. Her shoulders shook in silent laughter. ~Well, well. Pryenil was correct after all. I should know better than to question her in matters of the heart. I suppose I owe her now.~

Shance's mouth dropped open. ~Were you betting on my romantic prospects?~

~Only a little. And never with money. The holy scrit forbids it and I never go against the holy scrit.~

~Enough.~ He made a cutting gesture from chest out to the right for emphasis. He didn't care about the Four Corners holy book. ~Is this why you were suggesting I be a monk a few moments ago? In case you were wrong about Kesia? I don't need your pious judgements on my life, or the absurd punishments of the Four Corners.~

Wasn't his punishment happening in this room already?

Zilpath smacked his shoulder, hard.

~You hold your tongue. The Daughters of Allandra and the Sons of Olosael are an honor to join, and there is no guarantee they will accept you. I had to petition three times to be a novitiate. Something about 'language unbecoming.'~

Imagine that. Shance managed to still his hands before they formed the sarcastic words. Instead, he made a questioning gesture. ~And why should I try?~

~I don't know. Maybe because you've become so lonely that you fell in love with a dragonshifter you've only known for a few days? My religion aside, you're getting stupid, Windkeeper.~

~Kesia is a woman, a soldier, and one of the strongest individuals I have ever known. She has kept appropriate barriers between us and spoken with intelligence and forethought.~ And that only made him love her more, even with the secrets she'd kept from him. Even with the lies.

Even though she couldn't return his love.

Zilpath raised her eyebrows. For once, her hands were still. After a few moments, she began swiping through the air, her expression softer. ~You do love her, don't you? I didn't think it was possible. You actually care for her as a person, not as an escape.~

~She's not an escape. She's brought me closer to myself than anyone else. She's clever, she sees through my flattery, and she's fun to be around. She's relaxing.~ Shance released a sigh. ~And I wouldn't trade any of that, especially not for a religion I don't believe in.~

~You believe enough to have emblems on your ship.~ She jabbed his chest. ~You believe in the gods when they might save you. And now you are lying to your commanders while protecting dragons. You have nothing to cling to except a war record of death. What's stopping you from claiming a belief in something else?~

~Freedom. And I won't give that up.~ He pressed his palms down and out from him on either side. ~Stop. Kesia and I need to get back to the Central Market. High Command will notice our absence if we are away much longer. Now that plans are settled, there's no other reason to be here.~

Zilpath sighed. ~Go on then, Windkeeper. Act your part and treat that woman well, yes?~

Shance snorted. ~I do nothing else, Zilpath. She might kill me otherwise. And then Nightstalker would kill me again.~

~And that would ruin our efforts to ally with them.~ She studied him thoughtfully. ~All is not lost for you, Shance. Even if you choose not to take the path of the Four Corners, at least look a little harder before you jump into bed with the next woman you see. There are far worthier aspects to seek out in a companion than their breasts and hips.~

~But those are very important.~ He flashed Zilpath a smile. ~Wouldn't you agree?~

Her fingers flew in a complicated series of curses, then she clapped her hands three times.

All eyes fell on Shance as Zilpath gestured toward him. Even Kesia and Zephryn stopped. Shance's heart sank. Kesia's expression was softer and more open than he'd ever seen it. What had she said about heartflames? Bound at the heart, by life and by death. He should have known that was an unbreakable bond as strong as marriage.

The thought made Shance's stomach churn. No seducing married women. It was one of his few rules.

Although they still had to mimic betrothal. Firestorms.

Shance made a little bow, military-style, then translated the polite essence of Zilpath's gestures. "I'm afraid that's our notice. If we linger, the street officers will start searching for us. They watch us more than it seems."

Kesia nodded and glanced at Zephryn one final time, then stood and joined Shance, falling into pace with him as they walked toward the door. In the corner, the hooded man and woman moved aside to allow them passage. It would have been nice to see their faces, but as usual, Shance had to play by someone else's rules.

It was really starting to chafe. And Zilpath thought he should sign up for a religion with more rules? No. For all her wisdom, she really was doldrum-brained sometimes.

Kesia's hand slipped into his as they exited the shop and headed down the street. "That was … good. Thank you for offering to help me with the repairs."

"If I hadn't, you would have gone ahead anyway."

"True."

Shance chuckled. "Wouldn't a dragon say that there was no need to thank me?" He kept his voice easy, trying to lighten the serious expression on her face.

"Yes. That's true. But—" Kesia squeezed his hand. "I know you like hearing that, and I care about you. We're friends."

The word twisted in his stomach like soured food, even while it warmed a part of his heart. "Good. Friends are good, Kesia. I'm glad for that."

She cleared her throat with the barest smell of smoke. "Ah, so this afternoon at the gala, in the room where I was speaking to Zephryn. Before the green smoke. We shared information and then, well, I kissed him."

"And you decided you needed to try again tonight?"

"Of course." Kesia gave a sly smile. "There was a chance he had particles of green smoke inside him. It was an effective way of clearing it out."

"Oh, I see." Viorstan, the dragon woman learned fast. It sent a shiver through Shance. No. She was off-limits, and she knew it. He needed to know it as well.

For a moment there was only the raucous late-night sounds of the Low Quarter.

"Are you speaking with him right now?"

"Why wouldn't I be?"

Shance shrugged, his shoulders slouching lower. He'd been

a ground-cursed fool to have thought Kesia would consider him when she was bound to another.

"Shance, is something wrong?"

"Absolutely nothing." He cleared his throat and started walking more briskly. The edge of the Low Quarter was in sight. After that, it was only a four block walk to the Central Market.

"We should figure out who set off that bomb. Whoever it was had access to the Pinnacle and is probably part of the Curious Intrigue."

Kesia easily fell into step next to him. A woman who could match him in many respects, and she was with someone else?

Shance remembered how she'd thrown him against the shelves of Zilpath's shop when they'd first met. His heart sank further. No, she outmatched him.

It was just as well. Would've made life even more complicated.

"When I was burning away the green smoke, I saw the outline of a shape."

"Outline of a shape?" Shance steered them around the corner of a building "Outlines usually *do* have shapes, Kesia. Fiarston, woman, what kind of effect does kissing have on dragons?"

She snorted smoke. "Amusing. It's difficult to keep track of two conversations all the time. Add in trying to remember things, and it's enough to make me want to try that special liquid you drink."

"Ale?" Shance laughed. "That would make it worse. Maybe we can try it another time. It's been a long evening. We can talk in the morning."

See her as a friend. They were friends who were pretending they were madly in love, betrothed, and sharing quarters with all benefits. Why had that been a good idea? There had been a reason, but right now, he couldn't remember it.

Kesia yawned. "That *is* a good idea. For some reason, I am very tired. I feel worse than I did when I had to face the Pinnacle naked."

Fiarston, he did not need that mental image! Did she have any idea—no. She didn't. Shance ran a hand through his hair and breathed slowly, thinking of cold showers and bloody battles, anything to take his mind off Kesia naked. "Another thing you can explain tomorrow."

"No thanks." She reached for his hand again. "Shance? Can you carry me, like you did earlier?"

"What?"

"Just kidding."

"How do you remember that?"

Kesia's eyes sparkled with mischief. "Perhaps I wasn't entirely unconscious. It seemed like a good idea to feign it and avoid questions."

"You tricky little minxweir." Shance laughed as they entered the Central Market. "Where has this dragon woman been before?"

"I'm not sure. Beneath memories, perhaps?" She chuckled. "What's a minxweir?"

"A minxweir? Furry, four legs, a long, flat tail, round ears, narrow eyes?" Kesia shook her head. "I'll have to show you one. People sometimes catch them in the jungle and keep them as pets."

"Not food?"

Shance stopped at the elevator and pressed one of the bronze buttons. "No, they wouldn't yield much anyway."

"Fair enough." She followed him into the elevator.

"So now you're saying it?"

"Apparently I can adapt after all." Kesia stared at the wall for a long moment. Shance thought it likely that she was speaking with

Zephryn in her mind, but she continued. "Is there another human word for a male-female friendship other than 'friend'?"

Shanced scratched his head. "Sometimes the bond can get as close as brother and sister."

"Siblings—those are like clutchmates. I don't have one."

"Me neither. My parents wanted more children, but then the war happened. Now they're hardly ever in the same place, and wartime makes it difficult to raise families."

"I see."

The elevator came to a stop. Shance took a deep breath. Putting a new word to their relationship couldn't hurt.

"How about it? Feel like you could use a brother?"

Kesia smiled faintly. "Yes. I like it."

"Me too."

It was better than nothing.

CHAPTER TWENTY

KESIA LIKED BEING a clayborer beetle. Beetles didn't have complicated situations with their tactical partners that laid the groundwork for future conflicts. Beetles didn't have traumatic pasts or memories about being tortured by evil uncles. No, all her beetle form was concerned with was flying into the exhaust vent and straight into the engine furnace.

Fortunately, that was just where she needed to go. Kesia lifted off from the pile of tools and darted into the vent. Intolerable heat pressed her from all sides. She couldn't land on the interior, and she certainly couldn't indulge her beetle form's instinctive desire to zip into the flames. Instead, Kesia zoomed around the outside edges, checking the sealant. She'd melded the engine together seven days ago, but ever since, she'd been concerned about its integrity. Her eyes scanned the metal surface, searching for anything out of place.

Nothing. It was a perfect, seamless seal, at least as far as her beetle eyes could detect.

She grinned internally, then winced as a flicker of flame scalded her legs. Time to get out. Steeling her mind against the insectoid attraction to the flames, she flew back out the vent.

She buzzed in front of Shance's soot-stained face. He nodded.

"All done?"

How did he expect her to respond? She zipped around in frustration, landing on his nose. Shance knew exactly what she needed.

"Silly bugs, always gumming up the works."

Kesia huffed internally and wished clayborer beetles had a way of attacking humans. She circled his head once more and landed on the edge of his goggles.

"Oh fine. I'll turn around."

She flew off his goggles. As soon as his back was turned, Kesia shifted into human

form and grabbed her underclothes and coveralls. Never mind if another ship worker saw them, he'd assume they were having an intimate moment; being naked around hot engines was still stupid as poison.

She clasped the voicelator around her neck. "Everything looks good in there."

"Glad to hear it." He turned around, then paused. "What's wrong with your foot?"

"My foot?"

"You're not letting your heel touch the ground."

Kesia glanced down at her right leg. It sometimes took time for her human form to catch up with the sensory information from her other forms. She gingerly placed her right heel on the ground. Pain shot up her leg. She winced and sucked in a breath. Injuries carried over. Why did she always forget that?

"What happened?"

"I burned it a little. It's fine." Kesia tried to push past him, but his calloused hands stayed her. She looked up into Shance's face, smeared as hers was with grease, soot, and engine oil. He dared to hold her still, knowing that she could easily fling him off and throw him against a wall.

Because friendship meant she wouldn't.

"Let me see it. Please? You know I've learned medical care."

"All right." It was hard to tell him 'no,' especially when he looked earnest. "I'll take it off."

Kesia sat down, unzipped the boot, eased her foot out, and slipped off her sock. Humans wore so many layers! She allowed Shance to carefully inspect the blisters that had erupted along the bottom of her foot and across her ankle.

"Firestorms. This looks like more than a little, Kesia."

"I might have brushed up against a bit of flame in there." She shut her eyes against the pain as he prodded the wounds. "Anything you can do to help? I can't go to the medical facilities. On the outside, I look human, but if they use the zeroscope they'll know I'm a dragon."

"Right." Shance pulled a small container out of his pocket. "I have some healing salve that should take care of it."

The tension in her shoulders dissipated as he applied the brownish salve, easing the throbbing in her foot. "Why are you carrying that around?"

"Would you believe I'm precognizant?"

"No." She wiggled her toes at him.

He chuckled. "I keep it for my crew—or for me. When I first started serving aboard airships, I was accident-prone, even with my wind Talent. So I started carrying this around for when things happened. My first mission, I scraped my hands raw trying to slide down the main masthead. It was something I'd read about in a book. It didn't matter that my father had told me it wasn't a good idea. It only made me want to do it someday."

"I understand."

"You do?" Shance ripped off the inner sleeve of his coveralls and began wrapping her ankle and foot. "All right, now you need to share. I mean, if you don't mind telling me."

"It's fine. I was seven years old and my mother had just showed me how to use the bellows to control the forge's heat. She'd left the room, and, well, I really enjoyed using those bellows and I wanted to see how it would work with my own flame so—"

"How hot did it get?" Shance interrupted with a chuckle.

Kesia smiled sheepishly. "I melted half the tools closest to the forge before she returned. After that, she gave me another slatesheen treatment."

"Is that a bad thing?" His fingers tucked the last pieces of fabric into place. "I thought you said it made you impervious to everything."

"Oh, it's wonderful. But the first few treatments hurt badly, especially in skin form. After that, we develop an immunity to it."

Shance chuckled "So a treatment and a punishment. Very smart."

"She was."

Kesia grew quiet. His hand lingered on her foot. "Hard memories?"

"Yes, but good ones." She looked up at him. "I'd rather remember and know they loved me than forget about them."

"I understand."

She studied him for a moment, breathing in the fragrance of fresh trees. The scent still aroused her, even though Zephryn held her heart and desire.

She wrinkled her nose. It was time to get that dissonance sorted out. "Shance, do you wear perfume?"

"Perfume?" He chuckled. "No. I haven't even used hair pomade since your reaction when we first met."

"So why do you smell…" She searched for a word.

"Awful?"

"Irresistible."

He raised his eyebrows. "Oh, so now you're changing your mind about me? After how adamant you were before, I'd almost suspect a love potion at work."

Kesia latched on to the phrase. "A what?"

"It's a mythical elixir that makes someone fall in love against their will. Kind of like how the voice of a dragon woman is said to call airship sailors to their deaths by luring them over the edges of their ships."

"Foolish. Some humans can find dragon voices compelling, but we don't have any actual additional power to persuade."

"Yes, I know." He rolled his eyes. "But in my case, I was already falling to my death, so that myth doesn't apply. And the only elixir I've been drinking is this liquor Brody has been slipping me out of pity. Really strong stuff too. Has notes of different trees."

Kesia's heart raced, and she jumped to her feet, wincing as she pressed down on her right heel. "Trees?"

"Yes. Trees." Shance stood, looking at her quizzically. "What about it?"

"At the gala, I was strongly attracted to Zephryn. And he smelled like trees. Peak pine trees. Ever since then, that scent has been present before we kissed. Drawing me to him." Kesia glared at him, her throat heating up. "Do you always drink that liquor?"

Shance's eyes widened. "No. But I have it here with me."

He pulled out a small flask. Kesia grabbed it, unscrewed the top, and inhaled.

A rush of intense smells—tree branches and alcohol and other compelling aromas—flooded her nose and mouth. A perfect blend of Zephryn's scent combined with the alluring flavors of whatever spices were in the beverage.

Anger burned within her. How had they trapped Zephryn's scent? Who had given this to Shance? Did they know the effect it would have on her?

Whoever had done that needed to die.

"Kesia? Kesia! Your hands!"

"What?"

She blinked. Her hands were covered in scales and flames.

"Fewmets!"

She focused, trying to quell the fire.

Someone coughed behind her.

"Oh, dear me. Am I interrupting something?"

A deep alto voice laced with smugness broke into Kesia's churning thoughts. A woman with dark brown velvet skin and tiny braids falling down her back stood in the doorway, her full lips quirked into a smirk.

Countess Nula Thredsing.

What was she doing here?

"Civilians aren't allowed in the shipyard." Shance stepped in front of Kesia. Thank Viorstan the flames were gone, but smoke still filled the engine room.

Had Nula seen anything?

"Oh, but I would have missed the delightful show."

Firestorms!

"This is an engine room, Countess." Shance kept his tone flat. "Smoke and flames are hardly out of the ordinary."

"Except when they emerge from the hands of the Congruency's favorite First Mechanic." Nula brushed off her silvery corset-coat and stood on her tiptoes, fixing Kesia with a smile. "Or should I say, dragon mechanic?"

Kesia stepped out from behind him, smiling tightly. "Only a new device from the Scepter of Industry. A flame thrower that fits into the sleeve of the mechanic. It only appeared that my hands were on fire."

"Oh yes?" Nula sauntered up to Kesia. "Where is this miracle device?"

Kesia folded her arms and raised her chin. "That's a secret for mechanics only."

Shance clenched his teeth. "What are you doing down here, Countess?"

Nula shrugged. "I received special permission from General Brody. He's an old friend of the family, and most *curious* himself."

Brody? A member of the Curious Intrigue?

Nula continued. "He thought I should meet this rising star personally. Now I see why. She has many unexpected qualities, does she not?"

"Only tools." Kesia raised her chin and took Shance's hand. "I'm tired. The repairs to the ship are nearly finished, so I think my betrothed and I will leave. Unless you object?"

Nula's gleaming white teeth flashed as she smiled and stepped aside. "Oh no, feel free. Although, Captain Windkeeper, I don't think your coveralls are regulation anymore."

Shance glanced at his ripped sleeve and the loosened hem of his undershirt. "I didn't know you were knowledgeable in military regulations, Countess. Or that you cared."

He followed Kesia up the ladder to the main deck. Nula followed. "You're right. I don't. But they do."

"They?"

Countess Nula clapped her hands. Soldiers appeared and surrounded the ship. Kesia backed up until she stood next to Shance, her hands clenching and unclenching. "What is this?"

"I truly am sorry. You do seem like a nice one, but you incriminated yourself."

Winds swirled around Shance, ready to lift him and Kesia off the deck and over the heads of the waiting soldiers. "What do you mean by 'one'?"

The countess sighed. "A nice dragon. I'm sure you aren't, though, because dragons are murderous, reptilian devils. Or so the papers say. From what little I've seen of you and your partner, Kesia, I must say," her voice lowered as she turned her back to the oncoming generals, and genuine regret flashed in her gray eyes, "I wish things had been different."

She stepped aside, and there stood General Brody, his face tight and twisted. "Captain Windkeeper. You have been harboring an enemy spy, allowing her to enter our camp and learn our secrets. I hope, for your sake, that you were ignorant of her identity. If so, you will be tried for gross incompetence rather than treason."

"Treason? This entire war is a farce." The words slipped out before he could stop them.

"I tried to warn you. You should have taken the Countess's offer." Brody shook his head. "I hope this rebellion was worth it. Was it all for the novelty of having a dragon woman in your bed?"

"Sir?" Brody had never been this blunt outside of a tavern. Now, there was an edge to his face that Shance had never seen.

"You're not taking her."

Brody ignored him. "Captain Cryor."

The fresh-faced captain stepped forward, expression stoic.

"Arrest the dragon spy and Captain Windkeeper. Take them to separate cells for interrogation."

"Aye, sir."

"Viorstan piss on all of you." Shance reached out to summon a gale force when a hand closed over his arm, arresting his motion.

Kesia.

Shance glanced at her, but her gaze was fixed steadily on General Brody. There was no trace of the sweet, sharply curious dragon, only the deadly eyes of a soldier. She pressed something into his hand.

Her voicelator. She'd removed it.

Kesia leaned close to him.

"See that Zephryn gets this," she whispered. "Tell him to keep fighting, with or without me. I won't be afraid."

"Kesia."

"Tell. Him."

She backed away from Shance.

"Release him." Her voice vibrated with the resonance that had won him from that first rescue. Now it was directed at Brody. "Release us. Now."

He blinked, then gave a short laugh. "Do you think we came unprepared? We have ways of resisting dragon compulsion, spy." He signaled to the soldiers. "Take her out."

"No!"

As the word escaped Shance, a blast of wind from his hands threw everyone to the deck. A small canister landed next to him spewing clouds of green smoke. The wind ceased, the force he'd known since childhood gone again. Soldiers rushed the deck. He tried to see them through the clouds, tried to fight, but without the wind to guide his actions, every blow fell short. They bound his hands behind him and dragged him off to the side.

The smoke began to clear. Shance blinked. Kesia stood across from him, her arms outstretched, face pinched in concentration as she blew out streams of flame that eliminated the vapors.

"Very impressive. Just as your uncle told us, Kesia Ironfire. He's waiting for you now."

General Brody knew who she was? He was in league with the Pinnacle, a flame-cursed traitor to the Congruency.

Kesia growled so loudly the deck shook. "I see. Release Captain Windkeeper with a full military discharge, and I will come with you."

"You are in no place to make demands."

Kesia's eyes flashed to dragon slits. "If you don't, I will destroy everyone and everything in this shipyard."

Dread filled Shance as he realized she was serious. What had the Pinnacle done to dragons to make them so ruthless?

"Even your devoted betrothed? I think not."

"Kesia—"

"I have lost everything once. I'm familiar with having my life destroyed." Her voice was calm. "Captain Windkeeper is without his Talent and resources. He is no threat to you. And I can imagine your dragon ally wants me alive more than anything else."

Brody flinched, then his jaw set. "This is suicidal."

"I don't care." Flames erupted from Kesia's mouth as scales appeared on her face and arms, allowing the fire to travel down to her hands.

Brody swallowed. "Fine. I promise to secure his safety. He never had a stomach for warfare. He'll turn into a useless womanizer and drunkard within a few days. Might even be dead within a week. But you have my word."

Kesia gave a mirthless smile. "Your word means nothing to me. You will take me to a window where I can personally see him released without soldier escort. Then I will come with you."

"Agreed." Brody glanced at his timepiece. "Can we move on with this?"

Shance tried to catch her gaze. She couldn't do this! Kesia was the one person who could not get captured. She turned to meet his eyes, her lips moving.

Tell Zephryn. Find them. His muddled mind put the pieces together.

She didn't have to surrender; she wanted to.

Shance gave her a wink. He would find Zephryn and Zilpath and the rest of the rebels. One of the hooded figures had mentioned sympathizers in High Command. Surely they could get *The Silver Streak* out of the shipyard.

He would find a way.

Kesia had rescued him twice. It was time for him to return the favor.

CHAPTER TWENTY-ONE

ONE STEP. THEN ANOTHER. Slow and steady was the best way through the Central Market, especially with the heavy helmet blocking her vision. After she had seen Shance leave the Central Market unhindered, a rough cylinder with small holes for breathing had been forced over her head. Her footsteps sounded muddled to her ears, and her arms were cuffed behind her in tight manacles.

Apparently, they thought she would try to escape.

At this moment, Kesia wasn't sure she could get away. If she shifted into a smaller form, they could catch her in these confined hallways. Shifting to a larger form was even more unwise. And she had promised to go with them if Shance was free.

It was better to keep that promise a little while longer.

Meanwhile, there was the endless march to the roof. Keep plodding along; no point in running to her own funeral. Or would it be a funeral? Perhaps Lord Garishton had something worse planned. But if she were some kind of heir to his powers, maybe he'd keep her alive. Maybe he wouldn't go after Zephryn and Shance.

Unlikely. He had gone after her parents. There was nothing that would keep him from destroying her friend or her embermate.

Kesia swallowed. Never mind waiting. It was time to shift and attempt an escape.

Clayborer beetle.

She waited for the ripple, the tingling of her flesh. The vertigo of shrinking down so small, so fast.

Nothing.

Kesia focused harder.

Clayborer. Beetle.

There was only the sound of trudging footsteps and the whirring of an elevator.

Her heart sank. Fewmets! It must be the helmet. But how?

She was doomed, trapped in her skin form without her voicelator to communicate with Zephryn. Even if she'd held on to it, the soldiers probably would have taken it away from her.

She was alone.

In the end, she was always alone.

The words fed the fear churning her stomach. *Control, Rose-Wing. They can only defeat you if they can control your feelings. Bury them.*

Zephryn's remembered words settled her, but evoked a new emotion. Rage. Why had Brody given Shance that drink? What game was he playing, trying to draw her attention to Shance? Not even Zephryn would be able to find logic or reason in that.

But he would find her. He said he would always stay with her.

If only she hadn't been stupid enough to offer herself up. But what else could she have done? Too many lives had been lost trying to protect hers.

She could protect herself. *She* had challenged General Brody in the shipyard and negotiated Shance's release. *She* had broken into the laboratory. She could hold out until help came.

Even if it never did.

Kesia shook her head in the helmet. Zephryn wasn't stupid. He would understand and come after her. Even though it would risk his own life.

But Zephryn shouldn't have to do that. Not for her. He was worth too much, even if he couldn't see it in his master plan. She could see it for him.

But if she was captured, who would he have to talk with? Would that even matter to him? Images surfaced in her mind.

Zephryn offering to run away with her after the airship incident. Zephryn stroking her hair and scales when she was injured—and coaxing her through the pain of shifting her broken wing. Zephryn contacting her mentally to discuss problems and feelings.

Shock and certainty settled in her heart. She mattered to him. To Shance, her chosen brother. To that nameless, cloaked figure who'd kept insisting Kesia had value, even without her ability with the green smoke.

Wetness leaked out of the corners of her eyes even as she walked to her doom. A heavy hand of regret squeezed her heart. She had been foolish. So foolish.

A cool breeze rushed beneath the helmet, lifting her hair from the back of her neck. They must have reached the rooftop. Vibrations pressed through the ground beneath her, and she assumed an airship was docked nearby.

"Any chance you can tell me where we're going?"

The barrel of a rifle shoved her forward. "We're not going anywhere. You're going to that Pinnacle."

An answer! Albeit, a useless one. She'd already figured that.

Kesia swallowed hard. She couldn't undo her sacrifice for Shance's escape, and she didn't want to. But she could get more answers on her own. She was strong, and the Pinnacle wanted her.

There was leverage in that.

There had to be.

All she had to do was face them while she waited for Zephryn and Shance.

Fear and determination began percolating in her stomach, pushing more words out of her mouth. "What does Lord Garishton want?"

"Who knows? You'll find out soon enough though, eh? Can't imagine anyone will see you around here again."

Hands grabbed underneath her arms, yanking her up and shoving her face down into unforgiving metal. Behind her, doors slammed shut.

Something heavy smashed into her head.

The world turned dark and blank.

The Scepter of Commerce library might be deficient in books about dragon lore, but it had sufficient space for pacing. Not that Zephryn noticed any of the titles on the shelves. His mind was preoccupied with finding his embermate.

<Kesia!>

Still nothing. He stared at the voicelator in his hand. They must have her trapped in a device coated with tepstone.

Windkeeper was right.

"She's gone." Zephryn pivoted, glaring at Shance. "Explain."

"I told you. She cut a deal with them so I could get free and find you. And here we are. I'm not actually free, but I thought maybe you could help me take care of that."

The airship captain leaned back against a shelf and rubbed a bruise on his forehead. More bruises marred his face and, judging from the way he walked and held his rib cage, other parts of his body. Zephryn would expect nothing less from any efficient military.

It was far more surprising that Windkeeper was alive at all. Although, the new arrivals to the Obscure Antiquities part of the Scepter of Commerce library could only be there to locate Zephryn and set a trap.

A pity. He'd been looking forward to some peace and quiet after the last six days. He had gone with Pryenil, Zilpath, and the still-hooded man to a secret meeting every night, learning about the rebel cause and reassuring them that he and Kesia would stand against the Curious Intrigue. Locations included a Four Corners temple, a tavern back room, and something called a "dump." Because humans didn't or couldn't burn their rubbish.

Kesia would have been helpful at the meetings. She couldn't see how her presence disarmed others, but that didn't make it useless. Yet another reason they had to get her back.

"Why haven't you dealt with the humans?" Words were so clumsy. He would give anything to have Kesia's mind-speak in his head.

Windkeeper winced. "Green smoke killed my Talent for another twenty-two hours. Kesia blasted the smoke, but not before it got to me." Shance paused, eyes gleaming. "I suppose she could have kissed me to make it better."

"No."

Windkeeper laughed. "Such care for your comrade's well-being. I can still fight and run, but I can't promise much of either. I don't suppose you have anything great up your sleeves, besides your scales? Kesia's probably in the air by now."

"We need to disappear. Stop talking and follow me." Zephryn grabbed the airship captain's shoulder and focused. Bringing someone else beneath his Cloak was easy enough, but the Talent only extended so far. Close contact ensured the human wouldn't step outside the range of effectiveness.

Windkeeper opened his mouth to speak, then closed it and nodded. Zephryn began moving forward, slowly at first to allow the other man to sync to his steps, then faster, past the official military uniforms and the street officers in plain clothes with stances that made them even more obvious.

If the Scepter of Justice reinstated street officers after the war, they would have to be better trained. Something Zephryn would have to mention to his parents.

If he found them.

Otherwise, according to what Pryenil had told him, Zephryn would have to convince the Council, which could theoretically be led by Windkeeper and might be amenable to new ideas. *If* the airship captain assumed that role, which seemed questionable at best.

They had almost reached the end of the wide aisle that ran the length of the library.

Kesia, what were you thinking? He rubbed her voicelator again, recalling the way her face shone when he first gave it to her. Cloud lilies were her favorite. She even smelled irresistibly like them at times.

Had she given up? Is that why she'd turned herself in?

It couldn't be.

Sending out Windkeeper was a reasonably intelligent strategy. She had a better chance of taking on the Pinnacle than he, especially with her newly reclaimed abilities. They wouldn't have traded anything for Shance anyway.

Kesia had to have a plan.

If only Zephryn could still the ceaseless, mocking words in a corner of his mind. Words that told him she never should have returned to the Central Market with Windkeeper, that someone else should have made the repairs to the ship.

They exited the library, but instead of descending the last few steps, Zephryn pulled Shance off to the side beneath a small, covered alcove. "We should be able to speak here, quietly. Once we decide on a direction, I will have to release the Cloak. Slipping among busy streets while invisible is not easy with two people and would ultimately cause more problems. Speak quickly: what happened?"

"We were working in the engine room. Almost done with the last repairs." Shance winced. "And then Kesia got really angry. Something about this ale General Brody gave me, how it smelled like you and made me irresistible."

Zephryn frowned. "What?"

"She never had the chance to explain. Her hands started flaming, and Countess Nula surprised us. The countess seemed like she already suspected something, and once she had confirmation, she signaled to General Brody, who appeared with a squadron of soldiers. We were outnumbered. After they disabled me with the green smoke, Kesia stepped in."

"Yes, she would." Zephryn sighed. "Countess Nula? Then she is a part of the Curious Intrigue?"

Windkeeper shook his head, scratching his short beard. "I'm not so sure about that. Before she turned us in, she said she regretted it. That isn't what you say if you're happily signed on to an evil conspiracy. You've spoken with her before. Any insight?"

"None. She was human and annoying. Very driven. She has the ability to taste and perceive the worth of people, apparently." Zephryn paused, wondering how much he should reveal to Shance. He had already taken a strong and potentially unhealthy interest in Kesia and shown unstable emotions in other situations. On the other hand, Shance was intelligent some of the time, and Zephryn's options were limited. "She mentioned that Kesia tasted of incredibly strong value."

She'd also mentioned that he and Kesia had the most value together, as if that weren't already the case. They were bound at the heart. Nothing could change that. If he had to ascend the throne, it would introduce complications, yes, but she was worth it.

"Probably another one of Countess Nula's mind games. We need to get to Zilpath and the rest. It's time for this Congruency spy to come out of hiding." Shance rubbed the back of his neck. "Luckily, I know a back way through the Narrows. Fewer people means you can keep us invisible, right?"

Zephryn nodded. The street officers had exited the building and were scouring the passersby in front of the library. "As long as we move quickly and keep silent."

"Of course. As quick as I can."

Shance led them down one side street after another, some of them such a tight fit that Zephryn had to release Shance so they could squeeze through. Zilpath knew the same paths and had explained them through Pryenil once. Apparently, the people who built the Scepter of Commerce hadn't judged the spaces between buildings as carefully as they should have, creating a maze of tiny alleyways used by those from the Low Quarter to move around the rest of the city.

"Here we are." Shance pushed open the back door to the

clothing shop. "Zilpath, I have an emergency order for you. Expensive cloth."

Zephryn glanced at the front counter. Zilpath was there, but her hands weren't making their usual swooping gestures. Instead, they held her Berringer pistol, the barrel pointed at a figure across the counter. A human woman, with tiny black braids and calculating gray eyes.

Shance lunged toward her. "What the ducus are you doing here? You gave us away, you conniving—!"

"Touch me, and you'll never hear what I have to say." Countess Nula raised her hands. "And you very much want to hear what I have to say. You all do."

Zephryn tilted his head. "And why is that?"

"Because I can sway this whole city to your side, once and for all. If you give me asylum."

Chapter Twenty-Two

IF HE'D HAD HIS WIND POWERS, Shance would have blown the countess into the next Scepter.

"Asylum? Zilpath, how can you possibly trust her?"

Zilpath shot him a fierce look. She also refused to lower the weapon, leaving her unable to speak with him. Shance looked over at Nightstalker, but the dragon had disappeared.

"Zilpath, you can lower the weapon." There he was, between Countess Nula and the door. The dragon prince had drawn the curtains across the windows. "If she tries anything, I will take measures."

His voice carried the same finality Kesia's had earlier. Nightstalker didn't hide his predator nature as easily as Kesia did, but looking at him now, it was difficult to imagine him as anything other than a dragon.

The Countess raised her eyebrows and pursed her lips. "If you try to strike me, I will scream so loudly every officer on this street will hear."

"They won't hear a word."

Realization lit Shance's mind. "You can Cloak sounds too?"

"Yes."

"Why didn't you Cloak our sounds from earlier?"

Nightstalker smirked. "I prefer most people to remain quiet."

Zilpath's shoulders shook with laughter as she set the pistol behind the counter. Her freed fingers moved. ~He makes a point, Shance.~

"Thanks, Zilpath. That's so kind of you." Shance rubbed his knuckles, which were finally starting to scab over from his fight with the soldiers. Then he glanced at Zephryn. "Perhaps I shouldn't translate her words for you, then. That'll give you all the quiet you want."

Countess Nula rolled her eyes. "Or I could continue speaking."

"No." Shance and Nightstalker spoke at the same time.

Nightstalker continued. "If you do not translate, Windkeeper, I will show you just how far a dragon's flame can reach."

Shance chose not to respond, but studied Zilpath's rapid gestures. "Zilpath says the Countess has been an informant on the Curious Intrigue for years, but only when it suits her. The Lawless don't trust her, and most don't even like her—"

"Consider me broken-hearted," Countess Nula cut in dryly.

"—but she is often useful, especially with her powers of prediction and measuring value." Shance swallowed hard. "But she also turned in Kesia and I when we were working in the engine room."

"I had to. I'm a double agent, and the warmongers were getting suspicious because I hadn't returned with useful information in a while. Besides, it wasn't as if you were being careful; the dragon's hands were on fire! What were you thinking?"

Shance took a step toward her. "She got angry about some weird bilge Brody gave me, saying it smelled like Nightstalker over there."

"Nightstalker?" Countess Nula's shoulders shook with laughter.

"Oh my, they did find high-class blood for that potion. That explains why Nightstalker caught my interest."

His head felt light, and a sudden sweat prickled his skin. "Potion?"

"Yes." Nula flipped a braid over her shoulder. "You see, there is dragon blood in the Thredsing family ancestry. When I realized I'd have to marry you to gain some measure of freedom, I wanted to make it easier on myself. You're not exactly my type." Her ebony lips curled. "I arranged for an ... aphrodisiac, as it were. A dragon blood love potion made from their pheromones so I would be more attracted to you. Brody passed it to you as a favor to me. I guess it worked on Kesia Ironfire as well, though clearly not enough." The countess glanced at Nightstalker. "Your value has gone up considerably, but you're missing one final piece."

The dragon's eyes flashed to slits. "What do you mean?"

"Oh, that wouldn't be fun. Besides, that information isn't part of the deal."

She shifted her weight to her other hip. After all this, Shance still couldn't help following the curves of her fitted clothing. He quickly looked back toward her face and that mouth that wouldn't shut up. "I only revealed her as a spy. She did the rest. As I recall, Kesia had a clever way of releasing you so that she could save your life. Don't underestimate a pretty face, Captain Windkeeper. Her embermate certainly doesn't."

Shance swallowed. "Embermate?"

Countess Nula grinned. "Oh yes, I see you do know what that means. You fell in love with a very married woman. It really is a shame what the Pinnacle has done to dragonkind. I have heard stories about what fiery lovers they made in earlier decades."

She paused for dramatic effect. Shance hazarded a glance at

Nightstalker, but the dark lines of the dragon's face might as well have been carved from stone. Only his eyes gave away anything. Their cobalt depths glittered with glowing red-gold slits. "If you have nothing useful to say, I have missed roasting human flesh."

"Don't trouble yourself." Her words flew out quickly now. "My parents are life-long members of the Curious Intrigue, so I was raised within the inner circle and was privy to a lot of secrets. Being able to predict future patterns and taste value revealed that the Curious Intrigue's dominance in this war would come to an end. I chose to play both sides until I met those who were destined to take it down—namely, all of you. And it looks like it's time for me to claim a side." Nula smiled. "I'll get you into the Congruency to meet a few of the Lawless's insiders. I can relay any messages you want, and when the time comes, I'll turn my parents over and give you access to their nefarious plans. I'll even provide you with further predictions and value judgements—I have a ninety-nine percent accuracy rate. The only thing I ask in return is complete immunity and asylum, as well as my inheritance from my parents in full. I want to maintain my lifestyle independently."

Zilpath started slapping the counter. Once she had everyone's attention, her hands moved rapidly. ~Why should we trust you?~

At that, Countess Nula threw back her head and laughed, She gave Zilpath an oddly knowing look. "Oh, you shouldn't. I can be very untrustworthy. But I am your only option. You need to get to your precious dragon before her uncle tries to conscript her into his schemes—although I'm not sure he realizes the battle he'll have. Especially if that one," she pointed at Nightstalker, "flies ahead of us and makes sure he's there to give Kesia back-up and increase her power."

At that, Nightstalker's stoic expression broke into surprise and shock. "What do you mean by that?"

"You don't know? Mother and Father are right: they do keep you dragons dumb and ignorant." She paused. "What I've heard is that your embermate is a part of you. Your hearts are entwined, so your powers are a little more … fluid, somehow."

"How so?" Nightstalker moved closer, flames licking around his neck. "Explain."

Countess Nula shrugged. "I don't know. I wasn't officially invited to that meeting, and at that point, they realized I'd been eavesdropping and shooed me away. But let's not forget why we are here. Do we have a deal?"

Shance glanced at Zilpath. She made a few pidsyn gestures. He agreed. At this point, they had nothing to lose. Judging by Nightstalker's attitude, it seemed they were all in agreement. Hopefully he wouldn't eat the Countess, though Shance couldn't blame him if he did.

Maybe just a finger or two.

Shance nodded. "As long as you make good, we have a deal."

"Agreed," Nightstalker said. "Get your ship, Captain Windkeeper. I will track Kesia."

"How will I find you?"

"You'll be in dragon air space." Nightstalker gave a humorless smile. "I'll find you. Expect any other dragons to be hostiles."

Without another word, Zephryn turned and exited the shop. Headed toward his embermate. His … wife. Shance sighed. The next woman he fell for, he'd have to be extra careful she wasn't married and simply unaware of the fact.

Fingers jabbed sharply into his shoulder. Shance looked down in time to see Zilpath say, ~Still keeping a level head? You said you would keep focused on the task at hand, no matter what happened.~

"I am." Shance looked over her head at the Countess. "Take me to the Lawless insiders. There's no time to waste."

Nula pivoted and walked to the door. "Follow me, Captain Windkeeper. Stay close. Oh, and I know it's difficult, but try to keep your eyes on my head."

"Easily."

Shance followed her, trying and failing to keep a watchful eye on the street officers. Countess Nula kept a brisk pace, striding through the crowds of people as if she expected them to part before her. And they did. Even the street officers who caught sight of him were turned aside by her stare.

Such influence was impressive. Intimidating, in a different way than Kesia's soldier skills had been. Kesia appeared every inch the quiet woman, hiding fire and danger within. Nula wore her capabilities and intellect as openly as a soldier wore weapons.

It was little wonder she'd found no suitors. While the Scepter of Commerce allowed women to inherit, own property, and take part in business, men preferred wives who acted genteel and civil. Not that the countess was otherwise, but she seemed to be more than anyone could handle.

Shance certainly didn't want to, which left one question in his mind. He increased his pace to walk abreast with her as they crossed another street. "Why did you want to marry me if you wanted to be an independent woman? Why not just wait until you could strike a deal with the Lawless, as you have done now?"

"I don't foresee everything, Captain Windkeeper." She turned and gave him a quick, wry smile. "I only enjoy appearing so. At that point, marriage to you was the best way to ensure a place for myself when I had to turn on my parents. I judged that you would be fair and courteous, which suited my tastes. I do enjoy the physical aspects of life as much as anyone, so I attempted to broker an equitable situation for all parties."

"An equitable situation." Shance laughed in disbelief. "Is that how you see love? As something to be manipulated?"

Nula stopped in front of the Central Market and faced him. Her gray eyes softened, and her voice mellowed. "True love isn't meant for everyone, Captain Windkeeper. I of all people should know that. I cannot see any predictions for myself, nor can I taste my own worth, but in love I will not settle for anything less than something strong and lasting. I would rather have a just and open-handed marriage with someone who respects me and gives me freedom than to chase my feelings into heartbreak and unhappiness. I suggest you do the same."

"Have you seen something? Do you know something about me?" He shouldn't have asked. Countess Nula was just a Talent-aided fortune teller. And yet, his breath caught in his throat, waiting for her response.

The Countess paused, her eyes clouding over. Then she shook her head. "I cannot say clearly at this point. Your value is measured by a very unstable scale. I know that a few fleeting pleasures, however sweet, are not worth a lifetime of—" She broke off, turning and walking toward the front entrance. "We should hurry."

Shance strode quickly to catch up with her. "A lifetime of what?"

Her answer spilled out in a torrent. "A lifetime of wondering if you're missing something right in front of you in favor of cheap thrills."

"Are you telling me you haven't indulged in cheap thrills?"

Countess Nula studied him, eyes hard. "No. But even I admit they lose their savor."

She pivoted and strode ahead to the lobby, her boots clicking on the marble floor. Officers and merchants looked up from their conversations around the pillars. Nula ignored all of them and walked up to the front desk.

"Excuse me, but I found Captain Windkeeper in utter dissolution, making trouble at a tavern. As you can see, he's been in more than one fight." Nula gestured to Shance." I know he has been formally discharged, but I think he would be better off in your care instead of staining the honorable name of the Congruency fleet."

"I see." The receptionist, a third lieutenant, made a note. "I will send for an escort to take him to the cells, Countess Nula."

"Perhaps I should escort him personally to General Brody. This might be a matter of some sensitivity." Countess Nula's voice lowered. "For the sake of the *curious*."

The receptionist blinked, then nodded. "Go ahead, Countess Nula."

Another insider from the Curious Intrigue. Panic thudded Shance's heart, but he managed to keep silent until they were in the elevator. "General Brody?"

Nula grinned. "You really should trust more, Captain Windkeeper."

"You yourself said you were untrustworthy."

"True. Still, I think you have little choice right now." She smiled and exited the elevator, sauntering over to a doorway on the left side of the hallway.

Not General Brody's door.

What was Nula doing?

"General Markem?" Shance paused just outside the opening.

Nula gestured impatiently, adding a little pidsyn curse for good measure.

Fine then.

Shance walked into the room. It was General Markem's spare office with the same polished wooden desk, wireless commer, and suspension clipse-mirror. He glanced up at Shance, his expression sharp and unimpressed.

At his side stood Captain Tegan.

The general grunted. "Captain Windkeeper. I see you've managed to survive. I suppose that's a good thing. Now, let's get your ship out and stop this damn war."

Shance's mouth dropped open. "General? This whole time you were part of the Lawless?"

"Yes, despite those horrible night meetings and that curse-fingered clothing merchant." His eyes glinted with humor. "My Talent is disguising my voice—the Talent listed on my official records was falsified. There was no chance you would have recognized me."

The cloaked man. This whole time, it had been General Markem. Shance's mind froze trying to comprehend this situation.

Captain Tegan rolled her eyes. "Keep your mouth open, and a crenbird might lay an egg in it, Windkeeper."

"You're part of this too? But you're disgraced…"

She smiled thinly. "All is not as you see it, Windkeeper."

Nula cleared her throat. "Now that everyone has been introduced, I have a family to betray and a supper date, so let's get this breakout started."

"Here. I don't advocate much drink, but occasionally a little is called for." Markem pushed a flask across the desk and grinned at Shance. "I promise there's no dragon blood in this one."

Shance grabbed the flask and took a swig. There might be a day when he gave up alcohol, but today was not that day.

Chapter Twenty-Three

COLD AIR RUSHED OVER Kesia's skin as someone ripped the helmet from her head, freeing her hair to fall about her bare shoulders. She was naked. Again. They must have stripped her before waking her up.

She rolled over and stood. Light trickled in from the four corners of the room. A familiar bass voice spoke from one of them. "Kesia Ironfire. Murderer. Why do you not bow before your leaders?"

"I-I have no leaders here. And I am no murderer."

Fewmets!

No, she would keep steady and firm. For Zephryn, even if he didn't get here in time.

For Shance, even though he loved her too quickly and too much. For the Lawless resisting this war.

"You are not permitted to speak."

Kesia turned toward the voice, allowing it to wash over her and bring with it the memory of being brought here as a child, also naked in order to fully absorb the treatments.

Even then, was her uncle preparing her to be treated as worthless? Forcing her to devalue herself? Anger coiled in her stomach.

She had served them faithfully with everything she had, believing she was a criminal.

No more.

"I'm not allowed to speak because I killed my father? Is that why you named me murderer? Because a scared child defended herself against a monster, a monster that the Pinnacle created! Are you listening? I know what you did!"

Her voice echoed in the dark hall. Fire heated her skin, driving away the cold and feeding her courage.

"So you remember?"

Yes, she was a killer, and her father's blood was on her hands, as well as the blood of those she had killed in the war. But that blood was also on the Pinnacle's, especially Lord Garishton's. Far more on his than any other.

"Yes. I remember."

A pause. Did they expect her to be ignorant of the truth? Did they really think she was beaten? Kesia had been willing to take any punishment to earn their pleasure, and all the while, her uncle had stood there watching her quake and cower.

The fire spread through her veins, granting her boldness. She stepped toward the voice. "What? Are you without words now? You and your Curious Intrigue! Are you so sure of your victory in this war that you can't imagine anyone standing against you?"

"Be careful, niece." The light flickered around the location of the bass voice. Kesia's heart skipped as she recognized a dragon in scale form. They were all in scale form. She knew this. It was easier on her nerves if she couldn't see her accusers. "I have done all I can to protect you."

"Protect me? You used me as an experiment!"

"I honored you." Lord Garishton turned around. She felt the

scrape of his claws upon the ground, his every step vibrating the stone beneath her. "I gave you the power of Those Above, to give and to take away a basic right of human and dragon. The precious Talents."

Kesia tilted her head to the side. "Give? How could I give Talents?"

"Oh, how little you know, my dear niece. How much I have longed to teach you. But alas, I couldn't. Not while your parents hid you. At last, when they were dead, I thought to finally reveal your true strengths, but that weakness in you—that embermate bond—demanded satisfaction. I couldn't reach you while that prince held you captive in a heartflame bond."

She felt the wash of his commanding vocal Talent. Knew the compulsion was there, but only as rain splashing against a window. She wasn't affected. Because of her green smoke powers? Or her bond with Zephryn?

Perhaps both.

The claws scraped closer, like knives over a whetstone. Kesia longed to shift, to meet Garishton in dragon form, but that would be a move of challenge. With three other dragons in the room, she wouldn't survive for a moment.

She forced a laugh to hide the fear that shook her hands. "You blame Zephryn now? The embermate bond is undeniable."

<Zephryn, I wish you were here.>

If only she could shake the room. If only she could sing, wielding the incredible power she'd had in her memory.

Lord Garishton slithered closer to her, his words echoing in her bones. "Not anymore. I've found a way to break the embermate bond, to unbind your heartflames so that you may live."

Her breath caught, heart pounding.

"Why would you do that?"

"To free you, my niece. Just as I was freed." He sent out a tongue of flame. "I, too, was deceived into an embermate bond. A blessed honor among dragons. Until the most unexpected thing happened."

"What?" If he kept talking, it would give Zephryn time to get here. Maybe he could find her. "What is so wrong about the bonds?"

"That they aren't exclusive. My beautiful embermate, my heart-flame, was claimed by another equally. An exceptionally rare occurrence, as rare as the birth of a dragon with two Talents. Of course, this being the Scepter of Justice, there was a law governing such situations. The dragon of greater need was bound. The dragon-human council ruled that since the other potential embermate was the crown prince, he was far more important than I."

She swallowed, feeling a tiny twinge of pity. "A horrible law. Unfair. I agree."

"At first I tried to reconcile myself to it. You see, I deeply love my people. I loved the kingdom. I could bear the emptiness of a broken heart for the rest of my years. But the years are longer than you'd think, Kesia. Because I was denied a basic right of dragon-hood, I no longer felt kinship with my people. Thank the All-Maker I found others who had been equally deceived, others who had endured poor treatment from the famed Scepter of Justice."

He was so close now that each word shivered along her bare skin. "And so, you mistreated me? How does your grievance justify my torture?"

Garishton exhaled a gust of flames. She flinched but stood firm. "Don't you understand? I've fixed the system. Now there will be no more torment over lost bonds, no sense of affection to lose.

There is only order and discipline and our true primal natures to govern us."

"You've already lost everything. And I don't need you. I have Zephryn."

And so many others. Even if she died for them.

"Your fleetwing? Where is he now? I thought he would give everything to protect you, but apparently not. Maybe he finally realized your worthlessness."

"No." Zephryn would be here. He had to be. Even if she couldn't sense him, he wouldn't leave her alone to face her uncle and the Pinnacle.

<Zephryn!>

"As I said, I can unbind you." Garishton's voice deepened with sorrow. "I had hoped you would come willingly, but I see that you have heard too many lies. Only when you are at the point of death can you be unbound and remade into my true heir. If there was any other way, my niece—but there is not. And I will not lose my only remaining family."

"All of this, just to claim me as your heir?" Kesia scoffed. "You could have taken me in at any time when I was terrified as a child. Back when that Talent of yours actually worked a little on me!"

"I had to give my sister every chance! She didn't understand what she was turning away from."

"No, she just understood that she had to protect her only daughter from a madman."

"I saved your life." His words were dangerously calm. As they had been when she was a child and trapped. "You should be grateful."

Fear trickled up her back, cold water on the fire. Voice compulsion without a Talent. Calling up the small room, chilled to numb the pain. Kesia could almost feel the straps digging into her wrists and ankles.

No! She couldn't give in now. Kesia's hands clenched into fists, her fingernails digging into her skin. She had to give Zephryn more time.

"I-I didn't call to him, you know." *Firmer, Kesia. Firmer! Stronger.* She swallowed again. "I did not seek out an embermate. Zephryn Nightstalker found me."

"Oh, I know he did." Something slithered over the edge of her foot, hard and ridged with scales. The barbed edge cut into her flesh, and warm blood trickled to the floor. "He had been seeking you. Even the night you murdered your father, he tossed and turned in his cell, soaked in sweat and pain, using all his power to find you."

The night she murdered—killed the monster her father had become. Killed in self-defense. Kesia repeated the phrase in her mind. She couldn't let Garishton delude her again.

Then another part of her uncle's words struck her.

Zephryn, giving all his power. Even alone, in his cell.

"He was as selfish as his father, taking my own rightful kindred from me. What irony. The king takes my embermate, and his son takes my niece."

Garishton's tail coiled around her further. It was the coward's way, to take out another dragon in their skin form instead of meeting them in battle. Kesia tried to remember that, tried to hang on to it to still the shudders in her body.

She closed her eyes, willing herself to think back to that night in the cavern instead of burying it. Remembering the sudden swell of power within her that had shaken the cavern itself. It had been a power beyond hers, one that amplified her capabilities to frightening levels, even without a bond.

<Zephryn. Had you found me even then?>

"Embermates." Her word was a whisper.

Kesia could sense the heat building in Lord Garishton's body preparing to blast her with flame.

No.

She was not dying today without a fight. In her last, desperate battle, perhaps Zephryn might find her again. It was the only chance for success. Rage and purpose flared through her. Dragon scales speckled her skin, and her body flamed with fire.

Garishton gave a harsh chuckle. "Do you think this will deter me? I am made of flame and ash, and I have killed many more than you, my niece."

"I am Ironfire. And you have not seen the half of what I can burn."

She shifted, scales slipping over her skin with violent speed, her form matching those of the others in the room. She angled her long neck out of his hold, her wings pushing out behind her, creating a circle of protection.

The lights around the other figures flickered wildly as the dragons turned around, their eyes glinting dangerously.

Let them. She had nothing to lose.

Eleven years ago, a small dragonet had faced a monster in her cave and shook the walls. Now, Kesia called upon that same force, reaching out with everything in her. With all of her passion, all of her strength, all of her grief at what was taken, and all of her unspoken love.

<Zephryn.>

Inexplicable power filled her. More than herself. More than she could have ever been alone.

Kesia Ironfire opened her mouth and sang a song of high, bone-shattering notes and vibrations that quaked the ground beneath into fragments. A song of flame and power and hope.

Even if it was her last.

She was dying.

Zephryn flapped his wings faster, catching the powerful wind currents and letting them drive him toward the Pinnacle. The tower loomed in the distance, but his mind held only one purpose.

Get there in time.

He felt Kesia pulling on his heartflame, the same as he had when he was a child. The moment he'd seen her on the cell floor in chains, he'd known that she was the dragon who had stolen into his dreams and drawn upon his power.

Using it. Amplifying it.

Many had mistaken the Nightstalker ability for a simple Cloaking Talent, but the monarchy of the Scepter of Justice hadn't been established based on mere Cloaking. Their Talent could do so much more than simply bending light. His family's talent was a perception of the elements that bound the world together, elements that allowed dragons to shift their forms to and from the Nether. Their Talent had allowed the Nightstalkers to break the boundaries that held the very world together, even the energy that less enlightened individuals called magic.

Garishton had never discovered the truth.

Before they had even met, Kesia had called out to Zephryn and summoned the power of his Talent from his heartflame. He had responded, giving this unknown being every ounce of his strength and will, allowing her a full share in his inheritance and expecting nothing in return, except to stand by her side forever. To care for her, even though he hardly knew how.

Now, Kesia was calling on him again. He felt the power leave his heartflame and amplify her Talents. His Cloak left his form, exposing him to the eyes of any who would look. She would only do that if there was no other way.

Why hadn't he told her about it? Why had he hidden so much? To protect her? To protect himself? The only thing that mattered now was getting to the Pinnacle before she brought it down and buried herself beneath the rubble. His Talent was strong and terrible, and she had never been trained to use it. For that matter, neither had he, not beyond bending light.

<Kesia!>

No answer. Zephryn pushed on. Dragons patrolled the airspace around the Pinnacle, swooping in defensive patterns that allowed no one in except by permission.

He was the prince. He had permission.

<Nightstalker, the Pinnacle is interrogating your fleetwing. You are not permitted—>

<Move. Now.> Zephryn zoomed straight at them with all speed, daring them to challenge him in the air.

Another dragon with bright orange scales flew to intercept him. <Nightstalker, you forget your place. Stop now.>

<No. For the first time, I've remembered my place. And if you do not stand aside, I will be forced to harm you. The choice is yours.>

The intercepting dragon hesitated. It was a moment too long. Zephryn blasted him with a fountain of flames. They danced over his scales, flickering along the surface. Normally, Zephryn's Talent could undo any slatesheen protection, but right now, all of his power had to go to Kesia, which meant using less savory tactics.

He pulled his wings in and dropped down suddenly, dodging beneath the other dragon's belly. His claws cut through flesh, dragging long gashes into it. Then Zephryn retracted his legs and whirled into a barrel roll, flying away.

A shape loomed above him. The first dragon swooped down, claws extended. Zephryn didn't have time for this! <Rose-Wing, I'll be there soon.>

He pulled back on his power, just enough to fuel his flames into a slatesheen penetrating inferno. Whipping his neck around, he blasted the dragon with them. The firestorm captured the dragon in its fury.

Zephryn flew on, higher and higher toward the top of the Pinnacle. A large outcrop of rock suddenly angled toward him. He shifted to the side, the mass whizzing past his head. At the same time, a dragon song assaulted his bones, harsh and deep and beautiful. More debris fell around him as the arches of the great structure crumbled beneath the notes. Kesia was destroying the Pinnacle.

Two great dragons emerged from the rubble. Lady Oprisa Hailstone, her pale blue scales mottled with debris. Behind her, Lord Garishton Ironfire, with the same deep red scales as Kesia. Both of them struggled through the wreckage.

<Lord Garishton! Halt, on the authority of the leader of the Scepter of Justice.>

Garishton turned his head back, his eyes glittering. <The Scepter of Justice is dead, princeling. This changes nothing. We are many, and we are not tied to a single building. I will take no orders from an upstart whose embermate is dying because he couldn't

stand by her.>

<I'm. Not. Dying!> Kesia's voice broke through his thoughts, defiant but weak. <Zephryn ... wouldn't forget.>

More of the arches collapsed. Pain shivered through their bond. <Rose-Wing! Where are you?>

<Somewhere beneath. I'm sorry. I couldn't control it.>

He closed the last few lengths and hovered in the air. <You have nothing to be sorry for, Kesia. I'm sorry I wasn't here sooner.> Zephryn studied the rubble. <Can you shift?>

<I think so. Hard ... to focus. Wings ... Trapped.>

What did she need? Compliments. Telling her she was capable. Naturally, she was. But Kesia needed to hear it again. Her life depended on it.

<Kesia Ironfire, you are strong, you are capable, and you are immensely valuable. I want no one else by my side as a tactical partner and as a ruler. And ... I've always appreciated your appearance. You are always beautiful.>

<Beautiful?>

<Yes.>

A chuckle filtered into his mind. <Oh, Midnight, you are so—>

Her voice disappeared from his mind. No presence of her at all. Fear and disbelief punched at his gut. Had she died? Was he too late?

Zephryn flew through the deadly rainfall of debris, trying to catch a glimpse of her.

<Kesia? Kesia!>

Something landed on his back. Not heavy as the rocks, but light as a feather. Feathers. <Midnight, you're so cute when you're flustered.>

<And you are—Rose-Wing, if you do that again—>

The raven gave a few merry chirps. <You'll eat me? Fry me with your mighty flames?>

<No. I will never let you leave my sight.>

<I'm already out of your sight.>

Zephryn blew a stream of fire, joy overtaking annoyance. <That will change as soon as we meet the ship at the edge of dragon airspace.>

<The edge? The Pinnacle just moved a squadron to the front lines, Midnight. I heard it during the confusion. Ten dragons.>

He felt the lightness disappear as Kesia shifted again, returning to her deep red scale form. Zephryn flicked his tail toward hers.

<Then let's ensure the dragons lose.>

Chapter Twenty-Four

FLYING USING ONLY the ship's engines rankled Shance's soul.

Yes, *The Silver Streak* was the fastest in the fleet. Nothing could equal the strength of its engine, especially with Kesia's repairs. The hull had been remade with the newest wood and metal polymer alloy, designed to minimize wind drag as well as resist dragon fire. But the vessel was even faster when he controlled the wind currents that filled the auxiliary sails. Sails that weren't necessary on any Congruency airship except for his, because of his Talent. A Talent that still hadn't resurfaced and wouldn't for another eighteen hours.

Sunlight filtered over the edge of the horizon. Even without his Talent, they had made excellent speed to the edge of dragon airspace. Nightstalker was somewhere ahead of them. An unloaded dragon could best the speeds of even *The Silver Streak*, and the dragon had plenty of reason to speed on.

Shance walked the deck, running his hand along the railing. Doing so reminded him of the past six days, when he and Kesia had worked tirelessly on this ship together, inseparable and focused on the same goal. It had been magical—and he didn't believe in magic. Who knew having a friendship with a female was possible, much less enjoyable?

All that being said, he could use a good meal and a beautiful woman when this was over. A woman he didn't have to view as a sister. And preferably one who wasn't a killer.

The way Kesia's sweet, playful exterior had vanished beneath the threat of General Brody and his men had unnerved him. Kesia had become deadly, and it had fit her perfectly. Dragons were predators. Even the least of them were natural hunters. Balanced with a desire for justice, he supposed that made them good at watching over the other Scepters.

As long as there was a council to balance the bloodthirst. That was partially encouraging. Maybe his distaste of violence was rooted in something ancestral and useful instead of being a liability. Perhaps there was purpose behind it.

Maybe humans should be on this council as well as dragons, led by a Windkeeper.

"Captain Windkeeper?"

He blinked. Captain Tegan had been assigned by General Markem as his first mate. "Yes, Captain—Commander Tegan. How are the sails?"

"They are continuing to wave, sir." Was there an edge to her voice? He had to be imagining it. "The lookout has spied dragons."

So, the flamers had sighted them. Shance didn't feel bad about the slur. *These* dragons were on the enemy side. "How many?"

"At least eight, sir. Possibly ten." Tegan cleared her throat. "Are you able to use your Talent?"

"Not yet, Commander."

Tegan's eyes widened. "Then perhaps we should attempt a retreat. There was a cloudbank a mile back. We might be able to take shelter there before they reach us."

"Retreat?"

"Think of it as advancing in the opposite direction to minimize bloodshed and improve future chances of survival. Sir."

"Granted." As much as Shance loathed a fire-fight, skulking in a cloud cluster was equally repellant and cowardly. Still, what other options did they have? He wouldn't risk his crew. "All right. Do it. Once we're inside, everyone go full-silent."

"Aye, sir."

She turned to leave.

"Commander?"

"Sir?"

"You said 'bloodshed.' The preferred military term is 'casualties,' isn't it?"

She stiffened, and spoke in a soft, cold voice. "When people are injured and die, they lose blood, sir. Bloodshed. The loss of a ship is a casualty. It can be far more easily replaced."

Shance frowned. On one hand, he couldn't argue with her. On the other, she was impossible to read, which would make working together difficult. But he had no other options.

"Relay my orders. You are dismissed, Commander Tegan."

Tegan turned on her heel and continued to the voice-horn at the center of the ship to make the announcement.

General Markem had been as brusque about his Lawless support as he had been terse about everything else. But he was helpful. The general had managed to convince, order, and outright threaten anyone necessary to get *The Silver Streak* released on an early test flight. From there, it was simply a matter of Shance and his Lawless crew commandeering the vessel and turning off the radio in response to Markem's "official" orders to return to High Command. And Tegan was Markem's most valuable ally. Like it or not, she had to be aboard.

"Just as long as we stay on the same side," Shance muttered.

A few minutes later, *The Silver Streak* was surrounded by a dense fog. Water droplets condensed on consoles and the faces of his crew, slicking the surface of the deck. The air was a blanket of grayish wetness. All they had to do was wait for the impending doom and pray to Viorstan and Fiarston for a shipload of luck. Or pray to Bonilus and his emissaries. At this point, Shance sent up prayers to the whole lot of them. Surely, if one of them existed, they would look down and help.

If they could see through the clouds.

Shance tapped the pads of his fingers against the railing, his breath loud in his ears. Outside the cloud, the faint outlines of dragons hovered and darted back and forth. The additional benefit of moisture from the cloudbanks would make it more difficult for dragons to activate their fire spewing. Or so the myth went. If it bought them even a few minutes, Shance would be happy.

A dark figure dove closer, its long tail breaking through the clouds above them for a brief moment. Shance's heartbeat sped, and his mind filled with tension. The dragons had to be planning an attack. The only question was whether *The Silver Streak* would survive it, and take down a few of the beasts with them.

A small shape made a sudden plunge straight for the ship. Three crew pulled out weapons, and Shance did as well.

Tegan whistled low. "It's only a sun-dove."

"Kesia." Shance watched as the small bird fluttered through the mastheads to land on his shoulder with a trill. He stroked the top of her head. She pushed off his fingers and began pulling at his uniform. First gently, then insistently.

Clothes. Right. She needed to shift back. "I got it."

He jogged to his cabin and pulled out a pair of drawstring

trousers, a shirt, and a jacket. "I'll put these on the bed and face the wall, all right?"

The sun-dove trilled again. Shance turned away, trying not to think of her dressing and mostly succeeding.

Points for emotional growth.

"You can turn around now. Thanks."

Kesia's hair was loose and tangled around her shoulders. His clothes fit her decently well, with exceptions made for her more feminine figure. Her warm amber eyes smiled at him. "I knew you'd figure it out."

"I always had a thing for sun-doves."

"Me too. They make a delicious snack."

He laughed, wanting to lift her up in his arms and twirl her around. Was that something brothers did with their sisters? Not now, at any rate. Not with him in military uniform and her in his clothes. Her face was decidedly all dragon, complete with scales along her forehead and cheekbones and red strands in her brown hair.

"What does it look like outside?"

Kesia pressed her lips together and rolled up her sleeves. "Not good. Zephryn is out there Cloaked. He has confirmed the presence of ten dragons, all of them experienced warriors. The cloud-bank was a smart move, but it won't hold them off forever. We think the best choice is to make a break for it, using your cannons and Zephryn and me as cover fire. You have the coordinates for the Lawless outpost?"

"Yes." Shance motioned her over to a large table in the middle of the cabin where a map of Sekastra was spread. "The outpost is on the far side of dragon airspace, nearer to the Scepter of Knowledge. It's possible for a ship to skirt the edges of dragon and human airspace."

She leaned over him, her eyes blank for a moment, then she nodded to an unheard conversation. He suspected she was communicating with Zephryn.

A moment later, she confirmed it. "That will work. As soon as *The Silver Streak* is clear, use your alert siren at the loudest setting. Zephryn and I will land aboard, since your wind Talent is even faster than our flying."

"One problem. My Talent hasn't returned yet."

"What if I could try to alleviate the effects?"

"How? Is that part of your Talent? Some new development?"

"We'll say it's the latter." Kesia winked. "I can't make promises, but it's the best we have right now."

"That pretty well sums up our entire association."

"Yes. Give me your hands."

He placed his hands in hers. At that moment, a blast of fire pulsed outside the cabin window, glancing off the ship. "Was that—?"

"Zephryn's taking care of it." Kesia held his hands firmly in her own. "I'm sorry. This might hurt."

"More words that summarize our experiences together."

She squeezed his hands, just shy of breaking bone. "The only other time I did this was with Zephryn, and I'm not kissing you, Shance. I'll have to try another way."

She closed her eyes. Flames erupted from her hands. Shance tried to pull away, but Kesia held him fast with her iron grip. A penetrating burning sensation consumed him, as if every cell in his skin was splitting apart. After a few seconds, Shance felt nothing but pain. Sharp pins and needles rushed over his skin, stabbing into his very bones until his entire body was on fire.

He gritted his teeth. Sweat lined Kesia's face. Gradually, he noticed a greenish smoke emanating from his pores and smearing his skin. The more it prickled through his flesh, the more intense was the pain from the pins that tore him apart atom by atom.

At last, she dropped his hands. Her shoulders sagged and her eyes opened slowly, as if she'd been asleep. She stood in a cloud of green mist, the color tinging her skin and hair. "That's all I can do right now. Come on, let's see if it worked."

"And then you'll take a rest?"

"I'll rest as soon as you and everyone else does." Kesia managed a weak but defiant smile. "Try to make a breeze."

Shance reached toward the pillow on his bed, trying to collect enough wind to lift the cushion up. Nothing.

Kesia shut her eyes and rubbed them with her palms. "Try again."

A flash of fire and heat singed the ship. The dragons were close.

Shance gestured again. This time, the pillow shifted slightly, rising several inches off the bed. "Well, that's something."

"Not nearly enough for a ship. It was worth a try." She trudged over to the door, the green mist clinging to her. "I need to join Zephryn out there. We will try to buy you enough time to get through."

Shance strode past her, forcing himself between her and the door. "The last I knew, you both were priority figures in this rebellion."

"Meaning?"

"Meaning you shouldn't get killed."

"We don't plan on it. Do you have any other ideas? Do you want to go up there?" She glared at him. "Don't make me move you. I will."

"I won't let you get killed."

Kesia's eyes flashed to slits. "And I won't let you dictate what I can and cannot do, especially when it comes to the welfare of my embermate." Kesia grabbed his arms, forcing him away from the door. "Move, Shance!"

"No!"

A blast of wind blew her back three feet. Her mouth parted in shock. "Did you—?"

"I think so." Shance pivoted and ran outside, their quarrel forgotten. He raised his hands and felt the breezes come at his call. Gusts and gales swirled around the ship, filling the sails and wrapping around him like the embrace of an old friend.

The honor and pride of Windkeepers had returned to him.

Kesia grinned in relief, her green and brown hair whirling about her face. "Do your best, Shance. I'll see you when the ship is clear."

"Kesia, wait, your—"

She shifted into a sun-dove and flew away into the clouds.

"Sir." He glanced over at Tegan. Her brows wrinkled. "Her hair. Her file says she has red strands. But they looked—"

"—Green. I know."

Green like the smoke. Only deeper.

He pushed his thoughts aside. "No time right now, Commander. Let's get out of here."

Shance spun his hands, creating a funnel of wind around the vessel, one that would both protect them from attack and propel them forward faster.

"All hands on deck! Grab onto anything bolted to the ship." Shance beckoned Tegan forward. "Turn off the turbines, Commander."

"Sir?"

"Kill the turbines! You're about to find out the reason for those sails."

The ship wheeled around. Shance held out his hands, palms up, and felt the deck fall away beneath him. The wind carried him into a protective current where he could feel the breezes and hear their voices clearly.

The only place he was free.

A cheer rang out from below him. With the barest breath of wind, he could feel the location of each crew member and alter the currents to ensure each and every one of them stayed safe and secure on the deck, no matter how fast they went. Within reason.

A hideous screech broke through his calm. Shance squinted, the mist still partly obscuring his vision. A gray dragon careened toward *The Silver Streak*.

"Hang on!"

He pulled the funnel tighter around the ship, increasing the speed of the wind until it acted as a shield. Then Shance dropped his arms, and he and *The Silver Streak* fell through the air and flew in a diagonal evasive maneuver, narrowly avoiding the trajectory of the gray dragon.

It wheeled around, opening its gaping maw to flame *The Silver Streak*.

"Fire!"

At Commander Tegan's order, five of *The Silver Streak's* guns opened fire with bioelectric cannonballs, modified to track and zero in on dragon heartflame frequencies.

Shance held his breath.

Kesia, Zephryn, stay clear. By Bonilus, stay clear.

The gray dragon pulled up, but it was too late. Three of the bioelectric cannonballs hit their mark in an explosion of bluish-white currents, smoking scales, and dragon blood. Shance took hold of the winds again, sending a gale against the dragon to deflect the worst of the carcass.

"Good firing, Commander!"

"Sir! It's badly wounded, but still active."

Shance opened his mouth to order another attack, but before the words could leave his mouth another screech sounded through the mist, melodic and deadly. A moment later, a slender, deep red dragon drove through the air, flames bursting from its jaws.

The crew scurried around below, readying more cannons.

Kesia.

"Commander!"

"On it!" Tegan's voice blared over the voice-horn. "Stand down! We have a friendly dragon! Repeat, stand down!"

Kesia pounced on the gray dragon, claws out, teeth ripping and tearing. Both of them fell out of view, the gray dragon giving a final, pained screech.

Relief flooded Shance. Kesia could take it from there.

"All hands, brace yourselves! We're going faster!"

Tegan's voice echoed his orders on the voice-horn, and Shance took a deep, cleansing breath of winds. Never mind the carnage. They were fighting for something worthwhile. Finally.

A peaceful future.

He summoned more gales of wind, shoving them along the sails as much as he dared. The new synthetic canvas was meant to withstand any windspeed, but it hadn't been tested by a Windkeeper at full power.

The Silver Streak raced ahead, straight through three more dragons in attack formation. Screeches and deafening roars echoed through the air. Blasts of flame singed the edges of one sail. Below, Shance heard Tegan ordering sailors to shore up the canvas.

"Belay that!" Shance shouted. "We're going for the final push! Tegan!"

She glanced up at him. "Sir!"

"Sound the alert! Make sure everyone is strapped down. And sound the alert siren at maximum volume."

"Aye sir! Make sure you strap yourself down as well!"

A moment later the siren blared, blocking out even the sounds of roaring dragons. Shance stirred a few breezes, landing on the deck and starting to strap himself to the main mast. Ahead, he viewed open sky for miles. He tensed. A rare, clear path.

Come on, Kesia. Zephryn. Get your asses onboard.

Protocol demanded the safety of his ship and crew was paramount. But Shance wasn't leaving the dragons behind.

They were key figures in the Lawless. And his friends.

He finished strapping himself in, then pulled on even more wind currents, funneling some of them around the ship and holding others in reserve for one final acceleration.

"Incoming!"

His pulse jolted. Two dragons aimed straight for the ship. One was midnight blue, the other dark red with a greenish tinge to the scales.

Tegan shouted, "Friendlies! Friendlies! Captain, as soon as they're aboard—"

"Copy that!"

Kesia and Zephryn landed in a corner of the deck, both in skin form. Teagan rushed them into the cabin.

Dragons roared behind him.

Shance exhaled. Released the winds.

The Silver Streak shot ahead into the blue.

CHAPTER TWENTY-FIVE

KESIA'S HEAD ROSE AND FELL gently, as if on the slightest, softest breeze. A breeze that was as warm as the heartflame inside her. She snuggled closer, wanting to feel the warmth all over her, but something was in the way. Some horrible barrier kept her from the warmth. She took the wall between her fingers, tugging at it, a low growl rumbling in her throat.

<Rose-Wing? What's wrong?>

The voice was familiar. Safe and compelling as her own heart-beat.

Zephryn.

She opened her eyes. A small cavern room came into focus around her. A dresser and table sat against one wall, and a lamp hung beside the bed.

A bed where she lay curled up next to Zephryn, his chest beneath her cheek. Sort of. A loose shirt was in the way. Her face flushed. <Ah, that explains it.>

<Explains what?>

Kesia lifted her head and smirked at Zephryn. <Your clothes. I don't like them.>

He raised a black brow, his bronze face creasing into a small smile. <Interesting. As I recall, we were both too exhausted to notice earlier.>

<Flying for twelve hours will do that.>

She sighed. They had been trained in endurance flying at high speeds, but after the fight, every muscle in her body had been put to the test. They'd taken half-hour breaks in shifts on *The Silver Streak*, sleeping on the deck, ready for any fresh battles. By the time they'd reached the Lawless outpost near Edgefell Peaks, there had been no energy left, not even for mental communication. She barely remembered donning the sleeping clothes laid out and falling into bed next to Zephryn.

He trailed a finger along her cheek, lightly caressing her scales. <So, is it what you imagined, Rose-Wing?>

<Hm?> She leaned into his touch.

<Sleeping in skin form.>

<It's better.>

So much better. So much more intimate, being so close to her embermate. She ran her fingers over the cobalt scales at the open neck of his shirt.

His hand drifted to her hair. <What is this? So it is true.>

<That I have hair growing from my scalp?> Kesia winked. It was becoming one of her favorite human gestures.

Zephryn tugged at a lock with a frown. <Yes, but right here. A few strands are green instead of red.>

The pleasant warmth left her, and she pushed away from him.

<Green? What are you talking about?> Shance had been trying to tell her something when she left the ship. <Why? Why is it green?>

Her breath grew shallow.

Zephryn sat up too, his cobalt eyes intent. <You fell asleep before me. Before I slept, a dragon caregiver came in and gave us both

a cursory examination. He determined that the green smoke you've absorbed has begun affecting your physiology. It's harmless.>

<Harmless?> She fell back onto the bed, staring at the short stalactites dripping down from the ceiling. <Even after I face my uncle, he still manages to find a way to hurt me.>

<The caregiver said it would have eventually occurred anyway. Your physiology was fundamentally altered. Whatever Garishton did wasn't merely an experiment. He succeeded in helping you survive with two fully integrated Talents.>

She breathed out smoke. <So I should be grateful to him?>

Zephryn's frustration and concern filtered through their bond. <Not necesarily. Perhaps you should be grateful toward the All-Maker, or Those Above, or whatever deities the humans follow. Regardless, you are alive because of the smoke. You are using it to stop evil and do good. And that makes it … admirable.>

<Admirable?> Kesia's heart tightened with anger. <My father had red scales and hair strands, just like mine. Now that's going away too, just like my parents did.>

Wetness trailed down her face.

Zephryn squeezed her hand. <The caregiver said that, for a little while, you'll have both colors.>

<Still the same ending.>

<I know. It isn't the same, but … I lost my family as well.>

The quiet sadness in his mental voice prompted Kesia to look at him. Zephryn's face, normally calm and impassive, held a sorrow that wasn't evident in his scale form.

Open. Caring. Accepting.

Slowly, carefully, he pulled her into his arms. She burrowed her face against his chest, taking in his heartbeat until nothing mattered except the two of them.

Embermates.

What were the words Shance had said to her?

<I love you.>

His fingers crept beneath her shirt, tracing along her spine. The sensation both comforted and thrilled her. <I love you too, Rose-Wing.>

<What about when my scales are no longer red?>

<You will always be mine.>

She sighed, surrendering to the ebb and flow of emotions through their bond. Grief. Joy. Commitment.

Desire.

It was nothing like Shance's effusive words and extravagant gestures. Instead, it was a slow, steady trickle, as gentle as the mountain streams of the Cloudpeaks. Kesia pushed away just enough to ease her fingers beneath the edges of his shirt.

<Midnight?>

<Yes?>

She paused. How did one even say this?

<Would you—could we—>

He stared down at her, tracing her lips with the tip of his finger. <Continue to explore?>

<Yes. As long as that means having sex.>

Zephryn chuckled, his skin flushing darker. So odd that in the Pinnacle, she had feared being naked. Right now, anything less was unacceptable.

<Agreed. Would you like assistance?>

<Only if I can reciprocate.>

Slowly he slipped off her shirt, and she his. She ran her fingers over his bare chest freely, without fear of punishment, enjoying his touch in return. Anxious for nothing. There was only moment by moment closeness and pleasure.

Nearness. Security.

Need.

Until all they were was joined, and nothing more could part them.

And then, rest.

Curled up in each other's arms once more, Kesia rested her head against Zephryn's chest, tracing his scales, the rhythm of his heartflame keeping time with hers.

He traced the edge of her hip. <I agree. Sleeping is far better without clothing. At least, in this manner.>

She chuckled. <I told you so.>

Kesia settled against him, and her eyes closed in perfect peace.

"So, how was it?"

Kesia stared at the silver clipse-mirror in disbelief. Was Countess Nula really asking this? "Excuse me? I don't know you that well. And our sexuality isn't any of your concern."

"Oh, fine. I was only teasing." The Countess leaned forward, her gray eyes sharp even from a distance. She had called to ask Zephryn a question but seemed perfectly willing to speak with Kesia as well. "Of course, now you'll need to deal with Windkeeper. It seems he fell pretty hard for you, which is silly, considering you never were free to pursue. At least, that's what I've heard from dragons with embermates."

"Shance and I are on good terms. He isn't an issue." Kesia pressed her lips together. Why did her skin keep flushing all the time? There were many advantages to scales over skin, the masking of feelings topping the list. "I am not discussing this with you. I am waiting for you to tell me about the situation in the Scepter of Commerce, since that's what you called about."

Countess Nula looked disappointed, but she shrugged. "It goes well. After Nightstalker and Windkeeper left, General Markem brought forth the evidence he's been collecting against Brody. The Congruency had no choice but to prosecute him, along with my parents and several other key members of the Curious Intrigue. The balance of power is shifting. Naturally, there is some backlash, but the situation appears to be well in hand."

"And you're fine with your parents being imprisoned?"

"It needed to happen. I now have the freedom and security I wanted, and they're not supporting a sham war anymore. Everyone wins." The countess paused to take a sip of wine. "And I don't have to worry about marrying someone I don't want to."

"True."

Kesia sat back in the wooden seat and played with the ends of her hair, staring at the wall. The green strands continued to multiply. As it turned out, her ability to absorb the green smoke was sought after among the rebels at the Lawless outpost. As soon as she healed, her services would apparently be in much demand.

She could live with the color. Zephryn's quiet reassurance helped. So far.

What would Shance say? She hadn't seen him in a few days, which wasn't surprising, considering the size of the outpost. It was spread across different outcroppings of rock in the Edgefell Peaks, some of which were used for housing members of the Lawless, but the majority of which was a well-hidden hangar for ships.

At least, that's what the specifications said in the Lawless information journals. She and Zephryn hadn't left their small suite in the last few days. A time of uninterrupted rest was recommended by the caregiver. They had made the most of it, splitting their time between intimacy, reading, and sleeping. It had been refreshing, but after three days, Kesia was ready to explore. Thankfully, the general meeting was today.

In a few minutes. She needed to end this call.

"Kesia?" She turned back to the clipse-mirror. Countess Nula's expression was vulnerable, almost sad. "I'm sorry for what I had to do in the hangar. You didn't deserve it, and I admired how you stood up to the Congruency. It was stupid but very bold. And I wanted to let you know you could call me Nula, if you want."

"Why?" Kesia asked. Nula flinched as if she had been slapped. Kesia quickly added, "I mean, I don't understand the significance of this. I understand why you turned me in. And I don't mind using your first name."

The countess chuckled. "I forget that you are entirely a dragon, aren't you?"

"I believe so."

"I appreciate your bluntness. I wish humans were more like that. I don't really fit in with them. I don't mind it most of the time, but sometimes…"

Understanding settled in Kesia's heart. "I'd like to call you Nula. And you'll have some more experiences with dragons soon. Now that the tide has officially shifted to the Lawless in your city, additional dragons will be sent into the Scepter of Commerce to begin rebuilding relationships. The dragon council and human leadership are in full agreement. Tiers Sunscaler is nearly ready and will depart after the meeting today. He's been charged to work closely with you to ensure a successful reestablishment of open dragon relations."

"I see." Nula raised her eyebrows. "If I didn't know better, I'd think you were trying to set me up with a man."

"He isn't a man. He's a dragon. It doesn't work like that."

"True, he already has someone."

Kesia shook her head. "Not necessarily. Not everyone meets their embermate as young as Zephryn and I did."

Nula chuckled again. "Speaking of which, where is yours?"

"Zephryn is receiving a fresh coat of slatesheen. I'll see him at the meeting which is starting—" Kesia glanced at the timescreen on the wall. "In one minute. I need to go!"

She clicked off the screen, then paused. She had forgotten a leave-taking! Humans said good-bye or something else when they were leaving. There were so many customs to learn. Considering the new assignment she and Zephryn had received, she would have to learn quickly.

Kesia stood and smoothed the form-fitting buttoned shirt, corset, and long, narrow skirt that fell to her ankles. Her attire was practice for the fashion of the Scepter of Knowledge, and in its current state was completely unacceptable to her. She would have to speak to someone about adding slits to the sides of the skirt. Otherwise, it would be ridiculous to run or fight in.

She exited her quarters and walked down the hallway. Minerals lined the rocks on either side, their patterns interrupted by more doorways. At the end, the passage opened into a large meeting area with tables and chairs strewn about. A large window covered an entire wall and gave a scenic view of the Western Reach.

Kesia walked to the long table in front of the window, which was already filled with members of the Lawless. Zephryn had kept the chair next to him conspicuously empty. Shance sat across from the empty chair.

He smirked as she walked over, his blue eyes twinkling.

"Decided to come up for air?" Shance asked in a low tone.

She flashed him a smile. "I was breathing the entire time. Otherwise, it wouldn't have been enjoyable."

"Aha." He mock-sighed. "And to think when I first met you, you didn't even know what bedding was."

She blinked innocently. "Bedding refers to the sheets and blankets on a bed. Sex, on the other hand, involves—"

"Kesia, I don't need a lecture. As I was about to say the pupil has become the—"

She raised her eyebrows and let a flame dance in the palm of her hand. "The what?"

"The very wise colleague." He winked. "Who is always ready to defend her friend and brother. By the way, I see you've started eating more green vegetables."

"What?"

Shance tugged at a lock of her green-tinted hair. "I noticed on the ship. Is it because of the green smoke?"

"...yes." She sighed.

"I'm sorry."

His sympathy almost undid the careful barrier over her feelings. Kesia laughed shortly. "As you said. Too many vegetables."

"Indeed."

She laughed louder, rib cage pressing against the corset. What was wrong with human females that they agreed to wear such garments? Maybe it was fitted too tightly.

She felt a wave of amusement through her bond.

<Are you well, Rose-Wing?>

<Yes, I am.> Kesia smiled and shifted closer to her embermate. He and Shance both wore the clothing of the Scepter of Knowledge:

vests over high-collared shirts, tight pants to the knees, and long socks. <Your attire makes you look very … distracting.>

<Indeed. Some men wear wigs. Apparently, the Scepter of Knowledge is quite old-fashioned.> He gave her an aggrieved look, but his eyes smiled and his fingers brushed over her hand. <That dress seems entirely impractical for fighting. But it is attractive.>

<I agree. I might need some research help to see if I can make some modifications and still blend in with the Scepter of Knowledge's fashions. Care to help me?>

<In whatever way I can.>

Her smile widened.

Footsteps echoed through the chamber. A moment later, Commander Annabel Tegan sat next to Shance, stiff and quiet in her Congruency uniform of black tabard over a dark blue shirt. Officers weren't required to fit in with local Scepter fashions.

Kesia cleared her throat. This would be a good time to practice conversation. "So, you are not infiltrating the Scepter of Knowledge, then?"

"At this point, no." Her lips twitched, but otherwise her round face remained placid. "General Markem assigned me to keep watch on the ship, so that is what I intend to do."

"And she does a great job." Shance smiled, though it didn't quite reach his eyes. "Keeps everything in line well."

Tegan only nodded once in thanks.

Kesia mentally nudged Zephryn. <So this is Pryenil Slightshadow?>

<Indeed.> He paused. <She was a great deal more talkative before we left the Scepter of Commerce.>

<I see.>

<Make sure never to reveal her dragon half. She is still…

grieved.>

<Understandably so.>

Captain Tegan's eyes darted back and forth between them, aware of the presence of mind speech, but never able to comprehend or join it. Kesia's heart sank. The half-dragon lived in her own isolation. Perhaps, someday, that would be alleviated, and they could talk.

"Shall we begin?" The new voice was plain and firm. A dragon stood at the head of the table, smiling faintly, his narrow eyes calm. Golden scales patterned his tawny skin. Kesia fought to steady her heart. She hadn't even heard him enter the room.

She opened a private link with Zephryn. <Tiers Sunscaler?>

<Yes. One of the chief administrators of the Lawless.>

<Not a warrior?> He was certainly built like one, muscled and at ease. She had expected a far less impressive dragon to be sent on political duties.

<Apparently there were complications with his tactical partner. They weren't fleetwings, naturally, but they were close. And then his partner found his fleetwing. His embermate.>

<Ah, understood.> To see a close friend find that connection and be left alone would be discouraging.

Sunscaler cleared his throat. "I'll keep this short. Lord Garishton Ironfire's forces are already repairing the damage to the Pinnacle tower, and while we may be swaying the Scepter of Commerce, the Curious Intrigue is deeply entrenched in the other three Scepters. Only by gaining majority support in all Scepters can we issue a Declaration of Return for the Scepter of Justice. With the Scepter reinstated with proper authority and council, we can then officially end the war. This is clear?"

Kesia nodded, along with the others around the table. Sunscaler picked at his tabard. He was dressed for the Scepter of Commerce, and given his usual comfort in going around shirtless—typical for Lawless dragons in general—he was still getting used to his new clothing. At least Kesia wasn't the only one uncomfortable in her attire. "Our latest update on the Scepter of Knowledge is disturbing. It seems Cadence Folham, our strongest supporter in the courts and assemblies, has stopped promoting the end of hostilities. Without his leadership, many of his advisors have also stopped their protests. Without their voices in the city, the Lawless cause is greatly weakened."

"So we should find this Folham and learn what happened?" Zephryn asked.

Sunscaler passed out dossiers to each of them. "Yes, your highness. Please be advised, these are actual paper documents and are not at all resistant to water, unlike the coated documents from the Scepter of Commerce."

"Where's the intelligence in using lesser quality?" Kesia muttered, flipping through the files.

"Apparently paper is a large income for the area. Many tree farms are located in the vicinity of the city."

Shance raised his eyebrows. "Um, why does that matter?"

"You never know what details could be important, Captain Windkeeper." Sunscaler shot a glare at Shance, then cleared his throat again. "This is considered a top priority mission. The Curious Intrigue lost the first battle. They will increase their aggression, and we must be prepared."

Kesia glanced at her file. "An elocution acolyte?"

<I am one as well.> Zephryn paged through his own file. <Senior level.>

Sunscaler nodded. "They prize debate and public speaking

298

highly. That title should allow you and Zephryn into all major functions. Observe and if you must engage, take care to learn the expectations first. Princess Ironfire, you will also infiltrate the scientific community and investigate the green smoke."

His words seemed to come from a distance. Princess Ironfire. Not a convict. Not a criminal. The title was hers through her embermate bond, but most of the dragons she'd encountered since arriving at the Lawless outpost had simply avoided referring to her directly at all. When necessary, they had only said—

"Your highness?" Sunscaler studied her. "Did you hear me?"

Kesia nodded, shrugging off her thoughts. There were more important matters to consider, such as her association with the green smoke. The caregivers and doctors at the Lawless outpost were still examining her blood. They simply didn't have the facilities to analyze all that Garishton had done to her. And if he had experimented on her with the green smoke, it was certain that he had done so to others. His plans had to go beyond disabling Talents.

Sunscaler continued. "Captain Windkeeper will assist you as needed, but his primary duties are contacting and persuading the local military to join the Lawless cause."

Kesia frowned. "Won't they try to attack us?"

Shance shook his head, but Zephryn spoke first. "What happened in the Scepter of Commerce doesn't concern them. Each city-state has their own legal system and jurisdiction. In the Scepter of Knowledge, the ban against dragons has always been more theoretical than strictly implemented unless there is bloodshed. Even then, only the dragons responsible are prosecuted. Behave yourselves, and humans will overlook the possibility that you are dangerous, unless you are accused in an assembly. Even then, you have a right to defend yourself."

"He's right," Shance added. "The Congruency holds the four Scepters together in a loose alliance, but they've always had individual autonomy. Which is why the Lawless are seeking a cessation of support for hostilities through the assemblies. There's been enough killing already."

Tegan smiled faintly at the airship captain's words, but otherwise, kept quiet. Although Kesia wasn't one to judge. The idea of speaking out in an assembly twisted knots in her stomach.

<Rose-Wing?>

<You can do all of the talking in the Scepter of Knowledge.>

Concern emanated from him. <We're embermates. We will do this together.>

<You've had far more experience.>

<Only compared to you.> Zephryn nudged her hand with his. <And you stood up to the Pinnacle.>

<True.>

Somehow, an unknown assembly seemed far worse.

Kesia swallowed more doubt. As long as she could handle any spywork and fighting, she would be fine. And the green smoke. She could handle the green smoke, literally.

Sunscaler was speaking again. "Above all else, support each other. Don't let them divide your team."

Zephryn raised his eyebrows. "Divide us?"

"Every possible viewpoint has a voice in the Scepter of Knowledge. And each group is actively recruiting to make their collective voice louder." Sunscaler grimaced. "From our experiences, these groups will have no qualms creating discord in order to fill their ranks."

<And here I was looking forward to freedom of speech.> Zephryn snorted.

Kesia winced in agreement.

"Unless there are any further questions?"

Silence.

"Good. Meeting adjourned."

Sign up for Janeen Ippolito's newsletter and get exclusive bonus content from The Ironfire Legacy series, plus monthly giveaways, book recommendations, and excerpts:

Thank you for reading!

The Ironfire Legacy Series:
Outlaw of Smoke
Scion of Scales
Captain of Storms

ABOUT THE AUTHOR

Janeen Ippolito believes you should own your unique words—and make them awesome! She's a multi-published author of bestselling fiction, nonfiction, and poetry. She's also an experienced book editor and marketing strategist. In her spare time, she helps her missionary husband with his youth swordfighting ministry, indulges her foodie ambitions, reads whatever books she feels like, and explores a slew of random hobbies. Her life goals include traveling to Antarctica and riding a camel while wearing a party hat. This extrovert loves to connect, so join her on social media or at janeenippolito.com.

ACKNOWLEDGEMENTS

Thanks be to God. I create because I am fearfully, wonderfully created.

A huge thank you to my husband, Stephen Ippolito. Your support is invaluable and essential.

Major thanks to Julia Busko for being a tireless feedback machine during the early stages of developing this world and for encouraging me to put in all the things!

Much appreciation to line editor Sarah McConahy, who makes sure my stories are grounded, and formatter Sarah Delena White, for stressing out over all the little details and making sure I did too.

Shout-out to beta readers H.L. Burke, Kat Heckenbach, Sophia Hoxie, Rachel Kennedy (The Story Eater), Anne Jones, and Hannah Keeler. You made revisions so much more work, but I'm so much happier for the better story that resulted.

And last, a shout-out to all of my readers. Y'all keep me going with all the encouragement and quote love!

www.ingramcontent.com/pod-product-compliance
Lightning Source LLC
Chambersburg PA
CBHW031337020726
47499CB00005B/1296